a Christy novel

FATAL EXCHANGE

CINDY M. HOGAN

a Christy novel

FATAL EXCHANGE

CINDY M. HOGAN

O'neal Publishing

FATAL EXCHANGE

Layton, UT.

ISBN: 978-0-9851318-8-3

Visit her at cindymhogan.com
Google Plus: Cindy Hogan
Facebook page watched-the book
Twitter-@Watched1

To my sister, Tracie, who would have loved Paris

1

"The fate of the world hangs in the balance, and you're stopping for a baguette?"

I fought to keep a smirk from my lips as I paid for my baguette and started walking briskly toward the train station. Halluis knew I had plenty of time; he was just trying to provoke me. He and Ace were tracking my movements on the computer screen back at Paris headquarters, monitoring the operation and providing me information over the com in my ear as things progressed.

I couldn't respond, of course. I was undercover—for the first time since coming to Paris four months ago—and it felt great, despite the steady stream of mockery I was receiving from Halluis. I could just imagine the smug look on his mustachioed face as he watched my dot progress toward the train station, knowing the whole time that I just had to take whatever he'd throw at me. Well, I might not be able to tell him just how immature he was being, but that didn't mean I was completely defenseless.

I tucked the baguette under my arm—a distinctly Parisian move—and whipped out my cell phone. I texted a quick message to Ace, then slipped the phone into a hidden inside pocket of my skirt and ripped off a chunk of the delicious bread.

A second later I was rewarded with Halluis's sharp cry of alarm over the com. "Tiens! What was that for? *Oulà*, that really hurt!"

This time I did smirk, hiding the expression behind my chunk of bread. *Good man, H.*

I could hear the two of them scuffling, as Halluis tried to get revenge for the flick I'd asked Ace to deliver to his unsuspecting ear. Ace had obviously ripped off his headset, but I could hear laughter and the scraping of chairs coming in faintly over the com. Both of them were easily ten years older than me, but sometimes they were just like kids, and I loved them for it. Around Paris HQ, they were often lumped together and called simply "the boys," and the nickname was fitting despite their mega skills when it came to surveillance and information gathering. We'd all been transferred together from New York, and though I would never tell them to their faces, I felt incredibly lucky that we got to be a team.

I tuned them out and focused on my surroundings. I had just descended one hundred and twelve steps in beautiful and extremely hilly Montmartre to reach the entrance to the metro. Going down was never as bad as going up. Once I slid my card through the turnstile, I'd have to take another hundred steps down to reach my platform. Needless to say, it was dark and dingy, and I'd never get used to the faint smell of rotten eggs, but places like this were perfect for spy work, with lots of people moving quickly in and out. The only good thing was that it was a bit cooler down here. Paris in June was already hot and muggy.

"Now, now, children," scolded a female voice—that would be Rosabella, the team leader, with her gentle Italian accent. "Don't distract Agent Hadden. Put your headset back on, and keep an eye on Dufor." I knew she must be sitting rigid in her chair, staring intently at the monitor, her espresso hair shimmering in the light. Even though we'd only known her for four months now, it seemed we'd always worked together.

"I've got an eye on Dufor," Halluis grumbled, his voice growing louder as he placed the headset back on. "Agent Hanson said Dufor's on the train, and his tracker is live. He's not going anywhere other than where we want him."

Rosabella turned her attention to me. "Christy, I see you are at the station with time to spare. Good job. This is all in your hands now. You've got this. You're the best."

I nodded imperceptibly, knowing she couldn't see me, but acknowledging the compliment anyway. This was my first mission without Jeremy as my handler, and it made me slightly nervous knowing he wasn't there watching me, that I was under the scrutiny of a completely new team leader. Just a few days after we'd all arrived in Paris, Jeremy had been called away to complete a mission for an agent who'd been killed. It felt so strange to be without him, and even worse not knowing where he was. His mission was completely dark—no communication in or out. All I could do was hope and pray every day that he was all right. In the meantime, it felt good to know I had Rosabella's confidence.

"Now, listen, Metro Spy Barbie," Halluis started in again, his French coming across in a sardonic drawl. "Remember to approach slowly. Don't spook the informant. This man is incredibly paranoid—"

"Well, wouldn't you be if you worked for the most dangerous company in Europe, and you were about to spill their secrets?" Ace laughed, but I could hear the tension in his voice. He was nervous. Were his nerves for me, or our informant?

3

"Here comes the train, Christy," Halluis spoke in my ear. There was no trace of his former playfulness; he had his game face on. Despite all the mockery, I knew I could count on him for anything. "If Dufor is where he is meant to be, he should be on the fourth car."

My heart sped up as the train approached. Henri Dufor, our informant, was taking on a huge risk. As Ace had said, he worked for the most dangerous company in Europe, Sécurité Un. To the average civilian, Sécurité Un appeared to be just an Internet privacy firm, benignly protecting passwords and other mundane aspects of online life. But Division 57 had discovered that their real service was protecting secrets, especially dangerous ones. They were hired by the world's most nefarious groups to keep things hidden. And they had never once had a breach of security. If anyone knew what Dufor was about to do, his life would be forfeit.

That's why he'd been extraordinarily cautious about setting up this drop. He had contacted us just yesterday to say he had something important for us. He couldn't explain it over the phone—he was too afraid someone might be listening in—but it involved some incriminating evidence against a high public official. Not your run-of-the-mill affair or campaign bribes, he'd assured us—but something that needed our immediate attention. Something that involved the safety and security of all of France. He'd agreed to copy the encoded information to a flash drive and deliver it to an agent. But he insisted he couldn't do anything out of his ordinary routine, or his superiors would suspect him. Rosabella had made the arrangements for the drop to go down along his normal route home after work the next day.

Today.

I knew Rosabella wished she could be the one to make the drop—but she was no longer a field agent. She didn't like to talk about why, but I gathered that something traumatic had happened, and she had never recovered. She was a good agent, though, so she stayed on in HQ, running the operations.

I was good with disguises and excellent at sleight of hand, so I'd been chosen to complete the mission. I silently promised I would execute the job perfectly, not just for the fate of the world, as Halluis had put it, but for Rosabella.

For today's mission I would be Gabrielle, a young intern working for a fashion designer. With my billowing silk blouse, a sweet pink double breasted trench coat with flap pockets, and expertly tied scarf, I blended in perfectly with the Parisian business people in the train station. Yet, the tools of my true trade were close at hand. A knife fit nicely into my soft leather, three-inch heeled boots, and my light and airy, just-above-the-knee skirt easily hid the little .380 pistol strapped to my upper thigh. I hated wearing the long, brown wig, but it was all part of the game.

The job was simple—identify Dufor, retrieve the drive, then stick with him until he left the train. Two other field agents would tail him after that, ensuring his safety, but while he was on the train, he was my responsibility.

As the train pulled into the station, I counted the cars. I located the fourth one and subtly put myself in position to board there when the doors opened. I drummed my fingers on my leather satchel, hiding my own anxiety in my alias—a tired French intern, eager to board the train and get home. Finally the train stopped and the doors hissed open. I stepped lightly onboard, my heels making a sharp clack on the floor. I found a seat in the center of the car, a good position to assess the area for threats and locate my informant.

"Good girl, Christy. You're right on top of him," Rosabella whispered. I could hear the tightness in her voice. We were so close.

Keeping my face impassive, I carefully scanned the crowded car for the asset. I panicked slightly as my eyes flitted from face to face, not seeing him through the crowds of people. I only had two stops to locate him and make the pick-up. Dufor was exceptionally distrustful—understandable considering his line of business—and he'd only agreed to make the drop on the train. He felt that as long as he was moving, there was less chance of him being caught. If he got off the train with the drive still in his possession, he'd made it clear that the drop was finished for good. It had to go well. There wouldn't be a second try. I fought to keep my breathing calm as my search continued fruitless.

There. Finally. He was standing next to the car's other door, holding onto what I'd affectionately named the pickpocket pole. Seriously, most people would lose at least one thing standing at that pole as people jostled about with the train's arrivals and departures. Paris was a pickpocket's paradise. Even the Louvre was full of signs warning people of the threat. But I didn't think anywhere was as risky as the poles on the trains. Dufor, however, was a security man; I was sure he was aware of the risk. I spotted the signal right away. He was supposed to be wearing a gold tie pin in the shape of a tiger if he believed all was well on his end. I inwardly nodded my approval. For a civilian about to do a drop, he looked completely calm and collected. Then like a hunted bird that can't be patient long enough for the hunter to pass by and flaps his wings, rising to the sky, only to be shot down, Dufor patted the pocket that was supposed to hold the drive. His eyes darted about and his breathing sped up.

I pulled my bag onto my shoulder, making sure the pockets faced out and were easily accessible to me, then stood and made my way over to the door. To any casual observer, it would look like I was simply anticipating the train's arrival at the next stop and getting ready to disembark.

I came to a stop right next to Dufor, pushed my way between two others and gripped the pole above him.

"Excusez-moi, Monsieur," I said in perfect French. "Quelle heure est-il?" *Excuse me, sir. Do you have the time?* It was our code phrase. If he didn't have the drive, he'd look at his watch and give the time, and the drop would be aborted. It was the last chance for him to back out.

I held my breath.

Dufor glanced at me and pursed his lips. "Ma montre est cassée." *My watch is broken.* He'd completed the code perfectly—he not only had the drive, but he felt secure in passing it along.

I sighed in feigned disappointment, then shrugged and turned toward the door.

The train began to slow, and I steeled myself for the quick sleight of hand I was about to employ. The train lurched to a stop, and I allowed myself to be thrown slightly into Dufor. My left hand came up to his chest, disguised as an effort to steady myself, and while I was profusely apologizing, I slipped it stealthily into his right breast pocket and, quick as lighting, palmed the drive and something else—a thick piece of paper.

I flushed and pulled away from Dufor, playing an embarrassed young professional who'd been caught off guard. I patted my hair and rearranged my bag over my left shoulder, dropping the drive surreptitiously into the outer pocket and switching the paper into my other hand. Dufor frowned slightly and took a step away, to the other side of the pole. He played his part well. He looked like any other grumpy Frenchman, irritated at the disruption of his daily routine. In truth, from all I'd learned about him, he was a really nice guy.

The doors hissed open, and I turned my attention to the flood of people about to board the train, scanning faces for anything that looked suspicious. I saw nothing to worry about and relaxed slightly as I waited for the doors to close. This was a textbook mission. At the next stop, Dufor would get off, remaining under the care of Division until he got home, and I'd ride two more stops before disembarking and heading for headquarters. I could just imagine the excitement Rosabella must be feeling right now. A mission well planned and perfectly executed. I took a moment and glanced at the small piece of paper in my hand that I'd taken from Dufor's pocket along with the flash drive. It was a ticket stub for l'Orangerie museum. I tucked it into my jacket pocket. Just one more stop.

Suddenly, I felt a wrench at my side and an abrupt emptiness where my satchel should be. I gasped. The drive! It took me only a split-second to identify the thief—a young boy running swiftly away from the train, through the crowds and up the stairs, my satchel slung around his neck. His black jacket had an embroidered yellow sun on the back. I didn't have time to think—the doors were already closing. I glanced at Dufor and quickly scanned the people on the train once more. No threats. Dufor's eyes were wide with fright, but I couldn't focus on that. That drive could save millions. I could not lose it, and Dufor would be safe until he reached the next stop. I dove off the train, barely squeezing through the closing doors, and ran after the boy.

I pushed my way up the stairs, cursing my choice to wear three-inch heeled boots on this mission. It was a good thing that I had some nice thick stockings underneath. I pulled out the sheathed knife I had stashed in there, sliding it into my front waistband, just under my silk shirt. I kicked the boots off as I climbed, hoping someone who could really use the lovely things would find them. Ace and Halluis talked over each other, hurling agitated questions at me over the earpiece. I didn't have the concentration to spare to decipher their words, so I just gave my report through gritted teeth. "Pursuing thief out of the metro. Dufor safe on train, but solo. Requesting backup at Gare du Nord." Once up the stairs, I ran at top speed out of the metro tunnel onto rue de Dunkerque.

I spotted the boy only a few streets ahead of me, the yellow sun on his jacket standing out like a beacon. He was walking now, believing he had gotten away. The bag, now in his hand, swung at his side. I took off after him, people gawking as I passed. Only one more street and I'd have him. I wove my way through the crowds of tourists and only had half a street to catch up to him, when he looked back and spotted me.

He gave me a snide, taunting look before hauling off running. He slipped my bag back over his neck. That rotten kid really thought he was going to get away with it. That wasn't going to happen. A desperate ache spread through my gut as I thought of the team and how I'd made a mess of everything. I took a sharp breath in and squelched it. This was no time to wallow in self-pity.

My pulse pounded in my ears, making it hard to understand the voices raging on the earpiece, but the panicked tone came through loud and clear. I made out that Dufor's train had arrived at his stop. Over it all, I could hear the frustrated voice of Rosabella, and heat seared through my heart. I was letting her down.

I called out, "Two minutes. I'll have the drive back in two minutes." *Please let me get the drive. Please.* And then there was silence. I pushed on my com as I ran, my eyes focused on that jacket. Nothing. No sound. It was just as well, I had other things to occupy my brain and body right now.

The thief was fast. I had to give him that. But thanks to rigorous physical training, I was faster. I closed the distance between us with a burst of speed. Only a bit further. I reached out and caught a fistful of his jacket, but he simply shrugged it off and ducked behind a corner. I let the jacket fall to the ground and turned the corner after him. The alley's narrow walkway was packed with people. I looked around, frantic, running down the walkway, bumping into people as I went, searching for him and any doors or windows he could have entered. As I made it to the end, it was obvious there were none, only solid stucco walls on both sides of me. He was gone.

I rubbed my hands roughly over my face and shook my head. This was not good. My chest squeezed with what this would mean. My mind scrambled for solutions—I needed to find that thief. I gritted my teeth and fought back a groan. I'd had him—his jacket had been in my hands, that yellow sun taunted my memory.

There was nothing for it. The drive was long gone by now. I needed to get back to headquarters and start brainstorming with my team how we were going to get that information. We'd just have to convince Dufor to recopy it. I knew he'd be reluctant, but perhaps he could be persuaded. I took a deep breath, fighting back the wave of nausea and despair that threatened to crash over me. Dufor would have to help us. He was our only hope now. I ran back the way I'd come, bumping through the crowds to the metro, people calling out about my lack of footwear. C'est dégoutant, ça!

As I gasped for air, waiting on the platform for the train to arrive, Ace's voice sounded in my ear once again. "Christy. Christy. Do you read? Report to headquarters immediately." His voice was loud and clear. "Dufor is dead."

2

I called Ace as soon as I exited the metro and found a quiet spot.

"What happened, Ace? Tell me it's not true. He can't be dead." Heat seared my heart, and I gripped the back of a bench to steady myself.

"Someone stabbed him three times before shoving him off the train at his exit." His Canadian French was so distinctly different from what I'd learned during my three-month intensive training, I had to focus to catch every word.

I gasped. "This is all my fault. I never should have left him." I stood still, my hand grasping the bench tightly.

There was a slight pause. "You had to get the drive, Christy. Dufor knew the risk."

I tilted my head to the sky and closed my burning eyes to prevent the tears. "I didn't get it, Ace. The thief—he just disappeared."

For a moment, there was nothing but stunned silence. Then Ace said, "Come in, Christy. We'll figure this out." His voice was firm, but lacked its usual confidence when giving instruction.

"Okay." It was almost a whisper as I stood.

"Are you okay?"

I didn't answer.

"We're meeting in the conference room. It's all going to be okay. Don't worry."

"I'll be there soon." My head hung down as I walked toward the building that housed Division.

I walked to headquarters, barely registering my surroundings. My chest felt tight, and guilt ate at me. Dufor had been my responsibility, and he'd been killed on my watch. I kept seeing his face—the look of utter dismay right before I'd left him on the train. The decision to go after the drive played over and over in my mind and for a terrible second, I thought about running away so I wouldn't have to face my team. I trudged up the stairs. I was a failure in the worst way, and someone had died because of my error. I wiped my hands on my skirt before grabbing the door handle and entering the building. I wished I could talk to Jeremy.

After taking the stairs to the basement, I pulled open the first door on the left, marked Médecine Gaston. To a civilian, it appeared to be the entrance to a doctor's office, complete with receptionist, chairs, magazines, and crappy music playing. I looked up in hopes of clearing the tears that welled up in my eyes. I shook my head and glanced at the placard next to the door for a fraction of a second, allowing the hidden retinal scanner to scan my eye. The lock on the door slid open silently.

The door handle scanned my fingerprint and sent my identification to the receptionist's computer. Once the computer confirmed I was a valid agent, she buzzed me through to the scanner room. The full body scanner was the last defense against anyone trying to forge an agent's identity. I took deep breaths, trying to stop the shivers that threatened to overpower me. Once I was verified, a door unlocked, allowing me access to the enormous underground space Division claimed. Without a word, and angling my body away from anyone who came near, I made my way into the conference room. As I passed them, Halluis, Ace, and Rosabella rose silently from their desks and followed behind me.

As they filed into the room, a deep ache spread through my chest. I forced myself to look at them. Rosabella looked sick, a green tinge to her face and sweat beading on her forehead. Her normally bright blue eyes looked dull. Even her curly, brown hair hung limp, like she'd torn at it over and over in frustration and anxiety. Ace and Halluis were quiet and subdued, which was odd for Ace. I didn't think anything could get him down. Despite the ashen color that marred both their faces, they pulled out smiles for me. Ace tugged me into a quick side hug, a piece of his boyish, caring self bleeding through the stress. The new tattoo on his forearm caught my eye. The bright green color of the snake wrapping around the brown dagger was hard to miss. An angry, thin line of red surrounding the art was the only indication he'd received it recently. His earthy, sweet smell comforted me, but only for a minute. Anger welled up inside me. Anger at the boy who'd taken the drive and anger at the people who'd dared to kill Dufor. As I pulled back, Ace handed me a sucker from his pocket. He was the candy man after all.

I knew it wouldn't be long before Siron showed up. I had to apologize. "Look guys, I'm sorry. It was all my fault, and I'll make sure Siron understands that."

All eyes darted toward me. Ace's were soft and kind. Halluis's nervous and worried, mirroring his all black attire.

"I cleared the train. At least I thought I did." My frantic search through the train car played once again in my mind. "I didn't see a threat. And I knew Agent Heiner and Agent

Kawalski would have Dufor the second he arrived at the next stop. I thought he was safe. Obviously, I was wrong. I missed someone." I brushed at the tear that streamed down my face. How had I missed someone? Rosabella moved toward me.

"Oh, Christy, it could've happened to any of us." She clasped my upper arms, her soft hands cold, mirroring her cool blue manicure.

"No. No. It wouldn't have. I let my guard down. I was sloppy. And Rosabella, this was your op and so perfectly planned." Why was she being nice to me?

"It's not like you ignored protocol, Christy," Halluis said as he raised one dark eyebrow. "You had a difficult decision to make. You believed Dufor was safe. You double-checked. Only then did you go after the drive." His hand rubbed over his pencil thin mustache. It was hard for him to be kind after such a terrible blunder.

Ace said, "I know it can be tough out there, Christy, that's why I try to stay inside at all costs." He pushed his sleeves all the way up until they sat just above his elbows.

Rosabella interrupted, "But I think you should be prepared for Siron. She is hard as nails." She rubbed her hands down her tight fitting skirt.

I nodded, refusing to let another tear fall. "Thanks for trying to make me feel better, guys, but this...this was big."

"Come on, Rosabella," Ace said. "Siron was an agent once. She knows what it can be like." I wondered if Rosabella had botched a mission and that was why she stayed inside, too.

"But has she ever gotten someone killed?" I said. "Whatever happens to me, whatever punishment she gives me, I totally deserve it."

Ace straightened as Siron—the director of Division 57's

Paris chapter—entered the room and shut the door behind her. Her tall, lean frame set us in a flurry of motion to sit, though she remained standing, rigid. Her stony look gave nothing away. As always, she wore a perfectly tailored suit coat that leant her a look of importance. Her two inch heels barely poked out of the bottom of her dress pants.

Panic filled me, my heart racing like that of a scared rabbit. I forced my eyes to hers.

"I need a full accounting of what happened, Agent Hadden." There was no sympathy in her voice, only command. Rosabella had been right. It was surprising that at Siron's age— she had to be at least fifty—she only had a hint of crow's feet around her dark eyes.

I told her everything and took full and total responsibility.

One of her perfectly shaped eyebrows started to twitch when I admitted that I'd been unable to retrieve the drive after leaving Dufor. At my last word, she closed her eyes and took a deep breath in through her nose.

"You have been nothing but a disappointment, Agent Hadden," she said, her voice quiet and her gaze piercing. "When I received your file, I thought, this is too good to be true. Accelerated through training school, phenomenal test scores, astounding affinity for memorization and learning, fluent in seven languages, with comprehension skills in another ten! And so young—not even out of your teens." Her full lips curled in disdain. "So disappointing. I should have known that your talents on paper wouldn't translate to excellence in the field."

I opened my mouth to protest, but nothing came out— memories of everything that had gone wrong on my missions flashed through my mind. It was true that none of them had ever gone perfectly.

Siron's mouth twitched, and I suspected she was suppressing a smirk. She seemed almost pleased to have this chance to deride me in front my team. I didn't dare look at any of them for fear I'd see agreement on their faces.

"Your handler—Agent McGinnis, I believe—spoke particularly highly of you. He said you were exceptionally skilled at improvisation. So, let's hear it. What is your brilliant plan to redeem yourself and salvage what is left of this mission?"

I could tell by her tone and the scornful look in her eye that she didn't really expect an answer. She was expecting me to have nothing to say, and my humiliation would be complete.

But I did have a plan. When I'd learned Dufor was dead, that we had no hope of getting the information from him, my mind had immediately begun formulating.

I swallowed and mustered the courage to speak. "I saw the pickpocket's face. I can go undercover, find the thief and his gang, and retrieve the drive."

Her lip curled, and her small nose wrinkled.

"Ridiculous. To search for one pickpocket in a sea of thousands could take weeks. We do not have weeks."

"Respectfully, Director, it wouldn't take me weeks."

"Ah, I see you still think so highly of yourself, despite the utter lack of evidence," she waved a hand dismissively. "No, it's impossible. Even if you were as talented as your file claims, it couldn't be done. Find one pickpocket in the middle of Paris? If that was the extent of your plan," she spit the word at me like poison, "I am even more disgusted than before. If you had stuck with Dufor and protected him, he could have made another copy. Now we have no informant and no way of retrieving the information."

I chafed inwardly at her words, but kept my face passive. "Director, I know I made a mistake today, but—"

"A mistake?" Her voice was acid. "A man is dead, Agent Hadden. Where I come from, we do not have tolerance for such a *mistake.*"

The room was silent for a moment, Director Siron's recriminations ringing in the air.

Halluis cleared his throat. "If we don't go after the pickpocket, what hope do we have of retrieving the information? Dufor indicated that what he knew could have serious repercussions for Paris, for all of France. We have to get a hold of that drive."

I shot him a quick look of gratitude. He hadn't exactly challenged Siron outright, but his words did lend some support to my plan, and for that I was grateful.

But Siron only shook her head, her stylish brown hair sweeping her shoulders. "The drive is gone. Perhaps in the hands of Dufor's killers, but most likely tossed into the trash by a disappointed pickpocket. Our only hope of completing this mission now is to root out the original source of the information."

"You mean—infiltrate Sécurité Un?" I asked in disbelief. It had always been deemed too risky to break into the company itself. The place was a fortress.

"We need this information as soon as possible, and this is the quickest way," Director Siron said. "This happens tonight. I want the mission plans on my desk within the hour." She turned to go, then turned back and locked eyes with me. "Agent Hadden, I expect you will apply your *remarkable intellect* to the task. This is your chance—the only one you will get—to redeem yourself. While there is no way to bring Dufor back to life, you can at least give meaning to his death by retrieving the information he gave his life for. Our best course of action now is to find out what Dufor knew—and to do that we have to get into Sécurité Un. I will tolerate no more mistakes. I need perfection here."

She turned to Rosabella. "And Agent Cantu, don't underestimate Sécurité Un. Keep in mind that they found Dufor and killed him and quite possibly sent that pickpocket to retrieve the flash drive Dufor intended to give us. We have to assume they were privy to our plans and thwarted them."

"Yes, Director."

Siron left the room, saying, "Plans. On my desk in one hour."

"Getting inside Sécurité Un is no easy task." Ace's grim face turned a shade darker, more like his original color. He immediately started typing something on the keyboard in front of him, and the schematics of the target building appeared on the screen on the wall at the end of the table.

Halluis, on the other hand, looked a bit excited. "Their security is tight, Ace. I don't know that we can crack it."

The two of them started tossing out ideas, arguing back and forth about different entry strategies, but I couldn't get my mind to focus. I fought back waves of nausea as Siron's words repeated over and over in my mind. I'd ruined everything; Dufor was dead because of me; I was a complete and utter failure. Yet, underneath all the vicious self-recrimination, another thought was fighting its way to the surface.

Siron was wrong.

Trying to break into Sécurité Un was not only dangerous, but likely to prove futile. We had no idea where Dufor would have kept the information—or even exactly what information

19

he'd planned to give us. It was like hunting for a needle in a haystack, but without even knowing which haystack to search. On top of that, I couldn't shake the idea that Siron was wrong about the drive—she was working on the assumption that the pickpocket was either working for Sécurité Un or that he wouldn't know the significance of the drive he'd stolen.

It didn't make much sense for Sécurité Un to send both a thief and a killer, when just one could do the job. I was reasonably sure the kid was acting independently, and he'd had no idea what he was getting in the middle of. But I'd seen the look in his eye—he was clever, and he probably worked for someone smarter still. They wouldn't just toss away something that could be valuable. That information could easily make its way into the wrong hands. I glanced over at Siron; the door to her office was open, and she was sifting through paperwork at her desk. I thought about going over to her, trying again to make my case, but the futility of it struck me like a blow. She'd made her disdain for me and my ideas very clear.

I wanted to make things better, but how could I if the director thought I was useless? And she was right. Dufor was dead because of my mistake. We wouldn't ever know what information Dufor wanted us to have and there was no way to retrieve the information either. He had truly died for nothing.

But then again, Dufor had found the courage to seek Division out and ask for help despite his fear. If I gave up, it would be letting him down all over again. He risked his life to stop something terrible and I wasn't about to let that go to waste.

My team talked, but I didn't hear. They wrote plans on the whiteboard, but I was lost in thought. I curled my fists and set my jaw. Yes. I'd messed up, but I was not going to let this mission fail. I couldn't. Someone had been willing to kill to keep this information secret. There was no way I was going to let them win. But what could be done? A solution presented itself and I didn't like it one bit. I had to at least suggest it. If there was a problem with the plan, my team would find it. I stood up straight, took a deep breath, and thought to myself, *I can't change what happened, but I can influence the future.*

I cleared my throat, then said, "I think I know how we can do this."

Rosabella shifted in her seat. Ace leaned his head to the side, and Halluis stared at me, lips pressed tight.

"The only sure way in is through the vents. I know we very briefly talked about it before we started this mission, but just hear me out." I pointed to the schematics on the screen. I could see the questions forming in their minds. "Halluis will need to shut down the laser security running through them, and Ace will need to create something to disrupt the cameras that will hide me—er—whoever goes in. And whoever it is will have to be fast. We can't have the alarm systems down for long, or it will be noticed." They were all staring at me. I hoped they were analyzing what I'd said and realizing it was the only way.

"It is the only way we could circumvent the tricky alarm system," Halluis spoke up. "With the guards, the optical scanners, coded entry, and all that, there is no way through the main doors. This solves all those problems. Lasers I can take care of." There was renewed hope in his eyes.

"I have just the right thing for redirecting the cameras and security," Ace added. "And I know just the right *little girl* to get in that ductwork." He gave me a sly smile.

Rosabella raised an eyebrow. "And you know I'm the best leader around, even if forced to direct a troublemaker like

21

Christy." A smile played at the corner of her lips. "It's got to be you, Christy. I can't think of anyone else at Paris Division small enough to fit into those vents, and it would take too long to get someone else here who would fit. Will you be able to control that claustrophobia of yours?"

They turned to each other and Ace continued, talking as if I wasn't even there. "And Siron did say she wanted this done tonight."

Their eyes found me again.

A grin spread across my face. Smiles filled the room, and Halluis even chuckled.

Tiny flutters filled my chest. They were taking a great risk on me, and right after I'd totally botched the mission. I looked at my feet. "I think I can. I have to. And thanks, guys. Seriously. I won't let you down." My eyes flicked back up, and they all moved to pat me on the back and give encouraging words.

"We all mess up some times."

"No one's perfect."

"It wasn't totally your fault."

"I'd have probably done the same thing you did."

I didn't agree. It was my fault. And Siron had been right. Had I only stayed with Dufor, I could have protected him, and he could have made a new drive. It had been foolish to go after the drive and leave him unprotected. A terrible thought entered my mind. What if I had stayed with Dufor and hadn't been able to stop the murder? Which outcome would have been worse?

The mission plans made it to Siron's desk in under forty-five minutes.

3

Recorded satellite imaging of the building over the last week showed the guards doing somewhat random walkthroughs at quarter-hour intervals. Unfortunately, start times varied and they began their rounds at one of three times: a quarter past, half past, or a quarter to. It was smart to have such quasi-random security sweeps. I'd just have to be aware of the times the guards *could* come and get out fast. The real restraint was the laser security in the ducting. Halluis had been unable to find a way to override the system for longer than twenty minutes.

I donned a black cat suit compliments of Ace, enjoying the soft, elastic feel of the fabric on my skin and especially on my feet. The grip on the footies would help me climb down the two vertical portions of ducting I needed to get through.

"The suit will act as the jammer we need to hijack the cameras and put in our looped feed," Ace explained. I could tell by the slightly higher pitch to his voice that the excitement of me using the suit for the first time was making Ace a bit giddy.

"Can't wait to see your baby in action, eh, Ace? If this works, I'll have to take you to a café, and we can drink eight-euro sodas together."

"I'm going to have to take you up on that. Maybe then the mystery of it will dissipate, and you won't feel the need to mock the cafés of Paris."

"It's highway robbery, seriously."

"It's the ambience you're paying for, my dear. Not a meager soda." Halluis spoke in his native French language, and it sounded beautiful.

I crouched on the roof just to the side of the vent I was supposed to enter, waiting for word that the coast was clear. "Ah, I get it. You mean—"

"No heat signatures on any level above the third floor," Ace said, interrupting us over the com. "Lasers down. Mark the time." His voice was clear and confident; he had switched into mission mode.

I put the countdown on my watch. "Going in." I lowered myself into the ventilation system, using my grippy footies, just as we'd planned. I'd be cut off from all communication until I was in Dufor's office, which shouldn't take me more than five minutes.

I hated ventilation ducting. I'd had to crawl through a couple of different systems while in D.C. plus another in South Dakota, because I was the smallest and most likely to fit. It's not like there was training for that. I had to find my happy place and pretend I was in an open field of flowers the entire time I was in them or terror would crush the breath out of me from the inside out.

It was good they didn't have sound alarms, because I banged my way through the venting as fast as I could. Speed was more important than stealth right now, and I bonked my head three times trying to navigate one particularly tricky turn. Since there were no heat signatures of others within three floors of me, no one would hear. The patrols weren't scheduled to walk through the building for at least another fifteen minutes.

Once above Dufor's office, I unscrewed the vent cover and dropped to his desk using a rope coated in the same fabric I had on. Had Ace's new jamming technology not worked, the fabric would have at least made both the rope and me invisible to the cameras.

"I'm in." I leaned back and took several deep breaths.

"Right on time. Ten minutes and counting." Rosabella's sure voice encouraged me.

"Camera's masked. Feel free to move about the room in that awesome suit that just earned me an eight-euro soda in a Paris café."

It did bother me somewhat that they could see everything I did. For most people, it would be a comfort, but I didn't like the sensation of being watched. I tried to focus on the idea that they might see something I missed. I'd find Dufor's laptop or possibly a drive with a copy of the information he'd planned on giving to us as fast as I could and get the heck out.

Dufor's desk was clear of any clutter, and everything seemed to be in its proper place. In and out boxes, two books with bookends, and a small, shallow bowl with a lighter in it. No laptop. I pulled open the drawers and discovered the same complete and total order in the interior. Everything had its spot. Not a smidgen of dust was present anywhere.

Replicas of three Matisse paintings hung on the walls along with a thermostat and a few shelves with statues and other pieces of art from various countries. Dufor obviously appreciated art and seemed to collect various pieces as he traveled. I carefully, but quickly, searched every inch of wall space and the objects on or near it. Nothing.

"He didn't seem like a Matisse kind of guy," Rosabella said, obviously watching my progress along with the others. Getting into the building had been so easy, but nothing was ever this easy. No wonder I'd found nothing.

"Two heat signatures heading your way." Ace's voice was soft in the com, almost like he thought if he spoke louder the people approaching would overhear. I checked under the rug and two soft chairs across from the desk before voices filtered into the office from the hall. My watch told me it was one of the three possible times for the regular security sweep. I flipped off the flashlight. I had to hold still until they passed, wasting precious time.

Once the guards were past me, I flipped the flashlight back on and resumed the search. Not a single dust bunny floated in the corners of the room or under the chairs or desk. Dufor had been meticulous. I moved back to the desk. Not a piece of paper out of place. Seeing his things and the care he took to keep his space clean and organized made me see him even more clearly and mourn his loss. He'd been a good man. He'd risked everything in an effort to help his country, and I had to love him for that.

I looked in the trash, expecting to find nothing, but instead noticed a black residue on the bottom and sides of the can. I ran a gloved finger over it and then smelled it.

"Uh, C'est dégoutant, ça!" Halluis said. He was grossed out by stuff like that. It didn't bother me if I was on a mission.

I took some tape from Dufor's drawer and got a sample of the black stuff. I looked back at the desk, taking note of the lighter in the shallow dish. I examined it closer and thought I found traces of that same black residue on its plastic carapace. I snagged another piece of tape for a sample and then put both samples into an interior pocket of my suit. "The pockets were a nice touch, Ace..."

"I thought you might find a use for them," he replied.

"Think Dufor is a pyro?" I asked into the air, glancing again at the Matisses. They were the only things that spoke "uncontrolled" to me. No one replied, and I scanned the room again. "Can you think of anything that I've missed?" I hoped my team could see something.

Noes rang out in my earpiece.

"Please tell me I didn't get in the ducts for nothing."

Silence greeted me.

"In two minutes you'll need to get back in them. Sorry." Rosabella truly sounded apologetic.

Feeling a bit depressed by my inability to find what we needed, I sat in Dufor's chair and leaned back, knowing I needed to hurry.

If I were Dufor, would I record anything about the criminals? And if I did, where would I record it? I opened the thin drawer at my waist and pulled out a pen, channeling my inner Dufor. I opened the right side drawer and pulled out the top pad of paper. As I lifted it, my flashlight revealed indentations, lines on the paper, even though the paper had no ink or lead on it. My heart pounded in anticipation. I glanced at the ash tray and back to the pad of paper.

"Uh, we have bodies coming your way. They just exited the elevator." Ace sounded agitated.

I threw the pad of paper onto the desk and clicked off the flashlight. My spidey senses woke up and started bugging me. This was not a regular security check. I held my breath.

They stopped outside the door, and I was in motion in a flash. "Scramming," I said in a breathy whisper as I stood on the chair.

I turned from the cameras, unzipped the bodysuit, pressed

the notepad against my chest and re-zipped the bodysuit as I stepped onto the desk in one fluid motion. I began pulling myself up the rope just as the green indicator light next to the door lit up. They'd swiped the keycard. I gripped the rope more tightly and took two hard pulls. It would take me one more to climb into the vent. Good thing they had double lock entry into all the rooms in the building. Not only did you need to swipe a card, you also had to use a physical key. Even with that, I doubted I'd make it out.

Ace's voice rang over the com, "Hurry, girl. That suit won't hide you from real people eyes."

I flipped my leg over the ledge of the vent opening and yanked myself inside with a quiet grunt. I was now cut off from my team. I gathered up the rope in a flash just as two people entered the room and switched on the light. There was no chance to put the cover on the vent. I kept my breathing shallow, not allowing my lungs to get the massive amounts of air they needed at the moment. Instead, I peered through the hole to see who had come into the room.

The first was dressed in the clothes that identified him as a Sécurité Un guard. His powerful muscles pushed on the uniform, threatening to burst through. The other was also large, but in jeans and a T-shirt, his face unshaven. I pressed myself against the metal and focused on breathing shallow breaths, hoping beyond hope that they wouldn't look up. I was about to slide away when their words froze me to the spot.

"...wasn't on him?" a deep male voice said. I imagined it must have been the man with the scruff. Was he talking about the drive?

"I'm sure," a voice that sounded much younger said. It must have been the guard, though the voices didn't match either man's physique. "The boy said nothing was on Dufor."

"And there had been no contact with anyone before your man got to him?"

"He followed him on the train, but there was nothing, no one. We're sure no exchange was made before we disposed of him."

So, his company had put a hit out on him. They knew he was going to betray them.

"And you're sure the medical examiner found nothing on him either?" They had an in with the medical examiner, too?

I only had four minutes. I heard shuffling noises as they moved about the room looking for something.

"Yes. And this guy wasn't the type to put the drive anywhere not sterile. I mean look at his office. Does this look like the office of a guy who'd put a drive in his underwear?"

I expected to hear a chuckle, but nothing. They definitely knew about the drive. What would have happened had I stayed on the train? Could I even have saved Dufor? I hadn't sensed any danger. Had I become soft during all those months doing deskwork for Siron? Three and a half minutes.

"It has to be here then."

"Tear this place apart until you find it."

And the guy did. He threw the fake Matisses to the ground. He pulled the desk drawers out and dropped all the contents to the floor as he went through them. As he lifted the rug, a flash from my watch warned me that in two minutes the lasers would go live again, and I would be a sitting duck. Not to mention the two men would inevitably look up and notice the giant hole in the ceiling.

I didn't bother putting the cover on the vent. I didn't have the time. I moved as quickly and quietly as I could through the ducts, keeping my body off the venting, only allowing my elbows, thighs and toes to contact the metal in a flurry of motion. Something crashed in the room below me and I took the chance to push myself swiftly through the hard section of ducting, hoping the noise below covered my banging.

Just as I turned to climb up the last shaft, the alarms blared. I didn't hesitate. I rushed to the top of the vent and pulled myself out. Red lights twirled on the roof of the building, and screeching sounded all around me. I pushed on my com as I ran across the roof.

"West side extraction route. Heading for adjacent building." I would have to be super-fast not to get caught. I spoke up as I reached the edge of the roof. "I hope you're there when I get there."

I dug my fingers into the bricked exterior wall and lowered myself a few feet, using the grippy footies of the suit to help anchor me as I moved to the side and down three feet, under a foot-wide outcropping that housed something rumbling inside. I attached the same rope I'd used to lower myself into Dufor's office to some lag bolts that attached the machine to the wall. Ignoring the pain in my fingertips, I gripped the jagged bricks and wedged my toes in between them. *Now to lower myself down.*

The blaring sirens stopped, and an eerie silence settled over the area. I kept my body close to the wall, and while I moved quickly, I tried not to make any sounds. I had chosen the west side because it had no lights, which worked in my favor, considering I was in all black.

Two shafts of light blazed down the exterior wall, passing by me again and again. I kept my head down, counting on the black suit to help me blend with the dark red brick while I stayed in the shadows of the outcroppings, hoping my movements wouldn't catch their eye. A beam flitted over me. I froze and held my breath, but the light left me as soon as it had found me.

Three floors down, I waited for the lights to move far away from me. "Jumping to the neighboring roof," I said in the com.

"It's not far now." Rosabella's voice was calm and even. No wonder Division kept her on as a team leader. She had a calming influence on an out-of-control situation.

I knew my landing wouldn't be soundless, but if I could make it to the other roof, the guards wouldn't have a chance at catching me without a rope. Shooting me was another story. I would have to be down the fire escape ladder on the far north side of the building before they noticed me, or I'd be a blazing target running across the roof. I needed sort of a distraction. I glanced at the karabiner attached to my waist, and a plan formed in my mind.

A fifteen foot gap separated the building I was hanging on from the one next door. I pushed off hard, away from the building I was anchored to and over the narrow alley to the other building. I was glad the other building was only two stories high so that if I fell, I'd have a chance at surviving. It took me three swings to get enough power to fly out over that roof, but I eventually did.

As I landed with a loud thud, I released the karabiner from my waist, secured the rope around my flashlight, and swung it hard and fast back toward the building I'd just descended. The flashlight hit a window, shattering it. Just as I'd hoped, my pursuers' attention flew to the sound, and a spray of bullets pounded the area around the window.

I was already halfway across the roof when a barrage of

bullets followed me. My distraction hadn't been distracting enough. I zigged and zagged, and hoped I'd calculated the position of the fire-escape ladder correctly. I had the schematics of the building memorized, but I wasn't always able to use the dimensions of something to my benefit. Two feet to freedom, bullets rained down around me, sending rocks and debris flying all around. I had to act now or I would get shot—and this suit was not bulletproof.

I turned my body toward my attackers and jumped out feet first, off the roof, hoping I'd land on the escape ladder. I missed by a good six inches. I was in a freefall. The hard stones below would break my legs at the very least. In a last ditch effort to save myself, I swung my feet toward the rough stucco wall of the building and pushed upward in hopes of grabbing hold of the ladder. I missed and pushed again. My fingers wrapped around the cold metal of the bottom rung of the ladder.

The ladder descended with a loud series of clicks and rattles. About halfway down, I was able to put a second hand on one of the rungs. I said a quick prayer of thanks in my mind as the ladder continued to roar downward. The ladder yanked to a stop about ten feet from the ground, and I cried out in pain as my shoulders strained with the effort of holding on.

I let go, then tucked and rolled as I hit the hard asphalt, my shoulder aching and my feet stinging as I landed. Something sticky rubbed up against my cheek, but I had no time to wipe it away. I rolled into a standing position and hightailed it out of the alley only to be met by a white van. The side door slid open, and two hands pulled me inside.

4

Ace slammed on the gas as someone slid the door shut. It was Markay, a swing operative who jumped from mission to mission to fill any needs that might arise. I took a second to wipe the goo from my face with my sleeve and reached out to wipe the nastiness onto Halluis's hand before laughing out, my breaths hard and fast.

"Man, you guys really made me work for that one. Remind me next time to ask for helicopter extraction." I laughed even louder.

"You are the queen of cutting it close." Rosabella said. It surprised me a bit to hear Markay snort since he always seemed so darn serious. But it didn't last. Halluis passed me some wet wipes and wiped away the goo I'd smeared on him.

"We're supposed to be under the radar. Helicopters would never work," Markay frowned. I could tell he was nervous.

"Lighten up, Markay," Ace said over his shoulder, "the kid did good. No way would you have fit into those air ducts." He handed me a piece of mint gum and I popped it into my mouth.

"You call that good? The alarms went off! She was fired upon! We got nothing. The mission was a disaster." He shook his head and huffed.

"Things are never textbook when working with this one,"

Halluis said, swiping at my messed up hair. He stared me down, a slight smirk on his lips.

I sighed. "It's always an adventure with me, Hal, and you wouldn't have it any other way. Besides, it wasn't my fault—you guys saw those two goons that broke into Dufor's office. I couldn't make a clean getaway without alerting their attention to me. I'm sorry I triggered the alarms, but I think I got something!"

Markay looked at me sharply. "It was way too close for comfort." He shot Halluis a look of disgust.

"Hey," Ace spoke up. "It's not like I can read the hotspots' minds. I told Christy they were exiting the elevator. She's the one who chose to ignore them." He winked at me.

"And it's a good thing I did!" I shot back, blood rising to my cheeks. "Yes, they caught me, but did you guys hear what they said?"

"No, we only saw them for a few seconds before the feed went dead, and once you were in the ducting, we couldn't hear a thing."

"They were looking for the drive."

Halluis raised an eyebrow at me. "Yes, and?"

"*And* that means they don't have it." I let that sink in for a moment. "They were the ones who killed Dufor, but they didn't see the exchange—they didn't see *me*. That means the pickpocket had no idea what he was stealing, and he wasn't part of their team. We have a chance now—to get the information before they bury it forever. All we have to do is convince Siron to let us go after the pickpocket."

"Easier said than done," Halluis said, his pencil-thin mustache twitching as he scowled.

"It's the only way, and you know it. These guys are

desperate—they tore Dufor's office to shreds searching for that drive. You think they're just going to stop? They're going to find out what happened to it, and then *they'll* go after the pickpocket. We have to find him before they do."

We sat in silence for a moment.

"You said you found something?" Ace asked, finally.

I pulled the pad of paper out of my bodysuit after unzipping it. "Maybe." I tapped the paper. "I hope so." I truly hoped it was worth alerting the bad guys to our presence. "Does anyone have a pencil?"

Halluis fished around in his pockets and pulled out a stubby yellow pencil. He grinned.

"You're just like a boy scout!"

His grin faded, "A what? Excuse me?"

I laughed and turned to the pad of paper in my lap. I gently rubbed the pencil over the page, hoping my hunch was correct. As I scribbled, the barely noticeable indentations became swirls, boxes, letters and then words. Dufor was definitely a doodler. I smiled, thinking it comical that a man so rigid, formal, and precise could be a doodler, until the words spread all over the page grabbed my attention: *Liberté, égalité, fraternité* – the national motto of France: liberty, equality, fraternity. Each word had been crossed through with an angry slash. Vertically along the side of the paper Dufor had scrawled, "Poverty is the mother of crime, and he is the father." In one corner, he'd drawn a man with a dagger in his back. In the opposite corner, he'd written, "I am a dead man if they catch me." There was a circle around this statement and under the circle, the phrase "So what?" was written three times. Ice seemed to chill my veins. The name Henri appeared in several places on the paper, sometimes by itself, but sometimes as part of other phrases—"For Henri, I must," "Henri deserved better," and "Henri, I will not let him."

I frowned. Henri was Dufor's first name—was the man a bit loony? Why was he referring to himself in the third person? What did it mean?

The largest phrase on the paper, the one that stood out the best, as though Dufor had gone over it several times, read, "This cannot go on."

I held the page out for Halluis and Markay to study. Markay's eyes darted all over it before he finally shook his head in frustration. "This makes no sense!"

"Just a moment," Halluis murmured. He stared at the page, letting his gaze settle for a minute or two on each scribble before moving on. "This here," he said, pointing to the vertical phrase about poverty. "This is a famous French quote, but altered. The original says 'lack of good sense is the father.'"

"What do you think it means?" I asked.

"I have no idea."

I bit my lip. "I think Dufor was conflicted. He was using this doodle to try to work something out."

"Hmm. He was trying to convince himself to go through with it—informing us. That may be true."

"Yes, but it still doesn't tell us anything about what he had," Markay insisted. "All this tells us is that the man was insane—and really bad at drawing." He scowled.

"Perhaps," Halluis shrugged. "I still think we ought to send it to our analysts. Maybe we are just missing something."

I shook my head before lying back, sucking hard for air and rotating my shoulders, trying to ease the ache that swelled there. I'd hoped for more, some clue that would point us in the right direction. I stared at the paper a while longer, but all it told me was that Henri Dufor had decided the risk was worth it.

This cannot go on.

***

The chill in the air at Division HQ sent an ominous shiver through me. Something was up. Instead of greeting us, like usually happened as we entered the main room, people avoided looking at us. All the screens around the room were focused on one thing, a protest at the Palais Bourbon, which housed the National Assembly of France, the lower house of government. Perhaps that was why everyone was on edge. The French people were mobilizing, and that usually meant trouble.

The information ribbon at the bottom of the screen gave a snippet of the story. The people apparently wanted to oust the President a year early for alleged corruption. It seemed the second the elections were called four years ago, and the President had put Prime Minister Alden in office, the people had been out to get him. I shook my head in disgust. Politics were nutso everywhere. It was nice to work for Division, which did not hold any allegiance to any one country. We were there to help the good guys no matter where they hailed from.

Siron walked out of her office and caught our attention. She pointed to the collaboration room, her lips pressed into a scowl. Something told me she knew how close I'd come to blowing the mission, again. I ducked my head down and hastily walked with the others toward the room.

The unease in the room spiked as Siron stood at the head of the table and we took our seats. A terrible feeling of foreboding hit me hard. I needed to speak up and fast.

"I'll be reporting on the mission, Director."

Siron scoffed. "Markay already reported." Her eyes narrowed. "Your carelessness cost us the mission. If you had managed to find something, your mistakes could have been overlooked, but that isn't what happened, is it?"

Fire crept up my neck at her persistent stare, the heat spreading over my face. "But I did find things. Sécurité Un doesn't have the drive. It was only a pickpocket that took it. I can identify—"

Siron planted her hands on her hips and shook her head, stopping me. "You have no idea who those men were, or if they even worked for the company."

"Didn't you say one wore the company's uniform?" Ace asked.

"Yes. One was in uniform." I nodded my head so fast, Siron turned to a blur.

"And can you tell me with total certainty that this man in the uniform wasn't an employee of some other company that wanted the drive?"

The thought hadn't even occurred to me. Halluis's head jerked toward me.

"You were impulsive and careless in your conclusions. And we are left to pick up the pieces. Poor Dufor. He didn't have a chance, did he?"

I still had an ace up my sleeve. I held the paper up and said, "I have this." Siron peered down at the paper like it was a bug she'd smashed. It had been stupid to bring it to her attention. No one knew what the doodle even meant.

"You have a piece of paper with some indecipherable doodles and you think it holds all the answers?" She snatched it from my hand and crushed it before throwing it into the nearest trashcan. The quiet sound of paper hitting paper filled the room. No one moved.

"You are sloppy, impulsive, and careless."

"But, Director." Ace spoke up, a vein popping in his forehead. "The pickpocket could turn out to be the lead we need."

Siron sneered. Her eyes were dilated, her posture stiff, unyielding. "Seriously, Hadden, did you hear what Renauld said? You've poisoned your entire team, making them chase a fantasy. Creating an atmosphere on your team where unprofessional and ridiculous ideas are entertained is a poison like none other. You couldn't make a good decision if it hit you over the head. Such sloppiness is unacceptable in an agent for Division. You only think of yourself and not the consequences others have to face because of your poor decisions."

My heartbeat raced, and my stomach knotted, and a slight twitch developed just under my eye. It was like I could feel my whole team shrinking, feeling very, very small.

"Yes. I can't seem to find the words needed to express my complete and total shock that Christy was in the middle of a mission and quite nearly blew it." The sarcasm in her voice was readily apparent. She let her eyes pause on each of the team members in turn. My nails dug into my palms. She wasn't done yet.

"I want there to be no mistaking the fact that there will not be another chance at getting into Dufor's office." Her eyes then landed on me. "As for you, Christy. I have contacted your supervising officer, Jeremy McGinnis, and he will be overseeing your formal discipline once he arrives." Her lip curled, and her eyes narrowed. "I understand that in the United States you are considered somewhat of a star. Perhaps that has led to your impertinent and dangerous actions tonight. However, I will not allow you to waste any more Division resources on this absurd plan. You'll never find that boy. Ever."

She huffed, her eyes rounded orbs of fire. "Leave your weapon, phone, and any other Division devices you might have on you here. You are officially confined to your apartment until Jeremy comes for you."

I growled in complete frustration as I stood up, my mind feeling like a ton of bricks pressed on it. Then exhaustion took over and I set my hands on the table, leaning hard on them. "That boy couldn't have been involved with the company. If he had, they wouldn't have sent anyone to Dufor's office to look for the drive. They would have known where it was. Face it. Without me, you don't have a chance at getting that drive back and if you would take a step back, you'd realize that." Heat filled my chest. A large part of me wanted to take back what I'd just said and fall to my knees to ask for forgiveness, but another part of me rejoiced in being able to speak my piece. Besides, I was too tired to deal with this.

Hal lifted his head and said, "We really couldn't have done—"

One sharp look from Siron cut him off, and the other three who had been nodding froze.

To my utter joy, Ace spoke up despite her death stare. "She did get us info we needed. We now know who the targets are. I never would have thought to pull that pad out of the desk, and the residue—"

I reached into my catsuit and pulled out the baggies of material and set them on the table.

"Enough!" she snapped, and her eyes flashed. "She's out until Jeremy arrives and takes her in hand. We save lives, we do not take them. I will not have another Dufor on my hands."

The proud feeling I'd had at my team's words vanished as shame and regret washed over me and my face flamed. I turned on my heel and left the room.

***

After changing into regular clothes, I left HQ. Crestfallen, I made my way home.

Sitting on the train was not a good place for me to be. The memory of what happened to Dufor stomped through my mind. He was really dead. My actions had allowed his death to occur. Tears burned in the corners of my eyes and nausea settled in. I stood to disembark, hoping I wouldn't puke before the train stopped. As I moved toward the door, a young boy, no more than fourteen, his dark head down, sidled up to me. No way was this happening—I did not need this right now. Sure enough, he darted his hand out and scoped my pocket.

Quick as a flash, I had my hand on his wrist, wrenching it away from my pocket and behind his back. He didn't cry out, but a tear slid down his cheek and a look of anguish filled his face. I felt no pity.

"Get your filthy hands off me," I hissed in his ear, the French words sounding powerful. "And if I catch you doing this to anyone else, I'll duct tape your nose to your butt and put you back in the subway wearing a sign that tells everyone you're a filthy pickpocket."

He nodded frantically. I released his arm and gave him a slight push just as the train doors opened. He stumbled out and soon disappeared up the stairs. My blood was boiling. I'd endured these pickpockets for too long. Up until now, I'd taken precautionary measures like any good Parisian, keeping valuables well out of reach and always being on alert. Except for that one moment, one second when I'd been focused on identifying risks for Dufor—and I'd been taken advantage of. I hated Paris.

I stopped at a small park down the street from my apartment and tried to find some peace, some hope. I didn't know what was happening to me. Siron's words sat at the forefront of my mind. *Careless, thoughtless, unprofessional, poisonous, impulsive.* She was right, of course. Jeremy was going to be so mad, so disappointed. It was easy to see how ashamed and embarrassed by me he would be. He'd regret speaking so highly of me. The thought of seeing him made me feel queasy.

5

I'd been up half the night working on the Sécurité Un mission, so after a long, hot shower, during which I could barely stay awake, I walked the fifteen steps from the bathroom, past the kitchenette, and slipped into bed. The second my head hit the pillow, my traitorous mind began running around in circles. I stared out the crusty old window that helped give the apartment its charm, then at the small sofa across the room and then at the kitchenette, trying to get my mind off everything. At some point I fell into a fitful sleep, but I must have woken up a thousand times. Exhaustion ate at me until a breeze whispered over my face. I bolted upright. I hadn't left a window open. In two seconds flat, I located the intruder and was on him a moment later.

"Stop hitting me!" he yelled, and at the sound of his familiar voice, I reeled back, barely stopping myself from landing another kick.

"What?" I gasped in disbelief.

"Stop hitting me, girl. It's me—it's Halluis!"

I reached out and slapped the light on, revealing the tall, thin Frenchman dressed all in black, a look of utter disgust on his face. He had one hand pressed to his side where I'd kicked him. "This is how you treat your friends?"

"This is how I treat intruders! You know, the type of people who sneak into your apartment in the dead of night." I crossed to the window and yanked it closed, adrenaline still coursing through me and making my breath short. "My friends typically knock."

"Knock? I'm a trained spy; I'm not going to announce myself on the doorstep like some sort of civilian."

A soft rap sounded at the door, and we both turned to it in shock.

After a split second of hesitation, I walked cautiously over and peered through the peep hole, then yanked the door open with an exasperated sigh. "Come in, Ace." His face registered surprise when he saw Halluis already inside, and he rubbed awkwardly at the greying scruff on his jaw before shoving his hands into the pockets of his jeans.

"Hi."

Halluis snorted. "Civilian."

I rolled my eyes at the smug look on his face. "Okay, what is going on here?"

"I came—" they both started, then glared at each other.

"One at a time," I said, sinking down to sit on the edge of the bed. I suddenly felt very tired. "Halluis, why don't you go first?"

"I came to find out what your plan is, and to offer you my assistance."

"My—what?"

Ace came over and sat beside me, holding something out toward me. I took it before realizing what it was—a cellphone.

"*I* came to bring you this. It's completely secure, and no one at HQ knows about it, so you can communicate with me whenever you need to. The first number in the address book will reach me, the rest are dummies."

"But—"

Halluis scoffed, "Always trying to show me up, aren't you, Ace? Well, I did not come empty handed, you know." He unzipped one of his many pockets and pulled out something sleek and black. He sat down on the other side of me and held out a familiar-looking pouch—the same one I'd been forced to relinquish to Siron mere hours before.

"My knives?" I blinked in confusion. "Why did you—?"

"You didn't think we would leave you alone in this, did you?" Halluis looked hurt. "Ma petite, I am offended."

"Honestly, Christy, I thought you knew us better than that," Ace chimed in.

I looked back and forth between the two of them. The identical looks of consternation and reproof on their faces were almost comical. Suddenly, I understood.

"You guys think I'm going after the pickpocket."

"Of course," Halluis scoffed. "Wait—aren't you?"

"Are you crazy?" I stood and walked over to the apartment's nice sized kitchenette, keeping my back to them to shut out the absurdity of their expectation. I realized I was still holding the phone and the pouch of knives, and I set them down on the counter with a dull thud. "You heard what Siron said. There's no way I could—"

"Siron is wrong," Halluis interjected. I could hear the heat in his voice.

I turned to face them. "What Siron said about you, Hal—I mean, that was my fault, you know? She was just angry because you were sticking up for me. But what she said about me..." I bit my lip to keep the emotion from welling up again. "What she said was right—going after the pickpocket is a naïve plan, and

45

only someone as young and dumb as I am would ever think it could work."

Halluis shook his head and opened his mouth to speak, but Ace beat him to it. "I think it can work." He stood up from the bed and shoved his hands back in his pockets, pulling out a bag of sour gummies and handing them to me. "And I'm pretty much a registered genius, so—there's that."

Halluis stood too. "Look, Christy. If she were talking about any other agent, maybe I would agree with her. Finding one pickpocket in all of Paris is an impossible task, but not for you. The very traits Siron attacked you for—your impulsiveness, your willingness to follow your instincts—she thinks they are your liabilities, but I think they are your strengths."

I shook my head. "I followed my instincts with Dufor."

"And how are you to know that you did not do the right thing? How do you know that if you stayed with him, you would not have simply ended up dead yourself?"

I stared at him in disbelief. I had never thought about it that way.

"I don't know. A man is dead—I left him there to die."

"Dufor knew the risks," said. "He was willing to accept them. He believed it was important enough." Ace whipped out a crinkled piece of paper and smoothed it out on the coffee table. Dufor's doodles. And there it was. *This cannot go on.*

"You saved it?" Ace was the best.

"It's important. It's one of the many, many things I know." He flashed a mischievous grin.

"Thank you." I said it with as much feeling as I could. I didn't want him doubting how much I appreciated his help.

"Siron has us chasing our own tails—we will never uncover what Dufor knew if we continue down her line of investigation. The only way we will ever find out what he gave his life for is to find that pickpocket. Siron will never let us do that; she's made that very clear. Our only hope now, honestly, is you—since Siron was kind enough to remove you from her oversight."

I glared at him. The look on his face was just so unbearably smug. "So, you're telling me that my getting kicked off the team is a *good* thing?"

He raised his eyebrows and shrugged lazily. "Sometimes these things happen for a reason."

I didn't know what to say to that. "Does Rosabella know you guys came here?"

"Rosabella would deny all knowledge of our activities," Halluis said. "But she sent you her love."

His words reminded me of the danger of what they were suggesting. "If Siron knew you were here, we'd all be in a lot of trouble, wouldn't we?"

"You know that's never bothered us before." Ace grinned, his eyes flashing with impish pleasure.

"It's different this time, guys. Siron isn't a corrupt director—she's just doing what she thinks is best."

"But she's wrong. And you know it," Halluis said.

Before I could argue, he pulled on Ace's arm, dragging him toward the door. "Come on, Ace. We'll leave her to mull it over."

"Wait, you guys!" I felt a sudden wave of panic. Were they actually expecting me to defy Siron's authority, to go rogue?

Halluis pushed Ace out the door, then turned to me. "Do the right thing, Christy. Oh, and that residue? It was ash. We couldn't get anything from it, though." He winked and pulled the door shut behind him.

Do the right thing. Of course. If only I could figure out exactly what that was.

***

Hours later, sitting on the little veranda at the back of my apartment, I watched the rising sun turn the sky a hazy orange. The veranda overlooked an open, hilly courtyard full of trees, vines, and bushes. It was too steep to walk through, so it had become an oasis of nature—a little slice of green between apartment buildings. Sitting out there almost made me forget my situation. Almost.

I still hadn't slept. The doubt that had swirled around in my mind ever since Ace and Halluis's visit had finally resolved itself into one firm conviction: I couldn't let Dufor die for nothing. If that meant I had to go out on my own, probably risking my career and my future as a spy in the process, well so be it. I gritted my teeth. That's why I'd risked my butt in some cramped ducting on a plan that was destined to fail.

Henri Dufor was extremely paranoid and making one copy of the information was almost too much for him. He wouldn't have a second copy. And, he wouldn't have left a trail on his laptop even if we'd been able to get our hands on it. I glanced at the crumpled paper containing Dufor's doodles. At least I was able to uncover something. And, that man in the uniform. He definitely worked there. If Division couldn't get in Sécurité Un by imitating an employee, no one else would be able to either.

I'd been so sure that I could find the pickpocket, but where was I even going to start? I stared at the knives and the phone the boys had given me. At least I had a few tools—what else did I have?

I went back into the apartment and pulled open my closet,

revealing a full array of clothes, wigs, and accessories. At least Siron had not thought to remove my disguises. A flash of guilt pinged through my chest. Siron had not thought I would disobey orders. I fought back the wave of panic that overtook me—it felt so wrong to be going against my superiors, to not be following the rules. It was so unlike me. But Halluis had been right. The only chance to save this mission was to go under the radar. I'd just have to bite back nineteen years of habitual obedience and pull out my inner rebel. She had to be in there somewhere, right?

I wasn't sure what disguise to use, where I should go. My eyes drifted around the room, looking for inspiration. The clothes I'd worn the day before were still on the floor, so I gathered them up and pushed them into my laundry basket. A piece of paper fluttered out of the jacket pocket, and I reached down to pick it up. It was the museum ticket I'd taken from Dufor's pocket. He'd been to the Musée de l'Orangerie that day. I sighed and started to put the ticket stub on my nightstand, and a buzz of electricity shot up my arm. At the same time, a tingle spread through my chest.

I stared at the ticket stub. What could it mean? What could the museum possibly have to do with the information Dufor had wanted to give Division 57? It didn't make any sense. Still, I couldn't deny the feeling that had rushed over me. The museum was important. I might not know why, but I knew enough to trust my instincts. I put the ticket stub in my pocket. It was somewhere to start, at least.

I chose a minimal disguise—nothing that would make me stand out or make me memorable in any way. I decided against wearing a wig, and tucked my long blond hair back into a simple ponytail. I used makeup to make my face look paler and thinner, and donned a pair of glasses. Jeans and a non-descript t-shirt finished off the outfit. I tucked Ace's phone deep into the backpack I would use as a go bag for the day, along with an alternate disguise and some cash. I strapped a knife to each ankle and one to the small of my back, where it was out of sight, but could be easily reached.

I left my apartment out the back so no one would see me leave.

On the way to the station I bought a baguette, feeling a pang as I remembered joking around with Ace the day before. I pulled out the phone he'd given me and sent a quick coded text to the first number in the address book. *I'm on it.* Then I punched in Jeremy's number and sent him a coded message as well. *It's Christy. We need to talk. Contact me ASAP.* Hopefully, wherever he was, he had his phone, and I'd get through to him. As I paid for my bread, a storefront across the street caught my eye. I'd seen it before, of course, but never paid it much attention. It was an electronics store.

Before I could think about what I was doing, I slipped across the street, entered the store, and quickly located what I needed at the checkout—a flash drive. Division thought I'd sit on my hands and wait around for them to punish me—no way that was going to happen.

A second later, Ace replied. *I knew she couldn't keep you down for long.*

I slipped the phone into a hidden pocket in my jacket and ran down the stairs to the train station. I caught the crowded metro and had to hold onto the pickpocket pole, along with many other Parisians and tourists. That's when I felt a hand expertly probe for any valuables I might have on me. Again! That same rage boiled up in me. Could I not go one day without

50

having a bad experience here in Paris? It was such a breach of personal space and protection; I had to do something.

I grabbed the would-be thief hard, where I knew it would hurt, and squeezed. He conveniently bent over so I could whisper as quietly as I could on a clacking, roaring train, "If you promise to be a good little boy, and not pickpocket another living soul as long as you live, I'll let you leave this train with them intact." The threat seemed more ominous when said in French. He groaned and grunted, but I could make out a "*Oui.*" So, as the train jerked to a stop, I let him disembark. I put my hand over my mouth, hiding a smile as I watched the offender shuffle off the train, still bent over, obviously in a bit of pain.

It felt good to finally be fighting back. Sure, this kid would be back to it in a few days, we all had bosses after all, but at least I'd made him stop for a little while.

I disembarked at the Louvre instead of the Place de la Concorde so I had an excuse to walk through the sprawling masterpiece of the Tuileries Gardens on my way to the Musée de l'Orangerie. Exactly four fountains graced the garden, and trees lined the wide pathway to the staircase leading to the museum. It was definitely one of my favorite places in Paris and took my breath away. If anything could get my mind off my woes, it was the beautiful gardens, and the museums around them.

Once at the top of the stairs, I looked over the gardens and watched the thousands of people moving about and marveled that the park still didn't seem crowded. I discretely removed all the knives off my body and put them into my backpack before walking along the side of the building to the glass-lined entryway.

Inside, after waiting in a lengthy line, I went through the security check and had to relinquish my go bag, which I was prepared for. Leaving that area, I wondered if I'd entered the wrong building as the room opened up to what seemed like nothing. I grabbed a brochure off a desk. The map inside the brochure assured me that Monet's *Water Lilies* were indeed in the building, but downstairs. Two huge oval rooms housed the garden scenes. Along with lots of other visitors, I sat on the benches around the first room enjoying the enormous paintings. I had no idea what I might learn here, but opted to trust my feelings. Dufor had had a ticket stub from the museum in his pocket along with the drive. Had he come here before meeting up with me? Had his calm demeanor come from visiting this particular museum? I could use some calm.

People milled about, getting as close as they could to the paintings without getting in trouble from a guard. That's when I saw them. The pickpockets. My anger skyrocketed as I observed how brashly they took advantage of people. I glanced around for a guard and noticed four in the room. This was embarrassing. How was it none of them could see what the pickpockets were doing? The museum should invest in a class for its employees to teach them what to look for.

A boy walked through the room and I stood up, my body coiled tight like a spring. He headed for the stairs to exit the exhibit. I instinctively moved toward him.

It was him! The boy who'd grabbed my bag.

My mind raced. I really just wanted to grab him and bring him in for questioning. But I knew that could jeopardize everything. We didn't want the pickpocket, just the drive he had stolen. Besides, it could spook the people who had the drive if one of the pickpockets went missing, especially if this pickpocket had given them the drive. I needed to follow him, but carefully. I couldn't let him recognize me, but I wouldn't be able to retrieve my go bag as I left the museum. I'd lose him for sure. Hopefully he'd go straight to his drop, and I'd be able to get a level deeper into the pickpocketing ring. It could be the first step to finding the stolen drive.

He hurried down the narrow street to the left. Keeping my head down, I shadowed him at a distance from which I wouldn't be detected.

I followed him into the gardens in a roundabout way through one of the many entrances on the back streets until he sat in one of the green chairs that sprinkled the rocky pathways. He stared into the large fountain, setting his bag on the ground next to him. This was it—the drop. I could read the signs from handling hundreds of drops myself. Someone would come and pick up that bag. I was about to find out who was above him in the hierarchy. That person could lead me to the clearinghouse for all the stolen goods.

I pulled back and sat under some trees, my heart racing. The best thing would be to tail both of them—see the whole network of this pickpocketing ring. But of course, there was no way I could follow two people at once.

I thought about calling in Halluis, but it would take him too long to get here, and calling in would risk giving me away to Siron before I'd had a chance to gather any evidence. I'd just have to see how the scene would unfold, and choose which one to follow.

From my vantage point, I watched as a young man sat next to the boy, placing a bag that looked exactly the same as his on the ground next to him, except that it wasn't bulging. The newcomer couldn't have been more than twenty-five. A five o'clock shadow darkened his face.

Both boys sat for a few minutes, staring into the water,

before the first thief stood and took the empty bag instead of the full one. I watched him walk down the long, gravel path, heading for the street.

When I looked back, the other guy and the bulging bag were gone. I huffed and turned, catching a glimpse of him cutting behind some trees.

I tailed Five o'clock Shadow to the metro, watching as he pickpocketed a few unsuspecting tourists on the two trains we rode. I stood near the pole at one end of the car while he stood at the other. I almost missed the stop he got off at because he waited until the last second before disembarking. Luckily, I had followed my instincts and moved right next to the exit on my end. He must have grabbed something from someone on the train he wasn't sure he could lift without being detected, just like that boy had done to me.

Sure enough, when I spotted Five o'clock Shadow again I saw he was towing a bulky piece of luggage. He took it into the nasty metro men's room and came out only a minute later without it. His shoulder bag was extremely full now. I kept following him at a distance. I figured he'd be meeting up with another contact soon, so I put my hand on my phone, ready to take pictures.

Only he didn't meet up with a contact. Instead, he met up with friends in Halle, a suburb of Paris about a twenty-minute train ride from my apartment. I often took this stop to get a crepe at Mad Dogs—it was probably the best creperie in the city, despite its American name. The large seating area was surrounded by quaint shops and restaurants. Right in the center, a fountain tossed water within its basin and over the majestic bronze horses in the center. I watched as Five o'clock Shadow greeted the group, and one of his friends handed him a skateboard.

"Thanks, Daniel," he said with a grin, a slight Arabic accent shining through the French words he spoke. It was a strange moment—such a normal thing to do for someone who'd just spent his day reaching into the pockets of strangers.

"You owe me one, Kamal. I had to hike all the way to your place to get it."

Kamal—apparently that was Five o'clock Shadow's real name—laughed before throwing his board down and taking off around the fountain. He stopped momentarily by two other kids sitting on the cement bench and dropped off his bag. They did tricks and stunts on the twenty feet of smooth surface surrounding the big fountain. Creating a larger circle around the skating area were four sections of rounded cement seating full of people eating, talking, smoking, and watching the skaters. Two other skaters showed up, also with bags that they set next to Kamal's before taking a seat. The two who had been sitting, stood and began skating. I itched for my own long board, finding my feet tapping in longing. The last time I'd skated was when I was in Oregon trying to catch some kidnappers.

I smiled as I watched the skaters play to the crowd. A pickpocket who also craved an audience? Interesting. What was Kamal doing here? Were all six of these kids pickpockets? My eyes flitted over the square, and I noted the four distinct exits out of the area. Flowers, shrubs and trees graced the section above the seats in large planters, creating a feeling of intimacy in the large park-like area. On the other side of the flowers and trees was more seating facing away from the fountain. Constant foot traffic moved in and out of the four openings that allowed entrance to the inner seating and the fountain. If I needed to make a quick exit, I'd have to take those people into account. I hated to leave, but I had to return to the museum to get my go bag. It took me forty minutes, but not much had changed when I returned to Halle.

The rushing of the fountain helped create a feeling of peace even though the space was still filled with activity. It was like it blocked out the world beyond the massive planters, and only the things inside existed. I resisted the urge to sigh and lean back to relax. I needed to stay alert and find a way to get Kamal's attention. Once a spot near where some of the skaters sat opened up, I took it.

I pulled out my phone to give the appearance that I was busy texting someone. In truth, I was taking pictures and waiting to see if the skateboarders would discuss work, so I'd know if they were all pickpockets and where they were going to take their bags of loot. I sent the pictures to Ace. Maybe he could gather some intel on some of these guys, see who was worth following up on.

Two of Kamal's friends looked like they were close to twenty while the other two appeared to be in their early teens. It made me wonder how old Kamal was. I'd thought early twenties, but if he was hanging out with these kids and acting like he was their peer, then he must've been younger than I'd thought.

I recognized the two younger kids from l'Orangerie. They'd been making rounds in the oval room. I sat as close to the group as I could and listened in on their conversation as I pretended to be busy with my phone. Mostly, I watched Kamal. He appeared to be the leader, or at least the person most looked up to and wanted to be like. He'd try some crazy stunt, and the rest would follow. And while he would make sarcastic comments, I couldn't help but see that most of his comments were positive and even kind.

It started to get dark, but it didn't stop anyone from continuing to sit and talk, just veg out, or continue skating. Dim lights popped on and then, slowly but surely, the area began to clear. But the skaters remained. I walked over to Mad Dogs and got a hot Nutella and banana crepe, which I brought back over to the fountain to eat.

I wished I could order electronic trackers for all the kids so we could see where they were going and when. The more information I had to work with, the better. But even though I had Ace's support, I knew that if he started using Division resources, it could tip Siron off to what we were doing. I was going to have to play this old-school. That meant going in myself, undercover. Maybe after I found something useful, I could bring it to Siron and she'd sanction this line of investigation. Maybe when Jeremy got here, he could help me— if he ever did. He still hadn't responded to my text. I pushed back the worry I felt at the thought of Jeremy. Worrying wasn't going to help him, and it certainly wasn't going to help me.

From what I'd seen tonight, it was clear Kamal was the leader of this little group, so I was just going to have to focus on him. A plan started to form in my mind as I watched the skaters slowly trickle out of the square.

I would be Eva, an independent pickpocket who skated occasionally.

6

The next morning, I dressed as Gabrielle, the fashion intern. I wore an airy couture skirt that stopped just above the knee with a light sweater and, of course, a scarf. My feet were slipped into short, soft, brown leather boots that cost more than many people made in a week. One thing I would miss about being in Paris was the fabulous clothes I got to wear. It had shocked me when I'd first arrived to discover that even though it was the fashion capital of the world, everyday Parisians didn't bother with it—only those in the fashion industry, like my alias, Gabrielle.

I was planning to watch the pickpockets again today—I needed to know more about them before I tried to infiltrate the group. But if any of them spotted me tailing them as my Eva alias, the whole thing would be blown. I'd stick with Gabrielle for now. With the wig and sunglasses to obscure my face and the heels to modify my height, it'd be much less likely that anyone who saw me as Gabrielle would ever connect her with Eva. And I wouldn't have to do a lot of makeup or dress up in order to be Eva.

Since most of the pickpockets I'd seen and heard were not French, but immigrants with thick foreign accents, I decided I should have one too. I practiced speaking French with a

Portuguese accent. It was fun taking the language I'd learned in an intensive, immersive four month training program and molding it to what I needed.

Inside the Musée de l'Orangerie, I watched the pickpockets work. They definitely had a system, but I only saw four during the two hours I observed there. The other two from the fountain didn't show up, and there were two new ones I hadn't seen before. They had a rotation, I guessed.

Twenty-two percent of the people who entered the room sat on one of the benches at some point during their visit. Twenty percent took a trip to the restroom, and three of the guards were basically sleeping standing up for a good portion of their shift. There was only one escape route, and that involved going up a flight of stairs.

Perhaps Dufor had come here before going to our fatal exchange because he needed to find peace and calm before doing something super scary. Unfortunately, the façade of calm didn't remain long.

I moved outside and positioned myself on a bench near the museum, presumably to create an amazing fashion design by pulling on the inspiration of my surroundings. Unfortunately, I was a terrible artist. It was good that I was really only reconnoitering and not actually drawing. I had a perfect view of the entrance and exit through the floor-to-ceiling windows that made up the exterior of the museum's main floor. The sun played across my face and I could smell the baguette paninis sold on the street nearby.

The six pickpockets I'd seen during the day weren't hard to spot as they came and went, but I did notice that a few had some sort of disguise on, varying their look in hopes of fooling the guards inside. I took pictures of them all, which was easy with my phone. I sent them to Ace, not sure if he could really do anything with them. But at least he would be collecting a nice file of intel, in case anything happened to me. I shook the thought out of my head and focused on observing the pickpockets.

After several hours of watching, I noticed something interesting. There was one guy—taller than the rest, probably the oldest of the kids at the museum that day—who seemed to be lifting things off the other pickers. *That's odd*, I thought, as I watched him move by one of the younger boys and slide his hand into the kid's bag. I focused my attention on the tall kid and watched him do the same thing three more times. Each time, just before the pick happened, the younger kid had gone to a particular fountain, then stopped in front of Monet's water lily painting depicting early morning—they were signaling him, I realized.

He wasn't taking all their stuff—just one thing each time. It was possible they were handing off the most valuable or most sensitive items to him. That was something to think about. If the kid who'd stolen my bag realized the drive could be important, would he have given it to this kid? This was another path I needed to follow. Maybe Kamal wasn't the one I needed to focus on, after all. I definitely had to find out.

I tailed the tall kid for the rest of the day, and I saw him lift stuff off the other pickpockets a few more times. Once, I caught a glimpse of the item—it was an SD card, the kind used as backup memory in a camera. Not a drive exactly, but it did lend credibility to my theory that a drive might end up with him.

In the early afternoon, I watched him exit the building, walking casually down the stairs to the Tuileries Garden. I followed him down the many steps on the south side of l'Orangerie and onto the wide packed-gravel walkway of the gardens. This particular path led to the largest of the fountains, and he headed straight for it. I made sure to act like I was just on a nice walk in the park, looking for a bit of fresh air and relaxation, but in truth, I was watching for anything out of the ordinary and for anyone who could be watching me.

The tall pickpocket would speed up, then slow down and casually look over his shoulder now and then as he made his way. I walked around the small, perfectly manicured bushes and shrubs nearby, acting like I was just enjoying the beauty before me.

Before reaching the fountain, he took a left on a footpath and met someone at a café table in the gardens. The guy he met had his back to me. I switched seats so I could get a better look. I hadn't seen him before. He had a very distinct scar running across his forehead and through his eyebrow. I would definitely remember him if I'd seen him. If the tall boy had ended up with my drive, it was likely he'd passed it to Scar, here. Maybe Kamal had nothing to do with the drive after all.

They drank what looked like sweet tea and talked like they were old friends. I bought a panini from a vendor nearby, sat on one of the green chairs, and watched them. Two almost identical bags sat on each side of the table, only one lay flat while the other bulged with stolen goods. They laughed and chatted for a good fifteen minutes before Scar stood, taking the full bag with him. He left some money on the table before waving goodbye and leaving.

After the tall one left the cafe, I tailed Scar, following him to what I hoped would be the next drop. And he didn't disappoint. With a quick swipe the bag, all the stolen goods were quickly in the hand of the next person.

I smiled.

It was Kamal. Could he be the boss? No way. He was too young. I'd stay with him to the next drop and hopefully find out who he reported to.

I followed him to the main road, and watched with dismay as he walked up to a motorcycle. There was no way I was going to be able to tail him if he got on that thing. Sure enough, he shoved a helmet on his head, threw his leg over the machine and sped off. A hot rock seemed to sear my gut as he pulled away, but it cooled in a rush as I realized that I had a good idea where I could find him later. I was willing to bet he met up with his friends at the fountain every day.

It was time to become a pickpocket.

I made my way to the metro and to my apartment to change into Eva. I got rid of the long brown wig and the stylish clothes and put on a pair of Converse, some baggy jeans, and a baggy T-shirt. I pulled my hair up in a ponytail that I pushed through the back of my baseball hat so a thick blond wave bounced behind me and a flash drive into my front pocket. I had a half-formed plan of what I was going to do with it. I just hoped I'd know when the time was right.

I rushed to the fountain in Halle around four p.m., but none of the skateboarders were there. Instead, it was filled with younger kids and their moms, many with ice cream. The kids ran about and put their hands in the fountain, while the moms talked with each other, keeping one eye on their children at all times.

This time I sat on the back side of the cement benches so I wasn't looking at the fountain. Instead, I was looking directly at a McDonalds. The smell of french fries wafted past and an urge to go buy some hit me. I'd told myself that while in France, I would not resort to eating American food. I wanted to immerse myself in the culture. But it was tempting; McDonalds was everywhere.

The mothers and children left, most likely heading home to make dinner, and the older skaters slowly trickled past me into the fountain area. Even the tall boy came today. I could only hear them once they walked into the inner ring but even then not perfectly since there were bushes, flowers, and cement between us. However, I did catch a few interesting tidbits. They worked l'Orangerie and the Louvre most of the time and no one liked working l'Orangerie. There were also far more pickpockets than the ones I'd already identified.

I'd thought about bringing a skateboard and skating my way into their group, but that would take time I didn't have. Besides, I wasn't that great of a skater, and they were far more advanced than I was. What if they didn't let me join them?

Kamal was on constant pick patrol. It seemed his eyes and mind were always looking for the next opportunity to swipe something from someone, but while he skated, he never acted on it.

One of the younger pickpockets headed out. But before he left, he casually rummaged through Kamal's bag and pulled out a fresh bag. The boy then picked through the bag he'd brought earlier and shoved a few items from it into the new bag. Kamal watched him the whole time. So, this was how a lot of his crew got their bags for the next week. Another left, and Kamal watched him too. A plan formed in my mind, and I texted Ace to let him know about it. I knew he wouldn't be able to do much to help—he and Halluis were both busy with Siron's line of investigation—but what I was doing was risky. I needed backup or at least for someone to know where I was and what I was planning in case things went wrong. My body tensed in preparation.

The second I saw the next pickpocket take her bag, I stood and moved toward the girl. She put the bag with a moon embroidered on it over her shoulder and headed for the nearest exit, waving goodbye to the others. I caught up with her at the exit and pretended to stumble into her. As I did, she lurched forward, arms outstretched to catch herself, and I snatched the purse off her shoulder, and took off. I ducked my head down and prayed Kamal had watched her just like he had watched the other two.

I didn't have to go far before I heard pounding feet behind me. My instinct was to speed up and get the heck away from Kamal, but I had to let him catch me in order to get his attention and hopefully become a part of his team. To do that, I had to run until I was far enough away from the fountain that we would be alone, away from the others.

I hurried around several corners, leading him a few blocks away. He was right behind me.

Arms appeared and surrounded my chest, effectively stopping me in my tracks. Just as suddenly, I was thrown against the stucco wall of a building, hands pressing my back and shoulders against it. Air flew out of my mouth.

"What exactly did you think you were doing?" Kamal demanded, the spicy scent of curry on his breath. His fingers dug into me.

"I, uh, I," I stammered, wriggling, putting up some effort to escape. I looked side to side as if searching for someone to save me, but no one would be coming down this alley. It was a dead end.

He increased the pressure on my shoulders. There would

be bruising.

"Hey, no need to hurt me. You that girl's body guard or something?" I spoke French with a thick Portuguese accent, emphasizing the fact that I was not a native. How I wished Jeremy had eyes on me. Being completely alone was no fun as a spy.

"I asked you what you thought you were doing." He hit me into the wall over and over.

"Just trying to make it out here, that's all. She didn't have a good hold on it, ya know?"

"No, you tripped her, causing her to lose her balance." He bared his teeth and cocked his head to the side.

"Yeah, well, I wouldn't have had to do that had she kept it in her hand and not on her shoulder. Is she hurt? I-I didn't mean to hurt her. Her bag looked kinda full, and I wanted to see what was inside."

"You been doing this long?"

"Only about a week now. I just need stuff, ya know?" I looked frantically around. "I'm really sorry. Please. You're hurting me."

"Did you run away from home or something?" His hold on me relaxed.

"What's it to you?" Did being a street kid earn me sympathy points with this guy? I'd play that up.

His eyes dilated slightly as he looked me over. He was considering me. "Just asking. That was a pretty cool move you did there. If I hadn't been watching, you would have gotten away with it. It was pretty gutsy with all those people around."

I smiled. "It's one of the best ways to get bigger things off people, ya know?" I pressed my palms into the wall behind me.

"The problem is that you were picking in my area." His

look was once again menacing.

"I didn't know. I'm sorry. I won't do it again." I tapped my foot on the dirty asphalt.

"I've never seen you before." He stared at me like someone searching his memory for a recollection of someone.

He'd loosened his hold when he'd thought I was an orphan, so being on my own was a plus, maybe being a newbie would be too. "I moved here last week. I need a way to live, ya know?"

He nodded and his look softened again. "Actually I do know. You should come work for me."

Something told me not to give in easily. I shook my head. "No way. Uh, uh. I don't want to work for no one."

He tilted his head to the side.

"I'm a one-girl show. I don't need anyone." All sympathy left him.

His hands left my shoulders, still holding the bag, but he set them on the wall beside my head and then spread his legs to hem me in. "In that case, I'm going to have to hurt you." He flipped out a knife and brought it to my face.

I pushed hard against the building and sucked in a breath. I'd said the wrong thing. He didn't want me to think I had any kind of choice. I would join him or die. The wall seemed harder and the dank smell of the alley turned my stomach. Distant chatter and laughter filtered in from the main area outside the alley. "Well, I'm not sure," I stammered, time to show some vulnerability. "I mean, I don't want to get hurt and I've never worked for anyone before and…I don't know…I mean, what do you mean work for you?"

His forearm pressed me harder into the wall and my shoulder blades ached. Even speaking through clenched teeth, the smells of mint and curry met me. "I'm offering you something here. It's not something you can turn down. You're lucky I've given you as much attention as I have. You need to realize that and remember it."

I wanted to nod, but couldn't without having the knife cut into me.

"Fine," I squeaked. "But I really need this money."

"We all need money." He smirked.

"I need it for my family. My dad's sick. Really sick. I have to help him."

His eyes softened yet again. "I can supply opportunities you'd never get on your own, and I can keep you safe from other groups."

"Really? What kind of opportunities?" I blinked a couple of times and then gazed at him with extreme focus.

He put the knife back in his pocket and swung the bag in front of me. "You see this?"

I put my attention on the bag. "Uh, I stole it remember? Of course I've seen it."

"Ah, but you really haven't."

I stared at the light brown bag, the black crescent moon staring out at me. I raised my eyebrows in anticipation.

"This bag gets you into the best museums and keeps you safe while you're in them."

I scowled. "I can go into any museum I want already."

"Have you picked at any museums in town?" He jerked his head back, surprise in his voice. It told me what my answer should be. I could make him think I'd pulled off some good heists so he'd be even more determined to collect me.

"Of course." I stared at him with narrowed eyes.

"And you got away with what you stole?" His fingers went

to his parted lips.

"Yes." I drew the word out and put my hands on my hips. "Why wouldn't I?"

He tapped his fingers on the stucco wall, clenched his teeth and said, "Maybe because any number of rivals wouldn't hesitate to blow your head off and throw you into the Seine for filching in their territory."

I sneered. "You're kidding, right?"

He shook his head, slow and even. "No."

I gulped. "I didn't know."

"Listen, what's your name?"

I narrowed my eyes at him, making a show of considering if I should trust him. "Eva," I said slowly.

"Where are you from, Eva?"

"Portugal."

"Well, Eva from Portugal, I'm Kamal. People don't mess with me, and they don't mess with my employees. If you work for me, you won't have to worry about rival groups. I can give you the protection you need and give you safe territories to pick to your heart's content."

I gave him an exaggerated frown and nodded. "Well, all right. I guess I'll give you a try." I ran my hands over the stucco on the wall behind me.

"Not so fast." He stepped back. "First off, I'll be giving you a try and second, you only get one chance."

"But I thought you just said—"

"I need to see you do it again before I'll officially take you on. Let's head back over to the street by the fountain." He looked at his watch and I looked at the sky, the moon was up high now. "There should still be plenty of opportunities for you to do your thing with all those restaurants lining the street and people coming and going. It's only ten, so the place should be hopping."

You had to love the French and their late night eating habits. I glanced at the entrance to the alley, excited to be getting out of this dark place. "What? You want to watch me steal something?" I raised my eyebrows.

"Yes. How else am I supposed to vet you?" He raised his dark, thick eyebrows, his eyes piercing mine.

"Touché."

He threw his arm out, inviting me to lead the way, which I did. As we walked, I fingered the flash drive I'd tucked in my pocket. I walked slowly up the path, observing the people eating at the tables.

He came up beside me, and the heat from his body brought attention to the chill in the air. He put his hand on my arm, slowing me down. "See the woman with the red scarf?"

"I see her."

"Do you see what's sitting on the table next to her?"

"Her wallet?"

"Go get it."

Apprehension slammed into me. I'd wanted to fake-steal the drive in my pocket, not really steal from an innocent bystander. This lady's only crime was eating her dinner too early to be native to France.

"Very funny. You're crazy. She'd catch me, and I'd end up in prison." I tried to slow my racing heart.

"Here's how it's going to go down. I'll distract her, and you'll lift it."

I looked at my feet then glanced at him. "I'm afraid," I whispered. I had to make him see some weakness in me so he could see me grow under his tutelage.

"Good. That fear makes it more fun. Besides, if you get seen, we'll just book it out of here to the metro." He motioned to his board. "They'll never catch us."

I bit my lip and rubbed my hands down my pant legs as I looked around, watching people walk past, hurried and not paying anyone attention. He urged me forward. Did I want to do this? No. Would I do this? Yes. My stomach soured. I needed to get over it. This had to be done and the woman would be okay. But would I be okay? What if something went wrong? I had no backup. This would be yet another mark against me. Another item of proof for Siron that I was reckless. Another thing to make Jeremy wonder what he ever saw in me. I had to be perfect. No mistakes.

Kamal moved to the other side of the lady and started to talk to her. I couldn't hesitate, but I also couldn't breathe. I reached over and grabbed. I almost stopped once I was a few meters away, but Kamal was suddenly there, walking beside me. "Did you get it?"

"Yes." I said it in a breathy whisper, the wallet palmed in my hand. I looked back—a completely novice thing to do.

Kamal walked in front of my gaze. "Don't look back. Never look back."

"Ok."

"It was nice of her to leave it out for you, wasn't it?" He grinned.

I chuckled, slipping the flash drive into the folds of the wallet. We turned a corner and I said, "Let's see what we've got here."

The drive fell out as I opened the wallet, and I chuckled when I bent over to pick it up. "Great. A flash drive." After making sure I was standing in his line of sight, I threw it toward the trash can behind Kamal. He reached up with a swift hand and snagged it.

"Whoa! Never throw anything out. Give everything to me." He shook the drive in front of him.

"Oh, sorry. I thought a used flash drive wouldn't be worth anything." I feigned stupidity.

"You'd think that. But these drives can be very valuable depending on who they were taken from and what information is found on them." He tossed it in the air and let it drop back to his hand.

"Huh. Really?" A jolt of expectation ran through me.

"Yeah. I've got a guy who loves getting these things."

My heart sped up a little at that. What if he'd already passed Dufor's drive to his guy? If it had already moved on to the next tier, it would make everything that much harder.

"So are you going to give it to him today? Does he give you the cash right away?" I leaned forward eagerly, letting the strain in my voice come through as excitement about getting some money.

He laughed. "My drive guy's been out of town for a while, but *if*—and it's a big *if*—there's something on here, you'll get your cut in a week when he gets back."

Inwardly, I breathed a sigh of relief. Chances were Kamal still had the drive. A countdown started in my head—I had a week to locate the drive and retrieve it before Kamal passed it along. That meant next Wednesday was D-Day, the last day the drive would be in play.

I didn't want him to get suspicious, though, so I steered the conversation back to what Eva would be most concerned with. "My cut?"

"Yeah. Thirty percent."

I let my jaw drop and narrowed my eyes, like any savvy person living on the street would do. She wanted maximum results from her work. "That hardly seems right. I'm the one who did the work."

"The only reason the lift happened was because of me." He didn't tilt his head in a playful way, instead he leaned slightly toward me in a show of aggression. He was serious.

It took all my courage to stay rooted to the spot. Nervous energy caused me to raise an eyebrow and laugh. To cover it up, I said, "You got me there. I guess you'll be the one to sell it, huh?" He was good. He must be a lower level leader of some sort, that or he was mimicking what he'd seen the bosses do.

He nodded.

"I hate to have to wait that long, but I guess I don't have a choice." Trying to seem casual and still feeling nervous, I swung my arms out in a happy, awkward gesture and then clasped my hands together at my chest.

He raised his eyebrows and then snorted while he opened the wallet and pulled out what must have been a couple hundred US dollars.

I moved close. "And how much of that do I get?"

He handed me eighty dollars. I jumped up and down. "I'm rich! I'm rich!"

"You see, you pick the right wallets with the right protection, and the payoff can be superb." I wondered what his history was. Kamal was not your ordinary street urchin who fell into pickpocketing because of desperation. I could tell by the way he spoke, he was educated.

"Listen," he said. "I'll be in touch later about a possible job with the crew. There are no guarantees, understand?" He smiled and backed away a few steps before turning around and disappearing down a dark alley.

He hadn't truly disappeared; he was watching me. I could feel him. I knew he wasn't going to just let me go my way and take my "application" to his boss. He had to know I was who I said I was. Perfect. It was generally a strict no-no to let anyone know where you lived when on a mission. But I didn't have a choice. I couldn't call Division to set up a decoy apartment, and I didn't know anyone to use for cover. I'd have to make it work. For once, I was glad my apartment was nothing special, and in a shady part of town. It would fit with my Eva alias as well as it had fit Gabrielle's. Interns were also poor. I jumped the turnstile at the metro and took the train home.

One of the good things about my training as a spy was learning how to be still. I could still myself from the inside out and be hyper aware of my surroundings. That allowed me to feel for potential threats, including being followed, without changing what I was doing. I couldn't tell right away where he was, but I knew I was being followed. Kamal was pretty good at this.

I kept one part of my mind focused on Kamal's presence, then let the rest of my mind mull over what I'd learned. Kamal had a guy he sold the drives to, and that guy was out of town for another week. So, Kamal most likely had the drives in his possession, but where? I'd have to find his apartment, sneak in, and see if they were there. Sneaking into Kamal's apartment would be much easier if I had Division's blessing and their gadgets.

I texted Ace. *Drive still in play. Getting close.*

I was itching to turn the tail back on to Kamal after he saw me go into my apartment and get to bed, turning out all the lights, but I couldn't risk it. Not yet. If he was good, he'd wait somewhere outside my place all night. I'd lie low tonight, but I couldn't wait too long because his buyer would be back in a week. If the drives weren't in Kamal's apartment, I needed some time to figure out where else he might keep them.

7

I dressed as Eva the next morning, certain Kamal would be tailing me all day. I picked up some croissants at a boulangerie in the morning, not even bothering to act like I was happy. I ate a normal one and then indulged in a *pain au chocolat.* A croissant filled with chocolate? Yes, please.

I started lifting a few things from people as I walked along the sidewalk, tucking them into my shoulder bag as I went. I had to block off my nagging conscience with the knowledge that this was for the greater good. This would give me the opportunity to get the drive. Not for the first time, I wished we knew what information Dufor had had. Whatever it was, it had caused Dufor to risk his life. I thought of the doodles I'd found in his office. Something about them nagged at me. *Henri deserved better,* he'd written. *For Henri, I must.* Was he really just talking about himself in the third person? I wished I understood him better. I pulled out my phone and sent a coded message to Ace.

Can you do some digging on Dufor? Find out about his hobbies, his life, his family. I don't know how it will help, but it might.

A moment later, I got the reply. *I'm on it.*

I nodded, satisfied. I could trust Ace to come through for

me. It might not mean anything in the end, but I couldn't ignore any possible source of a lead. It had already been four days since the drive had been stolen. Too long.

I made sure to send out feelers for anyone other than Kamal watching me. Now that I was actually picking, I would hate to catch the ire of some competing gang. I picked my way to Mad Dogs, where I got a turkey crepe for lunch. My bag was getting heavy, so I headed back to the apartment, hoping Kamal had seen enough.

Walking out of the metro, I could feel Kamal moving in. I skipped up a few flights of stairs and then stopped to lean against a short wrought iron fence and watch some kids at the small park in the area. The entire park was in shadow thanks to the big trees lining it. Old men sat at a table and talked while moms sat together watching their kids run and play. A couple of dog owners walked past with their dogs. I felt Kamal approach me and stop.

"Hey, Eva."

I whipped around, pretending I was surprised to see him.

"Kamal?"

He stood tall, firm, like a boss. He'd cut his hair at some point during the day. He looked handsome. "Are you serious about wanting a job?" His stare was piercing, like he was trying to uncover any possible deception.

"Of course." I looked him directly in the eyes.

"Well, I may have one for you."

"Seriously? I passed?"

He rubbed his closely trimmed beard. "Look, I've been watching you all day and good grief. You picked in three different groups' territories today, including mine, and if you'd been seen by anyone but me, you'd have been dead. I told you that yesterday."

He looked at me like he wanted an explanation about why I'd risk it knowing what I knew. "Well, I didn't know if you'd really be getting back to me or not. I have to make a living, you know. I couldn't just sit around and wait for you. Besides, I was really careful." I thought about my team and how it might have been a blessing that I wasn't "hooked up" with them at the moment. Kamal and anyone who worked with him wouldn't be able to discover them.

"I can't argue that you aren't good. You are, and I think the only reason I was able to see what you were doing is because I knew you were doing it. But mark my words, if you keep going on your own, you'll be discovered and these leaders—they aren't forgiving. You'll find yourself dead or tortured in terrible ways if they find you. A kid, only twelve, was discovered stealing a bag in another group's area, and they stabbed stakes into his hands and feet and hung him on a wall. He was probably just some poor kid looking for a way to get some food, and they tortured him. You need to watch your step and follow the rules if you join our team."

I looked at my feet and swayed a little as if in deep thought. "So, why didn't you hurt me or kill me or something when you found me?"

His dark eyes narrowed and he pressed his thick lips together. "I'm not sure exactly. Maybe it was because you were so good at what you were doing. I mean, you aren't perfect, but you said you've only been doing this a little over a week and if you're this good already, I can hardly imagine what you'll be like in a couple of months. I picked up Daniel last year after he tried to steal from me. He's one of my best pickers now. You remind me of him. Do you want to join or not?" His face was unreadable.

"If you want me, you can have me. If there are people out there just waiting for me to slip up so they can kill me, I need to be on your team. I mean, I really need the money."

"You'll be on trial for a while. You've impressed me, but the big bosses need to be convinced. And you're pretty inconsistent right now, which makes me think maybe you're just lucky. We need to change that and take luck out of the equation."

"Well, maybe you should introduce me to the leader." I could only hope to meet the person above him.

"No. You don't need to do that. In fact, I'll be your only contact. Just do a good job and bring your stuff to me and everything will be all right. I'll show you where our territories are and teach you how it all works over the next day or two. After that, you should be golden."

"Wait. Are you saying I have to work for free for a while?" I threw my hands out to my sides.

"I didn't say that. I'll pay you and be your only contact."

I nodded. "Okay. Thanks for finding me. If you hadn't, I guess I could have been dead by next week." I pressed my lips together and pushed them out in a pout.

"You're good, but sometimes you're a little sloppy, a little reckless. We'll practice together. You're a natural. It shouldn't be too painful."

He seemed so nice. So kind. How could he be a part of a vicious pickpocket gang?

"But only if you acknowledge the fact that there are distinct boundaries and rules for each picking group. Even in our area, there are rules." His voice turned stern. "And you don't break the rules."

"How will I ever learn all those rules and the boundaries and stuff?"

"I'll teach you. And it's easy to know who is in what group. Each group has symbols that identify its 'members'." He held up an empty fanny pack.

I squished up my nose in distaste.

He pointed to the three gold stars on the pack. "Each group has its own symbols. Our symbols are the sun, moon, and stars. The symbols identify us and protect us, especially when we're in an area that more than one group picks."

A group of giggling teenagers passed us by.

I remembered the moon on the over-the-shoulder bag from yesterday and the sun from the jacket on the boy who stole my bag. I nodded.

"Oh, and while you're on trial, you get ten percent of what you pick."

"Ten percent? That doesn't seem fair."

"A lot of people need their cut of what you pick. Consider yourself lucky. Other groups don't pay anything during training." I thought it was interesting that he called the pickpocket rings groups instead of gangs.

I figured he was the one who collected the most because he would be training me. "Well, I guess I could give it a shot." I smiled, and trying to make him feel I was way more comfortable with him than I was, I slugged him softly. "But you better back me up."

He laughed, but it was forced. "That's all up to you. Why don't we practice a bit?"

After a couple perfect picks, I decided it was time to let him mentor me. He pointed out a small group of tourists sitting at an outside table at McDonalds. They were talking and laughing. I noticed that one woman kept glancing down at her phone as if she were waiting for someone to call or text. I figured Kamal would see that I was making a rookie mistake and stop me before I went in for the kill. I moved in that direction, and just as I expected, he grabbed me by the arm and pulled me to the side of the building.

"You can't just walk right up to take something without first making sure the owner is engrossed in something else."

"But how do you know? I thought she was distracted."

"Distracted is not the same as engrossed. It's something you just start to recognize and get a feel for as time goes on. If you aren't sure, then leave it. She kept taking quick glances at her phone. Couldn't you see that?" His smile was full of tension. Strange. It was like he was trying to hide his anger from me. Dark shadows lingered in his eyes.

I thought it was time to lighten the mood and crack a joke, but I had nothing, so I smiled instead.

Like he knew I was searching for levity, he said, "You know, you need to take this seriously." His eyes narrowed and they fixed on me, cold as stone. He stepped closer, the storms in his eyes making them appear almost black. "This is the way I make my living, Eva, and if you can't respect it, I don't know if we can work together."

I let my cheeks flame hot. "I'm sorry, Kamal." I reached out for his arm. He yanked it away. My hand hung out there for a bit while I talked until it slowly fell to my side.

The anger physically left his face but something like fear remained. "It's okay. I get crazy with people who think what we do is easy or a joke. It's hard work and it's the only way I have to earn a living." His sincerity rolled over me in waves. He spoke like he had some noble profession. There had to be something behind that conviction.

Suddenly I felt a little bad for everything I'd thought and said about pickpockets. I'd forgotten they were people with feelings just doing what they considered their job. I bet almost none of them chose this line of work because they thought it was a good career move. Desperation caused people to do desperate things. They had to eat and have a place to stay. Perhaps they believed the end result justified the means. It still had to stop.

"Fine. No more teasing." I wondered if the fear I'd seen in him was due to his boss and what that boss would do to him if he got caught because of me. I noticed the shimmer of the scar on his left cheek. I wondered if he got that scar from doing something wrong.

"You know, you really are lucky." His face had a serious, pleased look. "You're quite the lucky find."

I gave him a questioning look. I'd just messed up. "Present example excluded?"

He chuckled. "You just have a way about you. I can tell you'll get it fast."

I smiled, not sure how to respond. I didn't want him to think I was too good to be true. I couldn't have him suspect me of anything. "You sure know how to charm a girl."

He chuckled. So did I.

"Hey, you know, I…uh, I skate a little, too," I said, shyly. It would be great to find a few more opportunities to interact with Kamal.

"Really? You should join us at the fountain sometime. We're there pretty much every night." He smiled warmly.

"Thanks, I'd like that, but I'll warn you that I'm not very good."

He looked over the crowds, and I noticed sweat beading up along his brow. The sun shone hot on my exposed skin, and as I breathed in, I couldn't help but notice how the humid air felt thick in my lungs. "Want to get a drink?"

He checked his watch. "Sure, I've got twenty minutes before I need to head out."

I grabbed a bottled lemonade, and he grabbed a Coke from a panini vendor just down the walkway from McDonalds. We sat on a small grassy hill that had a big maple tree at the top, giving us some shade, and twisted the caps open on our drinks. Busy people walked by, not paying us any attention, but Kamal's eyes didn't miss a single one. The next thing I knew, Kamal's Coke dropped out of his hand, and he took off down the street. I stood up. "Kamal?" I shouted, but he kept running. So I ran after him, my lemonade in my hand.

He was fast, and I had to really push it not to lose him in the crowds. He took a quick corner off the main walkway, and I followed. He turned again at the edge of a building, and I sped up but stopped abruptly as a terrible scene appeared before me. Kamal had a knife at a boy's throat. I backed up and slid partially behind the stucco wall and a small dumpster. I looked behind me, no one was in the alley, and I slid further behind the dumpster so I wouldn't be spotted by passersby, but still had full view of the scene in front of me. The boy Kamal had a hold of couldn't have been older than fourteen. He still hadn't experienced his growth spurt and stood only as tall as Kamal's chest.

"I don't care if you are new. This is not your area, and now you have to pay. And you aren't that new. I've seen you before." His French took on a thicker Arabic accent in his anger. I swallowed hard, sweat dripping down my back as I watched.

At first I thought Kamal was going to kill the boy, but instead he did something much worse. He pointed the tip of his knife at the boy's cheek, using his other forearm to hold the boy's face against the wall as he started to carve. I closed my eyes and held back a scream. When I opened them, the hysterical boy had a bloody star carved into his cheek. My hand flew to my mouth. "Next time," Kamal said in a scary whisper, I take your hand." He let the boy slump down to the ground, cries of agony spilling from his mouth as he clutched his bleeding cheek. Kamal wiped the blood from his knife on the boy's shirt and after spitting on the boy, turned back the way he'd come.

I jerked back, duck walking from behind the dumpster and hurrying around the corner. Sucking in a hard breath, I stood and took off. Something told me it was better if Kamal didn't know I'd witnessed what he'd just done. I weaved through all the people on the sidewalks and retook my seat under the tree. I picked up Kamal's Coke and put the lid on, surprised only a little had spilled. It was my luck that he took his time to get back, so I was able to catch my breath and calm down.

I sipped my lemonade and tried to erase the memory of what I'd seen. Kamal, whom I'd thought had a soft spot for runaways, had cut that boy in a vicious way that was certain to leave scars, and then threatened to maim him permanently. My body buzzed with disgust, and a shallow fear welled up in my chest. What I'd thought was a petty, nuisance crime was much darker and more terrible than I'd imagined.

When Kamal touched me on the shoulder, I startled, jerking around to see him standing above me.

"Jumpy?"

"You scared me. Where did you go? I've been worried."

He sat down and picked up his soda, unscrewed the cap

and took a drink. "There was a problem I needed to take care of. Nothing you have to worry about." Strain registered on his face and the thumb of his other hand pressed on his chin while his index finger pressed on his temple.

"Well, you could have told me why you were leaving." My face flushed, so I finished off my lemonade and leaned back against the tree, knees up and the empty lemonade bottle tapping on my knees, pretending I was relaxed.

"I didn't know I would be leaving until I just did. And while you need to tell me about your whereabouts, I don't have to account for mine." He took a long drink of his soda and then twisted the top on.

We sat in awkward silence for a few minutes until his watch beeped. He immediately stood up and said, "Well, this is where I leave you. See you tomorrow. Upper entrance to the Louvre at nine." The sun was low in the sky, light hitting harshly off store windows.

"That's pretty late. Why not earlier?"

"The museum doesn't open until then."

"I think I like the thirty percent rate better than the ten percent rate. You could help me practice more before it's all official. We could meet just a little early, at eight."

"Wish I could, but I have somewhere to be at eight. An appointment."

"Okay. See you tomorrow." My life of crime would officially begin at the glass pyramid of the Louvre.

I headed down the street to go home, but quickly changed my course once I knew Kamal was out of sight and not following me. It didn't take me long to locate him. He was strolling home, in no hurry.

I followed him, making sure I wouldn't be spotted, which

wasn't easy considering he knew what I looked like and I had no disguise with me. We passed a few blocks of small businesses that had apartments on top and continued into an area of apartments without businesses. At least he was walking on a street that had a bunch of nooks and crannies I could hide in. I had to count my blessings even though I had to hide every ten feet.

He entered a small apartment building at the end of a long row. The blue, peeling paint contrasted sharply with the red trim as well as the attached building which was olive green. The flaking paint left large patches of exposed tan stucco. A small alley dead-ended on the exposed side of the building. A light on the second story blinked on. Bingo. I knew where he lived. Tomorrow I'd be visiting his humble home, hopefully in the morning when he went to his appointment. I watched for a while, trying to determine if he lived with anyone else. It appeared he was the only one there.

I stewed the whole way home. Having the knowledge of where he lived and when he'd be gone was huge. I'd be in and out of that little apartment in under ten minutes and hopefully have the drive, but what if something went wrong? What I really needed was a shadow and some listening devices to put into his apartment. That way, if I wasn't able to find the drive for some reason, I'd have a backup plan.

Once I was back in my apartment, I called Ace, hoping he was in a place where he could talk. The phone rang twice. Three times. A fourth. I almost hung up, but just when I was about to, I heard Ace's gruff voice on the line.

"Ace here."

I breathed a sigh of relief. "Listen, are you in a place where you can talk?"

"Yes, Halluis, I'm working on that right now."

Ah, so there were others who could hear him. I'd have to be quick and hope Ace wouldn't accidentally give us away. He could be really good under pressure, but he sometimes underestimated himself and got nervous.

I gave him a concise rundown of what I'd discovered then started to tell him what I needed. "I need help finding out where Kamal keeps the drives before selling them. I know he has an appointment in the morning, so his apartment will be empty."

"What do you want me to do about it?"

I balked for a second at his tone, then remembered he was supposedly talking to Halluis. "I need a lookout shadow. And in case the drive isn't in his apartment, can you get me a few drives with GPS trackers on them? That way I can give them to Kamal, and we can follow the signal to where he keeps them."

"I'm afraid you're on your own with that, Halluis," Ace said. "I can get you the tech, of course, but with you being so far away, I can't support it."

I cringed, trying to parse the meaning behind his words. From the sound of things, Halluis was gone somewhere—what did Siron have him doing? That meant he couldn't be my shadow. But Ace had said he could get the tech.

"No on the shadow, yes on the drives?" I clarified.

"That's right." He paused a second. "Just, be careful out there... man."

"Thanks, Ace. I'll be all right. Just get me the drives."

8

In the morning, I found three flash drives had been pushed through my mail slot, along with an envelope along with a bag of chocolate gummy bears. The coded note explained that two of the drives had the same tracking system on them, and the third had a different system. I was to give one of each type to Kamal, then try to plant the other one on another pickpocket, someone who might be likely to lead us to the drive buyer. The plan seemed solid, but something about it made me nervous. At the end was a postscript that read, *Siron's got Halluis in Calais, tailing one of Dufor's business partners. It's a dead end. We hope he'll be back soon. I found some stuff on Dufor, don't know if it will be useful.*

I slipped the drives into my pocket, happy to have some of Ace's handiwork, along with the two I'd bought the night before to use as decoys. I took some time to rough up a couple of them, make them look used rather than brand new. All five were different—I didn't want anything about them to expose that they'd come from the same person: me.

I pulled out the information on Dufor that Ace had included and glanced quickly over the page. 54 years old, divorced, no kids, a sister in Coulogne, but no other living relatives. Mostly kept to himself, but he liked art and books. He was a numbers guy, an accountant, and before working at Sécurité Un, he'd worked for a small financial firm in Paris.

That's it? I thought. It was no help at all. There was nothing there that offered any clue to explain Dufor's doodles. Still, Coulogne wasn't far from Calais, and since Halluis was already up that way anyway... I texted Ace on the secure line.

Can you have Halluis look into the sister? She might give us some insight.

If you say so.

I sighed. It would probably be a dead end. All the more reason to focus on Kamal.

I got to his apartment a few minutes after eight a.m. and confirmed that he had left and no one else lived there. I had no idea how long he would be gone or where he was going, so I needed to work fast.

I climbed the narrow stairs and found myself on a small landing. While the outside had been bright and colorful, the hallways were a drab gray. Each level only had two apartments. I picked the lock and walked in with only a bit of hesitation. The first thing I ran into was the kitchen. From there, the apartment opened up into a very small studio. The smell of acetone and paint hit me. I looked around the room in shock.

He was an artist. A painter. "Hmm," I said, frowning. Five easels with canvases on them dominated the room. In the far corner was a small cot-like bed, and on the wall with the window hung the TV. A small chest of drawers butted up against the bed, and that was it. Everything was in order, nothing out of place, almost like he'd been in the army or something. I turned around and looked back at the strip of a kitchen and headed in there. I opened all the oak cupboards.

When I opened the silverware drawer, it felt unusually heavy. I examined one of the forks, and it wasn't particularly sturdy and didn't weigh much. I pulled the drawer out the rest of the way and examined it more closely. It definitely had a false bottom. I found the catch and opened it. Inside was a lot of money, jewelry, a laptop, and various other expensive items— more than a young guy living on his own should have, and I was reminded that he was a pickpocket. I whipped out the laptop and booted it up, praying it didn't have a password. It did. Who was I kidding? This boy was a professional thief. Of course he'd protect against other thieves.

This was it. I needed Ace. I pulled out my phone and dialed the secure number I'd found with the drive this morning.

"This is Ace." His voice was clipped, tense.

I got straight to the point. "I found a laptop. It's got a password, and I need in."

"Tell me everything you see in the room." His voice was so low, I had to concentrate to hear him. He was alone enough that he could talk to me, but Siron must be nearby. I breathed a quick prayer that we wouldn't get caught.

"Five easels with canvases, some painted and some not. A very small bed. A chest of drawers. Three prints of paintings on the walls." Despite the increased tension, I couldn't resist teasing him a little. "I'm looking in his underwear drawer right now. Would you like to know his preferred color?"

"Not unless they're full of lace and frilly. That could give me ideas for the password at least."

"Nope, just plain white briefs. Sorry."

I thought I heard a faint chuckle. "Are the paintings on the walls his? Can you tell?"

I moved toward them. "Not by him. Looks like a Van Gogh

print? Yep. They're all Van Gogh's."

"Try Van Gogh."

"As the password or the username?"

"You don't even have the username?" He groaned.

"Nope." Now he sighed.

"Can you see an HDMI cable?"

"Yes."

"Great. Attach it to your phone and then to the computer."

"Is this going to take long? I have no idea how long he's going to be gone," I said, taking the cable in my hands.

"I need a good fifteen minutes."

My eyes flicked wide, but I said nothing. Fifteen minutes was a long time. I'd have to keep a good watch. I needed to get to Kamal's phone and copy and change his SIM card so we could get access to his phone calls. Too bad I hadn't asked Ace for listening devices yesterday. I'd have to get some of those soon.

Time crawled by as I waited for Ace to work his magic on the laptop. "I'm almost there. Give me three minutes, and I'll have your username and password."

I'd already been here too long. According to my watch eleven minutes had passed, and I'd wanted to be out in ten. I looked at Kamal's paintings. The two that looked completed were colorful and completely different from each other. One depicted a family of five sitting in a park eating a picnic dinner. The other was of the same family, inside a parlor, two of them sitting, comforting each other and two standing, looking into a small casket wherein the youngest of the family lay dead. I felt a sudden bout of sadness well up inside me. The emotion in both pictures, while in stark contrast to each other, was very real. Even I could tell he was good for being so young.

"I'm in," Ace said. "You have a drive for the info?"

I thought about the drives in my pocket. I was sure they were too small to hold everything on that computer. "I don't. Can you download it?"

"I can, but it will take a good thirty minutes to do it remotely."

"Seriously?" I huffed and without waiting for his reply said, "Let's get as much as we can. Hopefully we get the important stuff before I have to leave."

"Agreed. I'm going to hang up and work on something for Siron. Can you see the progress bar at the bottom of the screen?"

"I can." It read 8%.

"Just watch that and disconnect when it says 100%."

"Will do."

"Good luck."

"Wait, Ace. Thank you so much for helping me and risking so much. I truly appreciate it."

There was a pause. "You know I wouldn't let you down. And no pressure, but it's up to you to make sure I don't get fired. Find that drive."

I imagined the bemused smile he was sure to have on his face. "I will. Don't worry. I will."

The line went dead. I scoured every inch of the apartment again, even looking for hidden floor safes, and as I did, I made sure everything was in the exact location it had been when I'd entered the room. The front door would be out for an escape path if Kamal returned, so I made sure I could get out the window just above his small cot. I had to use a knife and pry the paint-sealed window open. I opened and shut it several times, using some oil from the kitchen to make the sliding action smooth and quiet. Just outside it was a small veranda where one person might stand. Unfortunately, had someone chosen to stand on it, his view would consist of nothing but the brick wall of the neighboring building.

I took up vigil at the door, listening and feeling for anyone's approach. At twenty-eight minutes, I checked the progress bar. Ninety-eight percent downloaded. Ace had been right on. I checked my watch. I was supposed to be meeting Kamal in ten minutes. I would be late. I kept my eyes on the screen. Ninety-nine percent. At least I felt secure that Kamal wouldn't be barging in all of a sudden. If he was meeting me at the museum, then he'd have to almost be there. It took another minute, but the bar flashed one hundred percent. I unplugged the HDMI cable from my phone and replaced everything in the drawer exactly as I'd found it. Then I gave the room one more cursory look and left the apartment, locking it before dashing down the steps and to the metro.

I made it to the museum five minutes late, which I thought was pretty good, all things considered. Kamal stood by a staircase on the outer rim of the Louvre, and tapped his foot impatiently as I walked up to him. There was already a massively long line of people waiting to gain admission. I couldn't wait for the drop off when I could give Kamal the tracked flash drive. I hoped we'd be able to follow the trail today so my pickpocketing days would be over.

He didn't waste one second in commanding me. His tone was sharp as he spoke. "You've got forty minutes in the Louvre. Here's your pass, you won't have to wait in that long line. Go right up to the guy by the glass enclosure." He pointed. "Meet me back here and we'll go over what you've done. Get as much as you can, but don't get caught. Here's the bag of the day." He handed me a leather satchel that had a long strap I could drape over my shoulder. It had a sun stamped on the flap, the sign that identified me as Kamal's pickpocket, and kept me from getting my butt kicked by competing gangs.

I wasn't sure if Kamal was watching me or if it was someone else, but someone would definitely be watching. If it was Kamal, I needed to be good—if it was his boss, I needed to be even better. I had to impress these guys and hopefully win a meeting with someone higher up the chain. If he didn't have the drive, I needed to get a good idea of where else I could look.

The sheer size of the Louvre was daunting, but when I'd first arrived in Paris, I'd spent a little bit of time for several weeks making my way through it. Today I walked into a massive hall with arched, painted ceilings that was lined with enormous paintings on both sides. Benches lined the center along with planters that had been placed exactly in between the benches. I spotted my first mark.

She stared thoughtfully at a painting of a war scene from the 1600's and her purse sat about an inch to her left. I could easily sit next to her and take my sweet time getting what I wanted out of it even though hundreds of people were passing through the area at all times. Just as I was about to pickpocket her, the hair raised on the back of my neck. I looked around and couldn't pinpoint the threat. There was too much commotion all around. That's when I noticed the camera. It was hidden at the top of one of the paintings to my left. Perhaps a security guard was watching me through a live feed. Even if that wasn't the threat, I knew better than to go against my feelings. I moved away from that mark and chose someone else, then continued on to take from five other unsuspecting tourists.

I exited the Louvre to meet up with Kamal after the

requisite forty minutes. As I walked toward him, I decided not to give him a tracked drive at our first meet. Instead, I gave him an empty drive.

We made the swap effortlessly, and then he sent me back to do the same thing again.

On the second drop, I got a big haul and handed him one tracked drive with all the other stolen property. It wasn't until the third drop that I could see faint signs of the smile he was holding back. I assumed he was happy with my take. One of the tainted drives was mixed in again, and I cringed just a little bit thinking about him having two tracked drives already.

It seemed a bit heavy-handed to even give him two, but we didn't have a lot of time. If one of the trackers didn't work, hopefully the other would. I had one empty drive left and one tracked drive, the one intended for another pickpocket. I fingered it in my pocket, thinking. There wasn't really a good candidate for it. I'd watched—all the pickpockets handed their stuff over to Kamal, one way or another. He'd just end up with it anyway. And two drives was suspicious enough, let alone three. No, I wouldn't plant this last drive. I'd keep it. It might not be a bad idea to have one in reserve anyway.

"You've done really well," Kamal said as soon as I met up with him the fourth time. "Let's just meet at the end of your shift at four and see what you can get in that time."

"Do I get a lunch break? I'm starving." I shoved my hands into my pockets and rocked back on my heels.

"Sure. Make sure you get just as much as you did this morning by four o'clock, and you can take as long a break as you'd like."

"Okay. You got it." I pulled my hand out of my pocket and a drive fell to the ground. It was the third tracked drive. I winced inwardly. Swifter than I thought possible, Kamal shifted his foot over the drive. Heat rose in my chest.

"The stand at the end of the path down there," he said, pointing, "serves a great panini and fries."

I nodded, working hard for a couple of seconds to hide my exasperation with myself and act normal. How had I been so clumsy?

After pointing me in the right direction, he reached casually down and grabbed the drive as he retied his shoe.

I mouthed the word *sorry* as I walked away, hoping he would think I'd just made a beginner's mistake.

I grabbed a turkey panini from the place Kamal had suggested near the entrance to the gardens from the Louvre and enjoyed the heat of the day on a shaded bench. At least, as much as I could. A little irritation niggled at me. I texted Ace with updates on what I was doing.

No one even gave me a second glance for entering the museum the fourth time in one day. It wasn't unusual for tourists to enter and exit the Louvre on the same day because it was a place you could spend a week in and not see everything. People would leave to eat or just to take a break for a while. I went to the halls of statues this time and had to concentrate on the task at hand and not spend all my time gawking at the amazing sculptures. After only a few hours, my phone buzzed. It was Kamal. *Meet me in Halle in the alley two streets south of the fountain.*

Got it, I texted back in a rush. Instead of letting the niggling worry settle in, I ignored it in my excitement. Maybe I'd be able to be done with work early for the day. I had to walk right past Mad Dogs in order to get to the alley Kamal wanted to meet in. It took a bit of restraint not to stop and quickly buy a crepe on my way, but I managed it. I turned the corner and spotted him smack dab in the middle of the alley. It was dark and narrow, and the smell of wet dog wafted over me as I walked toward him. He was looking in the opposite direction, so I thought I'd sneak up on him and give him a fright. I was tired of being so serious all the time. Maybe it was a sign I'd been separated from Jeremy and Ace too long.

Just as I was a few feet from him, ready to say, *boo*, Kamal turned to me. *Boo* hung on my puckered lips, but never came out as he came right at me, a scowl on his face. I had to resist the urge to sweep kick him.

"Where did you get these?" He held up four drives. Three were tracked.

Caught off guard, I didn't know what to say. In two moves I could have him completely disabled. Was it the right thing at this moment to give myself away? No. I had to ride this out. I had to find my way to the lost drive.

He rushed the remaining distance to me and pinned me against the alley wall, a knife against my neck. "I said, where did you get these?" His lips were only inches from my face and a light mist of spit coated me as he spoke. My eyes fluttered, trying to avoid the spray as dread spread through my veins.

I had to stay calm and think despite the abject fear that gripped my chest. *Stay submissive. Stay submissive.* "I lifted stuff from a hundred people, and you're asking me where I got four drives? Are you crazy?"

He pushed me harder into the wall, and I felt the prick of the knife on my neck. I tried not to swallow, but in the end, I had to. The chances of me escaping his grasp now that he had the knife at my neck were slim at best, even with my excellent skills. Had I acted the second he came after me, he wouldn't have stood a chance. But then I wouldn't have had a chance of retrieving the missing drive.

I forced tears into my eyes, needing to appear weak. "The Louvre?" I eked out. "The Louvre."

He released me just a bit. "Who do you work for?"

"I work for you," my voice was raspy, dirty sounding.

"Who gave you those drives?"

"I took them from people in the Louvre. Please. What's going on?"

"There were trackers on three of those drives. But you already knew that, didn't you?"

I shook my head—a slight motion—one that ensured my neck wouldn't be cut.

He pushed hard again. I let the tears flow. I needed him to have compassion on me so it would be easier for him to believe me.

"What's going on?" I whispered, my tears falling freely now. "Please. I don't know what's going on. Is this a test? Part of my interview?"

He backed up all of a sudden and brandished the drives in one hand and held the knife out with the other. "Some of these have trackers. Where did you get them?"

"Trackers?" I rubbed my neck and coughed. "I got them at the Louvre off different people, but I can't remember who. I just can't remember. I'm sorry."

"Are you sure? Think, Eva. Think." He moved toward me, and I shrank back, screeching, covering my neck like I was truly afraid. "Remember, you put one in your pocket, why?"

That's when I figured out a lie that could save me. "You told me drives could be valuable! I looked for guys with laptops, not students but people who looked, I don't know, business-like. There was a guy I got a couple off of, I thought I really scored. He was tall, in a suit, all official looking. I remember thinking he must be a government official or something. That's why I went after him."

"Are you sure?" he asked. One of his eyes narrowed.

"I'm sure," I squeaked. "I'm sure." I had to decide if I was going to stand up to him now or play the weak victim. In gang situations, it was important to be able to assert yourself so you weren't picked on, but only when it came to your equals or lessers. With a boss, it was important to appear submissive and indebted if you wanted to last for a while.

"Are you sure no one gave these to you?" He waved the drives in front of my face and grabbed my arm. "Because I will find out if someone did."

"I'm sure," I said, shaking my head eagerly. "I stole them. No one gave me anything."

He took a step back and looked off in the distance like he was thinking about something.

"What happened? Explain all this to me, and maybe I can help." I furrowed my brow.

His rigid posture softened slightly and he took another step back, letting go of my arm. It burned as blood rushed back in. "These drives you gave me, they're being tracked by someone, someone who wants to know where they are."

"Why would anyone track their drives? That's just crazy." I wanted him to think I was totally naïve and couldn't even think this through, but at the same time willing to help him out.

"Because wicked important stuff can be on a drive."

"Right, right, that's why they could be worth money. Like that Tom Cruise movie, uh…"

"*Mission Impossible III.* Yes."

"What was on those drives I got? Was it something, you know, worth something?" I knew very well that nothing important was on those drives, but I made my voice eager.

"Nothing important. I'm guessing whoever you stole those from hadn't had the chance to download whatever information they wanted to put on them."

I stood with my shoulders slumped slightly forward in a way he would consider non-threatening. Little did he know that in three moves, I could end his life, even from this stance. "So if these drives are so worthless, why did you just get all crazy with me? Aren't they the very things you want?"

Maybe if I kept him talking, I could get him to say his contact's name

"Yes and no. I mean, we want untracked drives." He leaned against the wall. "Or tracked drives from known sources."

"Well, who would put valuable info on a drive that wasn't tracked? Didn't you just say—?"

"Look. Some people put valuable stuff on drives without even knowing it. The guy I give these drives to knows what's important and who's important. The only thing is that he won't take tracked drives without knowing where or who they came from."

"Well how are you supposed to know if they've been tracked?" I threw my hands out to my sides as if I were exasperated. And I was. This system was crazy.

"Actually, I have a computer program that checks them. If they are, I chuck 'em fast."

"Hmm. No way around the tracking?"

"I think Marco has a way, but he's only willing to use it when he knows the source behind the information."

Ah, I got him to say a name. Marco.

"Huh. I'm sorry I stole tracked drives. I'll try not to do it again, but I'm not sure how to avoid it."

"Just make note of who you get any drives from. You could even snap a picture if you get the chance."

"I can't believe you were accusing me of working for someone. What was that all about?"

He sighed. "Look, I have to constantly be on guard in this business." He lowered his head and looked at me through one eye like he was still a little suspicious.

"Maybe I should just toss any drives I get from now on away."

He stood up straight and shook his hands out in front of him. "No. No. We get a ton of money from good drives. I just need to be careful where I check them. Today I was in a hurry and checked them at my apartment. It just made me nervous. It's been a few weeks since we've run into a tracked device. And get a picture of the people you get the drive from or at the very least a description of them. I am going to be watching you, though. Today seems like too much of a coincidence." He looked at me again, his face tight with suspicion. "Why did you have a drive in your pocket, anyway?"

I'd already come up with an excuse in case he asked me. I almost told him I thought about keeping that one for myself, but I thought stealing from him would be a pretty bad idea. "I was taking things right and left and didn't always bother to put everything into the bag. I just missed it when I put everything in there before I left the Louvre. It was small. What can I say? It won't happen again."

"I better not get any more tracked drives from you. That's all." All strain left his face.

It seemed like the situation had been defused. He noticed I

was rubbing my neck, and he moved toward me, a softness in his eyes.

"Sorry about that. It's only a small cut. I'm sure you understand."

"Would you really have killed me?" I narrowed my eyes and moved away from him.

"If you were a spy of some sort, yes."

I recoiled, my hands touching the wall behind me.

He put his hand out. "This is how I make a living. It's not the best, but it works for me. And I can't have anyone messing it up."

I didn't take his hand. I had to stay in character. I had to be afraid of him. "Have you ever killed someone, then?"

"No." He said it a little too fast, and then he touched his nose. He was lying.

"Good. 'Cause that totally freaks me out. I don't know if I could trust you if I thought you'd killed someone."

He shook his head and forced a smile. "No. I haven't. But if someone threatened me or my job, I would." There was determination and purpose behind his words. He had killed, and he would again. A cold, wet snake slithered up my spine. It took all I had not to shiver. I leaned hard on the wall.

His phone beeped and he pulled it out of his pocket and looked at it. "I gotta go. See you tomorrow. Louvre at nine fifteen sharp by the Mona Lisa."

I nodded. It still surprised me that he was so protective of this job. I wished I knew what his motivation was. Did he protect it because he loved it or was there something else? If I knew that, I would have some leverage over him. Until then, I was an open target and needed to be careful.

I waited thirty seconds, then I followed him. Inside, I was

still reeling from the attack—I'd been alone, no backup, with a knife to my neck. And now I was following that knife, again with no backup. *What is the matter with me?* I wondered. But I knew the answer. Nothing was wrong with me. This was just too important to let go.

I remained a good distance from Kamal as he walked purposefully over the sidewalks, blending into the crowds and disappearing when there were none. A constant stream of cars filled the streets and every metro tunnel was hopping with people rushing about. He picked up loot from four different kids at four different spots, all very open. Not a single Parisian seemed to notice anything amiss. He was smart, careful. I kept with him as he made his way to a business building I wasn't familiar with. Could it be the clearinghouse for all the stolen goods? I snapped a picture of the placard with the names of the business behind the door then took a few pictures of the buildings and the surrounding area and sent it all to Ace. I had to force myself not to go in and explore. I'd bring it up when I officially got back on the mission if it was still relevant.

Kamal came out with a different bag not ten minutes later. Things they wouldn't take? Payment? Or did he have a hiding place inside the building where he kept things? I'd have to find a way in. I wanted to get help from Rosabella, but that was too risky. What would Siron do if she found out I was still working on this mission? Probably toss me in a Division holding cell. There was no way I could let that happen.

Kamal went to his apartment. I stepped into the foyer and waited to hear his door click shut. Once it did, I crept up to the second floor, making sure no one was coming or going and listened. It sounded like he was typing on a computer. Was he checking new drives? Keeping track of what he had been given?

Divvying up money? I just couldn't tell. I needed to get some listening devices in there as soon as possible. Maybe tonight. I could probably find something I could rig up from civilian devices. Mentally, I thumbed through my training manuals from the Bresen Spy Academy, reviewing techniques for making and planting improvised bugs. Next thing I knew, there was silence, and I figured he was probably painting.

I slipped away and headed to the electronics store where I'd bought the drives. I gathered the necessary items I'd need for the bugs and headed back home to assemble them. None of them would be as good as what Division had, and as Eva I wouldn't even really have a chance to listen to whatever the bugs picked up. I seethed inwardly—it should not be happening this way. I should have my team around me. I should have the resources I needed. Instead I was on my own and stretched thin.

I'd put listening devices in his apartment in the morning and find a way to get the tracker in his phone. Maybe Halluis and Ace would have moments where they could listen in and track Kamal.

9

I set watch on Kamal's place at six am after a five-mile run. I sat on a bench across the street in front of another ratty apartment that had a full view of the entrance with a handful of magazines to pretend to read. No one would leave or arrive without me seeing. I felt invigorated and more alive than I had since arriving in Paris. In the early mornings, the city seemed to exude its historical charm because no one seemed to be stirring. No businesses were open and everyone was still in bed. I could almost see the Paris of my dreams with the Eiffel Tower, the Catacombs, the amazing gardens, and the Louvre standing in all their historical glory in the beautiful, awe inspiring city. But once the city and its people awoke each day, reality hit me in the face, reminding me that my dreams were a long lost fantasy.

I watched as Kamal left his apartment shortly after eight. He thought that was early? Perhaps it was if he'd stayed up all night painting. I waited five minutes to make sure he wouldn't return because he'd forgotten something, then I picked the lock and went inside. I didn't need much time. I'd be in and out in minutes. The inside of the apartment looked exactly the same as when I left it last time. Kamal was clean and organized—a man of habit.

I made quick work of setting my three improvised devices

and was about to leave when I had the urge to look in the silverware drawer again. I just wanted to see what he'd added or taken from it. I hit the jackpot. A ledger. I lifted it out of the drawer and set it on the counter. A piece of paper fluttered to the ground. I picked it up. It was a drawing of a girl, a beautiful girl with mocha skin and deep, dark eyes lined with long, inviting lashes. I couldn't help but smile back at her before setting the picture to the side and checking out the ledger.

I examined it, capturing the numbers on the pages in my mind. There were three separate accountings. Perhaps one was for the drives?

The last accounting was counting down from 300,000 euro. Maybe that was what his goal was to earn while picking. It was a lot of money, but he was already two-thirds of the way there— he only needed another 100,000 euro. Judging by the dates in the ledger, it had only taken him two years to earn that much. No wonder he lived in this terrible, rundown place. He obviously had a plan and was saving the money for something specific.

I moved toward the door, admiring one painting of a girl laughing, but stopped in my tracks when I heard a voice. And not just any voice. It was Kamal's voice. He was coming back. I'd lingered too long.

His voice boomed through the door. "Yeah. I think I have about ten of those right now. I'll go and check. Yeah, uh huh." Was he on his phone? His key jiggled in the lock.

I scanned the room for a likely hiding place. I was a dead duck. The only place to hide would be behind the door when he opened it. He did have a bathroom, but it was across the room, and I'd never make it there before the three seconds I had to hide expired. So, I stepped to the side of the door and stood, hoping the little alcove for coats would conceal me. I didn't even have time to put the coats over me before he entered the room, leaving the door ajar with me halfway behind it.

The seconds ticked by like hours. I didn't dare move—it would call attention to me. I tried to blink as little as possible. If he did happen to close the door, I would be completely exposed, but if I remained still, I'd have a chance to not be seen. At least I continued to tell myself that. I kept my eyes fixed. No twitching. No swaying. I had to be stone. Actually, I had to be a coat.

I had the worst luck today.

I glanced at the kitchen drawer I'd opened and had left slightly ajar. It stuck out a half centimeter farther than the counter. I was sure he checked it every morning before he left. I breathed the shallowest breaths I was able without passing out. Only inches and a door stood between us. The floorboards squeaked as Kamal passed right in front of me and moved into the kitchen. I had become stone. He paused a millisecond before pulling out the silverware drawer. His eyes lit somewhere in the middle of the counter. He must've been trying to remember if he'd closed the drawer the last time he'd been in here. He was definitely on the phone.

All he had to do was turn and look my direction and he'd see me. "For you, I'll make it work. You're my best customer." Kamal smiled that winning smile even though he thought no one was there to see it. I closed my eyes.

I could hear searching noises and then the sounds of the ledger being opened and thumbed through. "I'm pretty sure I have one like that, but I don't have it with me. I'll have to let you know."

My eyes darted to Kamal's hands. He held a key. Had I seen a key when I looked in the drawer? No.

"Are you serious? That much? We keep the same fifty-fifty split, right?" Kamal looked my way. This was it. I was busted. But he wasn't actually looking at me but at some unknown object in the air. I wanted to look behind me and see what he was seeing, but forced myself to remain a stone.

"Good." He tossed the key into the air and caught it. "I don't really care why this buyer wants to pay triple for flash drives collected in the next week, but I'll take it. I'll keep them for you." He put the ledger and flatware back into the drawer and shut it.

They had been talking about flash drives. I wished I could hear the other end of the conversation.

"I have a girl who seems to have the touch with knowing where those are. I'll encourage her to get more." Kamal's voice sounded truly thankful. "I could use the extra money for sure." He walked out of the kitchen, only an arm's length from me, staring at the key in his hand before slipping it into his pocket as he passed me. Kamal's laugh was pinched, forced. I could feel rather than hear him move toward the door. Kamal was going to get a lot closer to his goal, whatever that was.

He stepped outside and talked a bit more before bidding the buyer farewell. A bead of sweat trickled down my cheek, and I took the chance while he was outside and wiped it away. Kamal's fingers curled around the door. The question was, would he come into the apartment again or was he leaving? If he caught me, the mission would be a total loss. *Be the coat. Be the coat.*

He started to pull the door closed and then stopped and started talking again. "Marni?" There was a pause. "No. I'm happy you called."

He was speaking in Arabic. I didn't know a lot of Arabic,

but I had learned the basics while at Bresen Spy Academy. It was a required course. By the end of the month, I'd gone through the entire Arabic to English dictionary. And while I could recognize all the characters and had said most of the words at least once, I hadn't had someone speak it enough to understand everything.

He continued, and I was glad to discover I could understand enough of what he'd said to piece together a lot of it. He was surprised Marni had called because they had planned on talking that night. He told her about the possibility of getting extra money this week and talked about having enough money in ten months. That when he got it, everything would be all right and they'd be able to get her the help she needed. He also talked about a girl who was going to make it easy to make the money in ten months because she was twice as productive as his seasoned pickpockets. Apparently, they'd calculated it taking five years to get the money they needed, and he was hoping to cut that time in half.

He told Marni that he couldn't wait to be with her and even called her *habibi,* which was Arabic for *my love.* He told her he couldn't quit just yet but that he wished he could. It was a sacrifice, but it was also the only way. They spoke about his paintings, but I didn't understand it all. Then he told her when he came to her in ten months, he would be a full-time artist. Again he mentioned a girl that was making it possible to happen so quickly. Then he told her he loved her and couldn't wait to see her.

I wondered who this girl pickpocket was. Was he referring to me? It seemed a reasonable conclusion to draw. I assumed he ended the call, because his hand reached out and shut the door behind him. I heard his footsteps pound down the wooden apartment building steps. I exhaled sharply.

I stayed where I was. People forgot things all the time. I waited the two minutes and forty-five seconds necessary to make sure he was gone for good as my mind whirred with what I'd just heard. Someone was excited about buying drives and was willing to pay a considerable amount for them. This changed everything. Not only would Kamal be selling the drives, but someone was actively seeking them. I had competition.

I pulled out my cell and texted Ace. *Tonight. Meet.* No reply came and my mind wandered back to Kamal. He had a girlfriend or a wife, Marni, out there. Something was wrong with her, and that's why he worked so hard.

I wondered how many pickers had similar situations and felt they had to do what they were doing. It was true that it was still a choice. There were honest ways to make money, and lying, cheating, and stealing did not fit into that category. Sure, you had to be smarter than the average crook, but the path of least resistance was often fatal. I hoped Kamal would survive to help the person, the girl, on the other end of the phone. His scar flashed through my mind.

Still no response from Ace.

I listened at the door and took another look around the room. I assumed Marni had never been here. There was only a twin bed. He'd come here for the express purpose of making money for this girl. Maybe whatever was wrong with her made her unable to travel. I needed to get my hands on his phone so we could trace and listen to his calls. As much as I didn't want to, we might have to use this girl to get him to spill his guts about where the flash drives went. Did I want this to happen? While Siron didn't like torturing people or threatening them, it seemed this drive would be something that would make her look the other way. I'd tuck that information away for right now.

I made a final mental snapshot of the room so that I would be able to easily navigate all the easels and art supplies without light. I hoped he wouldn't move anything until after I came back to bug his phone.

It was weird how the knowledge of Kamal's motivation made me see him differently. On the one hand, it really bothered me that he was using me the way he was. On the other, I wanted to help him help the girl. If the police caught up with him, what would happen to her?

Before reaching my apartment, I got a text back from Ace. The meeting was on. I got dressed for a day of picking as Eva and met Kamal at the Louvre.

"I've got someone really interested in drives right now. Let's give him what he wants."

"Okay," I said and by the end of the day, I'd given him four.

"Good girl," Kamal said, "Let's get a repeat of today, tomorrow."

"Will do," I said before leaving to catch the train home.

***

I paced my small living room. Five strides in one direction and five back. At ten on the dot, Halluis and Ace walked into the apartment from the balcony.

"We've got a big problem," I said as the two took seats on the couch. "There's a buyer out there offering triple the usual payout for certain flash drives."

"What?" the two said in unison.

"I overheard a conversation between Kamal and his flash

drive buyer. The buyer told Kamal flash drives are going for a premium right now. Kamal promised him about ten."

"Not good," Ace said. "This changes everything." He put his elbows on his knees and cradled his chin with his hands.

"I'm going to need a lot of help from you two in order to beat this guy to it," I said. "In four days the drives are gone, which means we have less than that. But first, Halluis, tell me what you found out in Coulogne. Maybe there's something there to help us."

"Dufor's sister is a real sweetheart. She definitely needed someone to talk to. Dufor had a nephew named Henri. Yes, he was named after Mr. Henri Dufor. His nephew was killed in Paris a few years back in a murder that was never solved. The boy had gotten himself involved with some shadier elements and his body was found with its hands cut off and some symbol carved into his face."

I gasped. "I watched Kamal take a knife to a boy who'd stolen something in Kamal's area. Was little Henri a pickpocket?"

"I don't know. Like I said, the murder was never solved. Truthfully, I wasn't sure his mom would be able to hold it together long enough to finish the story, but she did. She had a really close relationship with Dufor. I mean seriously, the she named her only son after Henri. She's devastated, can hardly live a normal life now. Her son stabbed and what happens to Dufor? He's stabbed too. Besides misery for this lady, we don't have much information to go on. I basically got nothing more. I really felt for her."

"Shoot, I was hoping..."

"I know, but it was a dead end." Halluis frowned.

"Let's make a plan and hit this thing hard together

tomorrow."

"I'll see if I can't get us some listening devices and—" Ace rubbed his chin.

"I already planted some homemade ones." I leaned forward, excited to let them know I had already thought of that.

"And who's going to listen?" Halluis huffed.

"I will, I guess," Ace said, totally serious.

"In all that free time Siron's been sending your way?" Halluis scoffed.

"Touché," Ace said. "We'll have to find the time, though. We don't have a choice. And we need to replace the bugs Christy so deftly placed with better ones. No offense, Christy."

"None taken. You'll have all the time in the world once we get that drive," I said. "Since the things Siron has you doing aren't helping at all, put them to the side, ignore them for a couple of days. You won't be losing anything, right? Just tell her nothing is panning out."

Halluis scrunched up his nose. "You've worked with Siron, she's a hoverer. She's on top of what we are doing nine times out of ten. No. I have a solution and you're not going to like it. I think we need Division on this one."

"Siron has forbidden Christy from doing anything. If she were to find out…" Halluis interrupted Ace.

"We have no choice. This is not something the three of us could ever hope to do on our own. We need Division's backing on this."

"That's easy for you to say when it's not your prancing feathers on the chopping block."

"But it is and I'm willing to put them there. Christy is onto something, and I say we do it right or don't do it at all. I believe in the information you've found, Christy. We could totally do this, if we had the right resources. We need bugs. We need trackers. We need people to listen to the bugs, and a team ready to move when we uncover where the drive is. I hate to admit it, but we are over our heads on this one."

I stared at them, my mind running on fast forward. "I see what you're saying, but I still don't know if it's the right move to bring Siron in on this." What would happen if they failed again? Even if they were right, would she listen?

"It's really Christy's call, Halluis. It's her butt on the line."

As much as I didn't want it to be, Halluis was right. I was going to have to tuck tail and go to Siron. "Convincing Siron to listen will be a mission in and of itself, but we can't lose that drive now. Yes. We go to Siron. It's the only way to have what we need to get the drive before it's sold to the highest bidder."

"We have four days, right?" Halluis said.

"Less than four days. The drive will be sold on the fourth day."

"Listen," I said. "I'm going to go in to talk to her alone. I don't want you two anywhere near when I do."

"Pshhh!" Ace said. "Screw that. We're going to go in as a team. And, as you both know, we are the three greatest minds to hit the streets of Paris and can handle one little old Division head."

"We're in serious trouble if we can't."

Ace glared at Halluis, who loved to add skepticism to every conversation. "I guarantee Siron is a bit panicked right now because she's going to have to report to Central soon and she doesn't want to do that without something to show. She will be happy about a solid lead. We won't have to tell her everything, just a little truth and a little lie. She'll kick and scream, but in the end, she'll give in because she has nothing else. Soon she'll discover Christy should be commended for what she's accomplished on her own."

Jeremy flashed through my mind. I still hadn't heard from him. He would have been sick with worry knowing what I'd been doing.

"We can convince her!"

I loved that Ace was always so optimistic.

10

Bright and early the next morning, Siron walked into the conference room. When she saw me, her hands went to her hips and she turned back toward Halluis and Ace, who followed her in. "Tell me I'm not seeing what I think I'm seeing. Tell me this isn't the emergency."

Halluis said, "Hear us out."

"So, it's 'us', is it?" Siron's neck was red. "I hope you're ready to join Christy on leave."

Ace shut the door and I saw an eye roll. Halluis gestured to Siron to go further into the room. "You are going to love what you hear." He was trying hard to make the atmosphere relaxed. She sighed, but walked to the head of the table, staring at me on the opposite side. Once there, she said, "You have two minutes. Speak."

I glanced at the boys and they both gave me a slight nod. "Last Tuesday, I left the apartment to get food and stumbled onto something. I saw the pickpocket who stole my bag that had the drive in it."

Siron's eyes rounded briefly and then narrowed. "You were just out getting something to eat?" The derision in her tone was cold as ice. "So you contacted your team. The one I told you to stay away from?"

"Yes." I nodded. "Anyway. The pickpocket was there, and I thought I couldn't let this opportunity pass me by." I didn't pause to give Siron a chance to say anything else. "He led me to the person above him and I was able to find out that the drive is still in play and I know who has it."

Siron bit the inside of her cheek, eyes narrowing further as she stared at a spot on the dark mahogany table for several beats. Her head popped up and she stared at me hard. "You did this without sanction. Without protection or backup?"

I nodded.

"You know where the drive is?" Siron had finally digested what I'd told her.

"Not exactly. But, I know who has it."

She turned a skeptical eye on the guys and then peered back at me. "Tell me more."

"Kamal is the man who has the drive. He's a middleman of sorts. We hit upon some major luck because his drive buyer has been out of town and won't be back for four more days. Kamal has been collecting and saving the drives to sell him on his return."

"I don't understand. Are you saying you don't have the drive?"

"No. I've checked Kamal's apartment and it isn't there, but it is somewhere he thinks is safe."

"I'm surprised you didn't retrieve them before coming here today."

I swallowed hard. "That's actually what I was hoping to do, but things have changed."

"Now the bomb drops." Siron sighed.

"Someone is actively searching for the drive and has upped the bounty on any drives stolen for the next week. We can't let this buyer get the drive before we do. In order to do that, I need Division's help." I wanted to say I was sorry I'd let her down before, but I didn't want her to think about it if she hadn't already.

"Impulsive girl," Siron said. "You should have come to me the second you hit on the pickpocket."

"You wouldn't have listened to me. Not without concrete proof. Whoever the client is really wants the drive and fast. Like I said, they've tripled the bounty."

"And you're sure it's Dufor's drive?"

It was my turn to nod. This was a lie. The truth was that I wasn't sure, but all the signs pointed in that direction. To have someone, a powerful someone with deep pockets, suddenly triple the bounty for drives at the very time Dufor's drive went missing? It was too big of a coincidence. Despite that, I couldn't get my mouth to say yes.

"This Kamal. How have you been tracking him?"

"Following and befriending him."

"Of course. Following and befriending without backup." She shook her head. "This is against my better judgment, and if I didn't feel in my gut this was a good decision, it wouldn't be happening. But the search will continue on my terms."

I froze. Was she going to cut me out?

"The first term is that you, Agent Hadden, are going to get a shadow. I'd replace you, but we don't have time for that."

"That's me," Halluis volunteered. "I'll be her shadow."

"You think I would trust you to be her shadow? I don't think so. You're on my hit list right now."

Halluis's face reddened slightly. He did not like to be censured.

I didn't want to, but I nodded. "Fine." I couldn't help but

think of Jeremy. Where was he and why hadn't he already come back? If a Division director wanted him to come in and he hadn't, he must be in deep. I hoped he wasn't dead somewhere. I couldn't think that way. Instead I imagined him working miracles and saving the day.

"Come up with a plan while I go find Christy a shadow. Ace can work on new drives that can't be tracked and we'll try to follow these drives to the one Dufor was supposed to give us. In the meantime, Christy will keep working the personal angle to try to find out where Kamal is keeping the drives. Ace, you get Christy whatever tech she needs, and Halluis, you try to find out who else is looking for the drive. Bring me the plan when you've got it down."

Siron left the room and the three of us got to work on a plan to get the drive: How many listening devices we'd need and where to put them, how many agents to have on standby to swoop in and retrieve the drive once we found it. Three hours later we had a proposal ready for Siron. The first thing on the list was to check out the suspected clearinghouse I'd seen Kamal go into yesterday.

"I'll take it to her," I said, looking over my shoulder toward Siron's office. The door was shut.

"You don't need any more punishment. I'll do it," Halluis said.

"All right."

"I've been working on a solution already." Ace said. "It will blow your mind. Se magnifique!"

"Can't wait. I need to get out there and steal some stuff." I rolled my eyes.

"You are my favorite thief, darling," Ace said with a southern American accent as he left the room. "Come see me later today."

I will. "And you're my favorite tech magician."

"And I'll get information gathering and see if I can find who wants the drive so bad they're willing to pay three times for it." Halluis went straight for Siron's office and I watched as he knocked on the door. When it opened, I saw Summer Barnes.

I squeezed my eyes shut and looked away. I turned back. The scene hadn't changed. Summer was in Siron's office. A heavy feeling landed in my gut, and I forgot what I was supposed to be doing. I stared dumbly as Halluis explained a few things to Siron as she looked over the proposal. She shook her head and then spotted me. I quickly turned away and headed for the exit. I had no intention of learning why Summer was there and could hardly bear the thought of having to talk to her. Things were hard enough as they were right now, I didn't need anything taking my head out of the game. In two steps I'd be gone, down the hall that led to the exit and it wouldn't matter, but Siron's voice cut through the air. "Agent Hadden!"

I froze. My lower jaw jutted forward, and I closed my eyes with a sigh. I didn't think things could get worse, but I'd been wrong. I pulled in a big breath and straightened before turning around and walking to the office, shoulders squared. I put on a fake air of confidence and even managed a smile before arriving at the office, but inside, I trembled.

I kept my eyes on Siron. "Yes, Director?"

"Come in, Christy. Your shadow's arrived."

I flashed a look at Summer, whose jaw was slack, eyes rounded. Guess this was a shock to her as well. As our eyes met, her look of surprise or maybe horror vanished and her eyes narrowed slightly before returning to normal.

"Close the door, please," Siron shuffled through some

papers on her desk. I stepped farther in and shut the door.

"My shadow's arrived?" I asked, hoping beyond hope things weren't as they seemed.

"Yes," Siron said, looking up. "Agent Hadden, meet Agent Barnes."

Summer's left eyebrow raised. No. This could not be. "Director, I'm not sure this is such a good idea."

The director's head popped from Summer to me and back again. "Oh, you two know each other already? Great. That will make things easier."

"No. Seriously, with our history—"

Siron interrupted me. "I don't care what kind of history you have. From this point forward, your history will soon include the fact that you were both professional Division agents who worked together on a case and triumphed."

I opened my mouth to explain, but she cut me off again. "Summer was kind enough to leave her training in Germany to be with us today and from what her handler says, she's a great shadow. You are lucky to have her. The next closest available shadow is ten hours away. Put the past in the past and leave it there. You two will be a cohesive team from this moment on. Suck it up. Lay it aside. We are moving forward. Understand?"

We shot each other a look and then both nodded. "I can't hear you."

"Yes, ma'am," we both said in unison.

"See that, you're working as one already. I'll introduce Summer to the rest of the team and brief her on the plan and what has already happened. I saw in the proposal that you're supposed to be at the Louvre. Head out. Summer will find you at some point during the day to start shadowing you. You'll finally have the protection you need, Agent Hadden. I'll see both of you tonight for your report. Oh, and Hadden, I want every bit of intel you've collected over the past few days."

I nodded, hating the fact that I'd have to give her the file that had the contents of Kamal's computer on it, and after opening the door, I left the room. I couldn't believe Summer would be watching my every move. My nose wrinkled and my throat burned with disgust. Not fun. If only Jeremy were here, this would not be happening. A desperate ache filled my gut thinking about his absence. I said a little prayer for him as I walked through the office. He had to be safe. He had to continue to be safe. Memories of my past with Summer flooded my mind. We did have a history together. A history I wanted to forget.

We'd met on a school trip, became witnesses to a murder, and ended up in witness protection at a spy school in Belgium. Summer had made it clear that she thought I was the cause of her having to leave her perfect life and family and on top of that, blamed me for the death of her boyfriend, Josh.

I didn't know how I was going to do it, but I was going to have to make it work. From the look on Summer's face when I'd entered the office, she was going to have just as hard a time as I was. It had been over three years, it should all be forgotten, but I knew it wasn't. I was supposed to trust my shadow. I didn't trust Summer.

I went straight to Ace to see what new tech he had for me. I hoped he had something good enough to help me out of the gloom Summer's presence had brought.

Ace was in the sprawling lab with ten others working on various projects at different stations around the room. I walked to the very back corner where Ace liked to hide out. He'd even made the area his own by hanging paintings of colorful and dynamic superheroes.

"Looking for a lost team member?"

He turned, grinning like a mad scientist. "Not any more. I'm shocked at how quickly Siron took to our plan."

"No kidding. But I could do without my shadow."

"Is he already here?"

"Yes, but he's a she."

"Seriously? And you don't sound impressed."

"Let's just say I have a history with this girl and don't trust her as far as I could throw her. Siron said she's going to introduce her to you guys. Just don't fall in love with her, okay?"

"No worries there, my beautiful thief. I only have eyes for you."

"Seriously, though, be careful with her."

"I'll keep my electronic eye on her for you."

"I'd appreciate that."

"Check this out, Christy." He held up a thin piece of plastic dangling from tweezers, his face tight with excitement.

"Playing with plastic, eh?"

"Tracking plastic, actually." His eyes gleamed as he stared at it.

"Tracking plastic that's somehow not detectable?" My voice cracked as I spoke, I really wanted it to work.

"I think so."

I didn't like hearing the *think* part. "I'm really amazed that skin of plastic somehow tracks, but it's no good to me if it can be detected."

He nodded. "Theoretically, this will work, but it hasn't been tried and tested. You will be doing this. I'm assuming the pickpockets are using a program to identify the RFID trackers that the previous drives had attached to them. They were constantly transmitting, albeit in completely different ways.

We're going to use trackers that we activate from our end. It will only transmit once activated, and this plastic-like coating protects the drive from activation by anyone else and detection of the device itself."

I thought about the tracking device Division had put in my arm to help me catch a kidnapper. I was the one who had had to activate it. That seemed like forever ago.

"So we'll be able to activate it whenever we want to?"

"Yes. In theory. If they have any jammers, however, we will not be able to activate from a great distance."

"How would we know when to activate it?"

"Seems to me the best time would be at night when people sleep, but there is no good answer to this."

"Kamal told me he tests the trackers right after he acquires them. So night sounds good. Is it ready, then?" I thought about Kamal's hesitancy in taking drives and decided that I would not be the one giving this drive to him. I would have to get that drive into one of the other pickpockets' hands.

"Give me five minutes, and I'll have it for you."

The sparkle in his eye made me happy. "You know, we still need to get our eight-euro sodas at a café to feel the amazing *ambience* of Paris." I winked.

"Yes, we do. Yes, we do."

As I turned to leave, he grabbed my arm. "I'm really glad you're back. Now, let's go kick some pickpocket butt." He handed me a bag of chocolate smarties.

I smiled and chuckled before slipping into the evening air, humming. Things were looking up for me.

I headed to the Louvre—I had three new tracked drives to plant, and the thought of it made me nervous. The fact that Summer would be following me everywhere I went made me more nervous. At least I couldn't feel her, which meant she wasn't following me just yet.

This time, I was smarter about how I went about getting the drives to Kamal. Immediately after entering the museum, I headed for the bathroom where I stripped off my clothes to reveal a different outfit, pulled a wig and some makeup out of my boots and put them on to change my look completely. I was Gabrielle again. I picked the lock on a small cabinet where I stuffed my other clothes so I could get them when I needed them. I tracked down two of Kamal's pickpockets who were in the Louvre with me and anticipated where they were headed after watching them for a few minutes.

I slipped the first drive into the side pocket of the jacket of a young man who was in the direct path of the first pickpocket. Sure enough, the pickpocket brushed against the man at the same time someone else bumped into him on his other side. I watched the pickpocket's hand flash through the young man's pocket and palm the drive, setting it casually into his side pack with two small stars and a crescent moon on it. I watched him, wanting to see him take the drive to Kamal so I could be sure it got into the right hands.

I felt someone watching me. It bugged me, but I was glad I was at least able to feel Summer. I guessed I'd rather feel her than not.

To my surprise, the tall kid that I'd seen at l'Orangerie showed up in the romantic collection of paintings near the *Raft of Medusa*. He signaled the pickpocket, who moved in front of one of Eugene Delacroix's paintings and the tall kid took the drive and a few other items from the pickpocket's side pack and put them into his own. Afterward, Tall Kid moved in the direction of the other pickpocket in the Louvre. His area was all the way in another wing called the Richelieu wing, where the most ancient pieces of art are kept, and I knew another way to get there. I hoped to beat Tall Kid there and find the pickpocket, plant the second drive, and get it picked before Tall Kid arrived.

I walked as fast as I could without some guard kicking me out for running. When I found the second pickpocket, I watched him for about thirty seconds before planting the drive on a woman dressed in professional clothing. Two minutes later, the drive had passed through the pickpocket's hands, into his side bag, into the hand of Tall Kid, and finally into Tall Kid's side pack. I stuck with him like a bear to honey. I had to see the drives pass to Kamal.

It was a big risk for me to exit the museum and get anywhere near Kamal. He could make me, and that would end my career as a pickpocket. With extreme care, I stepped out of the Louvre into the sticky hot air of the courtyard only moments after Tall Kid, but I hung back, letting him show me the way. I moved to some steps that led to doors that had long been sealed to the public and watched Tall Kid sit next to Kamal near some flowers in the same courtyard. The exchange was smooth, with Kamal taking the full side pack and leaving Tall Kid with an empty one.

After giving myself a second to celebrate, I headed back inside the Louvre, using the entrance inside the mall this time. After changing back into the clothes I'd left in the bathroom cupboard, I went to work.

Tall Kid visited my area twice during the morning, but he didn't approach me. Had Kamal sent him to check up on me?

I shook it off and headed out of the museum to get some lunch. I knew the only thing that would make me feel settled was a crepe from Mad Dogs, so despite it being a bit out of my way, I headed to Halle. I couldn't feel Summer anymore which made me feel even better.

Today I branched out with a butter and cinnamon sugar crepe. The fountain area was packed, and I was lucky to get a seat. After lunch I'd have to hustle just a bit in order to get Kamal enough stuff that it would look like I'd worked hard all day.

My phone rang, which was unusual. I typically got texts from everyone. My heart flooded with glee as I heard the voice on the other end. I thought I might spontaneously combust.

"Hey." It was Jeremy, speaking to me in French. So sexy. "Get your body to HQ if you aren't already there."

11

That's when it really hit me that I was talking to Jeremy. I had to concentrate not to sob. Jeremy was safe. He was back from his covert mission and I would be able to see him soon. Then I remembered where I was and a hard lump formed in my throat. I needed to get back to the Louvre as soon as I got done with my crepe. I'd been gone too long already. "I can't." The words felt like sandpaper in my mouth. I had a lot of picking to do. Division had used a lot of my time this morning.

"Seriously? I've been gone for four months and you can't make it work?"

"I've taken too long of a lunch already. I've got to get back to the Louvre." I cleared my throat. The moment of our first kiss in New York filled the screen of my mind and I relished every second. "If I had known you were coming…"

"I heard you got yourself in trouble. I'm supposed to come and slap your wrist or something."

I paused. "So, you haven't been briefed yet?" A new surge of relief washed over me.

"Well, I got a four page email from Director Siron, but I chose not to read it until I'd heard what you had to say first. I'm on my way to HQ now." His voice lowered a register, and the worry in it gave my heart a tiny flutter.

"There have been some…developments since then. You can probably disregard it."

"Of course there are." A curious disappointment sounded in his voice.

I spoke quickly to beat his outcries. "It's all squared away now. Siron's still raging mad, but she let me back on the mission. Turns out I know what I'm doing after all."

"She took you off the mission? Tell me you didn't go undercover on a mission without any backup, without any support…" His voice was a soft growl.

"How do you know I went undercover?" I demanded.

He sighed. "Well, I know you, don't I? You always do what you have to do no matter what anyone says."

I smiled. He did know me. That felt good. What felt bad was that there would be no more kisses between us. The conversation we'd had about our relationship still felt sour on my tongue after all this time. We'd agreed that his job and my job were more important. He was my handler and there couldn't be romantic feelings between a handler and his agent. But intense feelings swirled around us anyway. We had to fight them and not give in no matter how hard it was. "I have a lot of things to tell you, both terrible and great. Don't let Siron make them all seem terrible. You'll never believe who my shadow is."

"Lay it on me."

"Summer."

"Summer Barnes from Washington, D.C.? Summer Barnes who hates your guts?"

"That's the one."

He whistled. "I'm here now, so that won't last long."

His words felt like a balm to my soul, but I couldn't have him challenge Siron. Not now. "I'm hanging by a thread with

Siron as it is. I would love for you to get rid of Summer, but I don't think it's the right move right now. Siron brought her in as a condition of my return."

"She really expelled you?"

"Not for long. Are you at Division now?" I had to change the subject. I didn't want our first conversation to be an angry one.

"Not yet."

"What took you so long to get here?"

"You know I would have been there had I been able. The mission I was on was one held one minefield after the other. I sure am glad we have the team we do here."

I wanted to gush and tell him how glad I was that he was back, but I couldn't. He was my handler. I hoped that he would hear in my voice how I felt about him since I couldn't say it. I had to be a bit sarcastic to hide my disappointment. "Sure you are. All I am for you is trouble, right?"

"Far from it. Is that a fountain I hear?"

"Yep. I do believe you have a picture of said fountain." I'd sent him pictures of various things despite knowing he wouldn't see them until he came back. It was so amazing to hear Jeremy's voice again, and yet so painful not to be able to touch him.

"I did get those pictures as well as the fifteen other texts as soon as I turned on my phone today."

"The kids in the pictures are all pickpockets."

He groaned. "Of course you wouldn't send me random photos of you having fun in Paris. You were working the mission. I should have been here a week ago."

"You said it, not me."

"I've got to go. I'll see you later."

I frowned. "What?" I didn't want to say goodbye. "See you

soon."

A strong smell of moss and water wafted throught the air. Watching the water flow over the fountain soothed me. I felt his presence before he actually sat next to me. Then I smelled the musky scent that belonged solely to him. I kept my eyes forward and instead of giving in to my desire to grab him into a hug, I took an involuntary breath in as relief washed over me. All the massive worry and fear I'd been carrying around and not allowing myself to think about burst at knowing he was right next to me. An ache settled in the back of my throat.

I let my peripheral vision sweep over him. He had on long black dreads—it had to be a wig—a rainbow crocheted hat, and very baggy clothes. Even though he didn't look anything like himself, I knew this was Jeremy. The corners of my mouth turned up, and I bit into my diminishing crepe. My insides felt like smooth melted chocolate with him next to me. I looked forward, not wanting him to know that I knew he was there. When I couldn't hold it in anymore, I said, my lips barely moving, "You know it's risky having you here."

"No such ting, man," he whispered in a thick Jamaican accent. "No' here. No risk. Just enjoying da afta-noon rays. We don' know each udda."

My insides vibrated like a tuning fork. He was the most beautiful sight in Paris, even in disguise. I wanted to look at him straight on. I wanted to touch him.

I leaned back so I could see more of him. It was just the two of us. I could talk to him. How I loved his fake accent. "We don't have to pretend. No one's here." I'd know it if they were. My spidey senses never let me down when it came to people tailing me. I'd lost Summer when I left the Louvre.

"We never know who's there."

I finished my crepe, wishing the whole time that I could share it with him.

"I should have known when you sent me those pictures that you were already working on this. What were you thinking?" He'd dropped the accent. Too bad, it had been kind of cute. Did he want to hold me as badly as I did him?

"I already told you, time was of the essence. And it's all worked out."

"You drive me so crazy how you put yourself in danger all the time. And without me to protect you. Christy, the most important thing is that you stay safe, and without Division behind you, you weren't safe. What happened with Dufor—?"

"Was a terrible mistake," I hissed, trying to keep my voice down. "Please don't rub salt in the wound." A horrible heat started in my belly and rushed to my chest, anguish filling me.

He reached for me, but pulled back before his hand touched mine. I wanted desperately for him to grab me into a comforting hug. I'd told him we were alone. Why wasn't he holding me?

"I'm sorry. I wasn't going to chide you. You should know me better than that. I can't imagine what you've been going through." He wrung his hands in his lap.

Just do it, take my hand. No one will see. He didn't. "I'm going to fix it. I saw the pickpocket—I knew I could find him again, but Siron refused to even listen until now."

"I'm not denying that you were treated badly—but still, did you have to go rushing into danger? You have a gift for persuasion. Couldn't you have persuaded her?"

"She wouldn't let me talk." I could feel the pulsing heat coming off his skin, so close to mine. I took a quick deep breath to help slow my heart.

He was here. He was finally here. I suddenly didn't care about Siron. The only thing I wanted was his hand in mine. I almost reached over and took his hand, but he turned to me and said, "Just...don't be reckless. Please don't be reckless." His body slouched slightly, and his pleading voice tore at me. Hadn't Siron told me I was reckless?

"I'm not reckless."

"Uh, this, what you are doing right now, is reckless. Where is your backup?"

Instead I said, "Right next to me." While it was kind of a buzz kill to have him lecture me, nothing could douse the total excitement that I felt now that he was with me. He moved like he was getting ready to leave. "Before you go, grab a crepe." I wanted to share something amazing with him. "Mad Dogs."

"All right. Heading for the Louvre, then?"

"Yes."

"I just re-programmed your phone. Number one on speed dial is me. If you're in trouble, press it and I'm there."

He'd reprogrammed my phone? I hadn't even felt him take it. He was so good. Or perhaps he just distracted me so much I couldn't notice. I'd have to get him to show me how he'd done that later.

"I know you don't want me to say it, but I can't not say it. Please be safe."

I nodded.

"I'll see you back at HQ later." Then he was gone.

I hated that our first true meeting would be at HQ.

I pulled out my phone to look him up. I had a message. From him. *I can't tell you how good it was to see you. I missed you.* My heart raced.

On the train back to the Louvre, a pregnant lady sat close

next to me. I had an open seat on the other side of me and thought about sliding over to give her room, but she sighed and turned to me. Summer. I slid to the next seat and she slid into the one I'd vacated. I stared across the aisle. I had had no idea she was there. "That was a beautiful little reunion. Glad I was able to pick you up when you left the Louvre. I wouldn't have wanted to miss that for the world."

"I don't know what you're talking about." I clenched my teeth. Wait. Had she said she picked me up after the Louvre this morning? I thought I'd felt her following me inside the Louvre. I must've misunderstood her.

"You and Jeremy. Even from a great distance, I could see your longing."

"Shut up, Summer. You don't know what you're talking about."

"I know unrequited love when I see it. How old is he anyway?"

I didn't answer.

"There's got to be about a ten year difference between you two. He could never be interested in you." She snorted.

Only eight, I thought. I stared hard at the people across the aisle, my jaw tense. I wanted to get the heck off the train.

"I'm sure there's someone out there for you," she continued. "I met some nice guys taking a nap in the train station that would be perfect for you."

"Look, Summer, you're supposed to be my shadow. Never seen or heard."

She snorted. "It's kind of ironic, don't you think. That I'm here to keep you safe?"

Heat flushed through my body as I stood to take my exit.

"He has such a smooth and inviting voice—even as a

133

Jamaican."

I couldn't help it, my head jerked back to her. She'd listened in on our conversation.

She grinned a wicked grin and I rushed off the train, the sounds of her laughter following me. It took all my strength not to turn back and let her have it.

It was a good thing Jeremy had held back.

***

I stopped off in Division's restroom to freshen up before the debriefing. I was about to see Jeremy. Jeremy as himself, with no disguise. Would he have changed in the last four months? My heart thumped in anticipation as I looked through the windows of the conference room. The team, Halluis, Ace, Rosabella, and Jeremy, all stood around the table talking. I focused on Jeremy. My whole world seemed to stop as a great relief once again rolled off me. His striped, button up shirt fit snugly against his toned body and I imagined what it would be like for him to hold me tight. His hair was a bit longer and shaggier than usual and my soul was set aflame. I stared a little too long, giving Summer an opportunity to needle me.

"He looks so good, doesn't he? I'm excited to see the fireworks."

"There's nothing going on between us."

"And I'm good at pretending too," she hissed before heading to the room, entering right after the director. The room seemed to fill with energy when Summer entered it. I forced myself not to look her way. She'd always had that gift, while mine had been to go unnoticed. Now it seemed she had both. I hurried in behind them and shut the door. The meeting was over in what seemed a flash. Summer had already reported everything I'd done, so I simply asked if they needed clarification of anything. It took me a total of five sentences.

"So, tonight should be the night, then," Siron said. "If those tracked drives work, we should be able to determine the whereabouts of Dufor's drive and retrieve it. Good work, everyone."

After leaving the conference room, I went to look at blueprints of the suspected clearinghouse and surveillance tapes with Ace for a little bit before noticing that Siron, Jeremy, and Summer were still in the briefing room discussing something.

I frowned. I hated that Summer was in there with both of them, probably undermining me. But I knew there was nothing I could do about it.

I was about to leave headquarters when Halluis said, "Siron wants you back in the conference room."

I lifted an eyebrow. So they had been talking about me. I fought back a sudden desire to stomp into the room. He took my arm. "Don't make any assumptions. Ace told me what you said about Summer. We're watching her, so don't worry. Play by the rules and everything will work out." He smiled softly and I returned it.

"Thanks for that."

"Anytime."

As I walked in, Director Siron said, "Check other agencies and see if anyone else is working pickpocket cases right now. I mean, they're always working them, but see if there's a connection with Agent Hadden."

"I already did," Jeremy spoke up. "No one is working on anything that has to do with our girl."

"Okay, then. Glad you're back, Jeremy. Maybe you can knock some sense into this rogue agent." Siron's eyes fell on me.

Summer curled her lips into a conniving smile and said, "Maybe we should pull her until we find out who they are."

I was sure she said that just to annoy me. I ignored it.

"That's really not practical." Siron's eyes searched mine. "As much as I don't want to reward Agent Hadden's insubordination, we are on a time crunch here. We need her to continue."

Summer stood just to the left and slightly behind Siron. She gave me a mocking smile.

"What were you talking about just now? What's going on?"

"You're being followed." Jeremy ran a hand through his hair.

"I know. Summer is following me."

"Someone other than Summer," Siron angled her head toward her shoulder and then looked at the huge monitor on the wall. Two surveillance photos of two different men filled the screen. One was bulkier than the other, but both wore big black glasses.

"Those guys are following me? How did—"

"Summer took these pictures today. She spotted these two taking turns watching you. What do you know about them?"

I stared hard at the faces. "Nothing. The bulky one on the right looks slightly familiar, but I have no idea why." Along with the huge black glasses, both men wore caps. They obviously didn't want to be recognized. "But why would they be watching me? No one made me the other night at Dufor's office, right?"

"Not that we know of. Summer saw them follow you through the museum this afternoon. Could they be the henchmen for Kamal's boss?"

Summer put her hand over her mouth and coughed. She loved making me look bad.

I stayed calm and asked, "Do we have anyone following them?"

"Not yet. We just found out. I'll put someone on it." Siron nodded. "It may be nothing to worry about, anyway, especially if we can recover that drive tonight."

"It's been seven days since Christy lost that drive. What are the chances that the drive hasn't already been compromised?" Summer asked.

I shook my head. "No, Kamal said his drive guy would be out of town for a week. That should give us three more days before the handoff. That means he probably still has it—we just need to figure out where he's keeping it."

"What if the tracked drives don't work?" Jeremy insisted. A line of worry creased the space between his eyes. "The last ones didn't—these may not either. We can't count on that. What's the backup plan?"

Siron pursed her lips, then turned to me. "Well, as a last resort, we can bring Kamal in, possibly use that girlfriend of his against him."

I chafed at that. I'd hated having to tell Siron about Marni, but once the contents of Kamal's laptop had been given to the analysts, it couldn't be kept from her. Marni was completely innocent in all this, and most likely suffering enough already. I'd do everything I could to keep Kamal and Marni out of this.

Siron went on, "We'll get our best agents working to discover the identity of the men following you, as well as tracking the drives you gave Kamal. I have a team ready to steal into the building you suspect is the clearinghouse tonight. Maybe the drive is there, who knows? One of these avenues is bound to lead us to the information. In the meantime, see if you can't put a little bit of a squeeze on Kamal. Try to get him to tell you more about how he runs his business. Maybe he'll give us some kind of clue."

I nodded. I knew how to get Kamal to spill his guts—the perfect thing. I knew he was pocketing all my profits, rather than taking them to his boss. He was making a lot of money off of me—if I threatened to leave, he'd have to pull out something spectacular to get me to stay. It was risky, but it could work. If we had any luck on our side, the drive would be in the building Kamal had dropped some stuff off at, and the craziness would end. I huffed. That would be too easy. Tomorrow was going to be a busy day if none of the other leads panned out.

Summer and Jeremy moved toward Ace. I took one last look at Summer, wishing I could tell her to shove off but knowing it wouldn't do any good, and headed out.

I was being watched by someone other than Summer? I couldn't imagine why anyone else would be watching unless I'd somehow given up my identity to the thugs from Sécurité Un. But Division had blocked all the cameras when I'd gone in that night. And a cleanup crew had scrubbed the feeds from the three cameras that had caught me on the other rooftop and alley. Besides, no one had been close enough in the dark to get a good look at me. Then a horrible idea climbed into my brain. What if Summer took pictures of some random people and then claimed they were following me just to make me look stupid?

I continued to the metro, and after I transferred trains, out of the corner of my eye I noticed Summer get on the same one with me. I hadn't even known she'd gotten on the first one. When had she stopped talking to Siron? Seriously, how was that possible? I was spidey senses personified, yet here she was again, and I hadn't even known it until my eyes saw her. It bugged me to no end that I had not sensed her the whole day.

Instead I'd most likely been sensing the other guys Summer said were following me.

Sitting on the train, I zeroed in on her, trying to assimilate her into my mind, my body, or my soul to force myself to pick up her shadow somehow. Maybe she *was* the best. I hated to even have the thought, but I couldn't help it. I'd never had to do anything like this before and had no idea what I was doing. I just knew I couldn't let her keep shadowing me without my knowledge. It made me feel violated.

Heat started in my belly and radiated out through my body. I had to figure something out and fast because I had things to do that I didn't want her to be privy to. Once off the train, Summer turned left and I went right. Relief swirled around me, glad that she didn't live on the same block as I did. At least I was free of her the rest of the night. Feeling extra rebellious and very insecure, I got back on the train and headed for Halle. I wouldn't wait for tomorrow. I'd start my squeeze on Kamal tonight, and Summer would not witness it. Maybe I'd luck out and get the information on the whereabouts of the drive.

12

I showed up at the fountain in the same clothes I'd had on earlier in the day, jeans and a t-shirt with the addition of a zip-up hoodie, without my board and slumped onto the cement bench, placing my elbows on my knees and holding my chin in my hands. The smells of rich sauces wafted out of the various restaurants in the area. It was still muggy, but the hope of relief during the night filled the air.

Kamal was the first one to notice me. He put his arm around my hunched back and said, "You ok?"

I angled my head to the side, pressed my lips together and just stared at him.

"What's wrong?" One of the others in the group asked.

I covered my eyes with my hands and rubbed them over my face and sighed.

Kamal crouched down and took hold of my wrists, moving my hands away from my face. A genuine look of concern graced his face and he said, "So, what's up? What happened?"

I shook my head. He still held my hands. I let the tears come. By this time, the whole group surrounded me.

"Talk to me, Eva. Talk to me."

I shook my head all the harder, stood up abruptly and ran away. I hoped Kamal would tell the rest of them to stay and he'd follow. If I'd read him right, I knew he would. He needed me.

I was rounding the corner of a restaurant when he caught up with me. He grabbed my arm. "Hey. Hey. Slow down. Let's talk."

"No. You won't understand. I just don't know what I'm doing." I shrugged off his hand and ran away again. I wanted to get to the park just up the street. It was a good place for us to talk. He caught up with me again when we were about a block from it.

"Whoa!" he said, grabbing me into a big bear hug.

I squirmed in his arms, but he held tight. I finally gave in and relaxed, melting into his hug. I let the tears pour out of my eyes and made sure to sob loudly and violently. He relaxed his grip on me and rubbed his hand from the crown of my head to the middle of my back, shushing me the whole time. I burrowed my face in his chest, and he rested his chin on the top of my head until my body no longer jumped with my sobs.

"What's this all about, Eva? What happened?"

I pulled back from him, wiping my nose on my jacket sleeve. I closed my mouth and shoved a breath out my nose before squeaking out the words, "I can't do this anymore. I have to go back to Portugal."

He frowned. "I don't understand. What are you talking about?"

I threw my hands out to my sides and put my chin on my chest, hoping I looked completely dejected.

A group of people passed us, staring the whole time. He took my arm and said, "Let's get to the park where we'll have more privacy."

I nodded and wiped my nose again.

He put his arm around me, and I leaned into his side as we

walked the last block to the park. I totally had him. And a part of me was sad about it. I was about to play on his love for his girlfriend or wife or whoever she was. It was cruel, but necessary. And definitely better than Division having their hands on her.

The gravel crunched under my feet as we passed through the small gate marking the entrance to the park. We sat on a bench as far away from anyone else as possible. A few men were still playing various games with balls in the dirt on the far side of the park.

He angled his body toward me and took my hands in his. "So, what's this all about?"

"My dad is super sick. I came here to get money to help and I have. I mean, I send them money each week, something I couldn't do back home, but now—my mom fell, and my dad's having a really hard time taking care of her. I can't afford to get them a healthcare worker, so I'm going to have to go home." I leaned back in the bench.

I could see the panic in his eyes. He was working hard to find a solution.

"But you're doing so well as a picker. You should wait a bit. I can give you an advance on your earnings to get someone to help your parents."

I shook my head. "It will never be enough. It will never be enough."

Desperation crossed his face. He was starting to think I was going to jump ship and quit.

"I mean," I continued. "I don't want to be ungrateful. You were the only good thing that's happened to me since I got here. But I'm sorry, I have to be there for my family."

He was struggling to keep calm. "Listen, I'm going to tell

you something that very few people know."

I sat up and took in a hard, shaky breath. Had he fallen for it?

"My parents wanted me to take over the family business back home," Kamal said, "and I wasn't about to. So I left. And becoming a picker was the best decision I ever made."

I thought he was going to tell me about Marni. "No one leaves a good home to become a picker. Why would you choose that over a good job?"

"I have an artistic bent, and my father didn't like it. He wanted me to spend all my time doing stuff I hate. I will never become like him. I will never be an accountant or a lawyer and sell my soul for money."

That made absolutely no sense to me because I thought that was exactly what he was doing. "What about taking over the business and becoming the boss?"

"No. It's not me. I'm an artist and if I'd stayed, I'd never have been able to do it. With picking, I get good money and I get to paint."

"But you're a leader here. Why not in the family business?"

He raised his voice a little, his cheekbones becoming more angular, rigid. "It's just not me. That's all. I'm an artist. Anyway, this isn't about me. It's about you. You have a gift. You're the best picker I've ever had on my team. You're smart enough to see that this could be very lucrative for you. Do you realize you've earned over two hundred euro this week already?"

"It's not enough. Not if I have to hire someone to care for my dad full time." I pouted.

"That's the other thing. You're official now. You get thirty percent." He was pulling out all the stops. He was desperate.

"Big deal. Triple of a tiny bit is not that much." I shook my head in disgust. I wasn't sure how hard I was going to have to push to get him to tell me about his girlfriend, but I had to keep going no matter what.

"It is, considering how well you do and," he lowered his voice, "in less than a year, you could be earning a lot more than that."

"What are you talking about?" This was a turn I wasn't expecting.

He looked around the park as if someone might be listening in. I took a gander too, wondering if I'd catch a glimpse of one of the guys supposedly tailing me.

"Well, you work for me, and I plan on taking off in less than a year. I'll give my spot to you if you want it."

"Like you get to make that decision. I'm sure your boss will want to know who your replacement is, and what if he doesn't want me?"

"No one will be vetting you. I'll disappear and you'll take over. It's as simple as that."

"What, they won't notice that you're gone and I'm doing your job all of a sudden? I want you to tell them when it comes time. I don't think they'd like me surprising them like that."

He shook his head. "No. You don't understand." His voice was a whisper. "No one quits this job. No one. Once you're in, you're in for life. But I can't be in it for life. I have plans, and they don't include picking forever. And listen, Eva, you can never tell a soul about this." His eyes narrowed and he tipped his head toward me, emphasizing he was serious.

"But then how do I get out when I'm ready?" He'd given me something even better than Marni. It would be good not to involve her. Now I could get him to talk about the business side of this picking operation. If I was slated to take his place, he'd have to train me and give me all his knowledge.

"You do what I'm doing. You set up someone to take your place." He leaned back.

"Why would I or anyone else want to take your place?" I leaned back too.

He leaned into me. "Because I have seven pickers under me. I make almost 150,000 euro a year doing this."

My eyes popped wide in pretend surprise. "You're kidding right?" So, he lived on fifty thousand euro a year. Pretty nice.

"No. You see, I get forty percent of what I pick and ten percent of what you all pick. I'm like midlevel management."

"Why don't I just go to the source and start getting all the money for myself?" I didn't know why I was pushing so hard. I didn't want him to rethink his offer.

"Because I'd kill you if you tried." His face was suddenly hard.

Hot oil seemed to bubble in my gut.

His index finger shot out, and it bobbed in front of me. "I brought you in and trained you. You are mine. Double cross me, and you won't like the consequences."

I scooted away from him, but he slid next to me, quick as a flash. "I'm a nice guy, Eva. I'm nice as long as you do what you're told. I have big plans for you, and they make both of us rich, very rich."

I nodded, furrowing my brow. I needed to reel him in, let him think I was ready to accept his offer. But he started talking again.

"Don't look at me like that. It's not like I like this job. I hate doing what I'm doing, but it's a means to an end. It will get you what you want—and fast. Just like it has for me. And if all you want is a caregiver for your parents, you could get that in a month or two and as you get faster, you'll have extra, all for you. Save that up and when you have enough to get out, all you have to do is secretly train your successor and then disappear. You will have to disappear, but you could go back to Portugal. Your parents wouldn't even have to work." He was really selling me now.

"So, you're going to train me to be you, then?" It was time to put the squeeze on him.

"Yes." He nodded vigorously.

I'd get the information we needed without having to follow the drives to their destination. "So, when we give you what we pick, you take it to your boss and he pays you?"

He nodded. "I take it to the sorter and they pay me, then I pay you guys your cut."

"So if I get a bunch of drives, I could get the money even faster?"

"If they have good stuff on them, yes."

"And do you turn them in everyday?"

"Normally, yes, but like I told you my guy has been out of town. He gets back tomorrow, though. I think I've saved up about fifteen drives over the past two weeks that he's been gone. I should get a good amount of cash."

Dread pulsed through me. "Tomorrow?"

"Tomorrow."

This was terrible news. My three days had just become only a night and part of a day. It had turned out to be a very good thing that I'd met up with him tonight. "Can I come when you deliver them?

"No. It's too early to involve you in that."

"Well, where do you keep them until you turn them in?

Your apartment?"

"No way. They go to a safety deposit box at the bank. You can't keep stuff like that lying around. You're likely to get caught or robbed if you do. You'll have to get an account for stuff like that."

The key he'd retrieved from the kitchen drawer the other day. It must be his key to a safety deposit box. "Does it cost money?" I needed him to tell me which bank he used.

"No. I mean, the account doesn't. I pay a little each month for the box."

"And you'll show me how?"

"Of course. It's not difficult. You'll see." Sparkle returned to his eyes.

"Is there one bank that is best to use?" We could raid the bank tonight, and it would all be over.

"I don't think so. You'll just have to pick one."

I couldn't detect any hint of him trying to keep information about his bank from me—he really didn't think it was important. "I think I'll use yours. Which one do you use?"

"Don't get ahead of yourself. I'll teach you everything you need to know. We have time. Just relax."

Ugh! This was not going to be easy after all. "It's not one of my strong points," I sighed. I had to get it out of him. "What would it hurt for us to go set up my account in the morning?"

He shook his head. "You really don't need it yet."

I wanted to drop kick him and force him to tell me right there and then, but there were too many people around. "So, you meet the guy in the morning?"

"Yes, and he's pretty high-strung. Don't ever miss a meet with him or try to suggest he change something he does. He will cut you off."

I nodded. "Got it. Don't piss off the drive buyer." After a short time I said, "I wish I'd gotten some clean drives today."

"I got four drives today. Only two were clean."

Great. Now I wondered if the drives I'd given to the pickpockets were the clean ones. "Huh. Is that usually how it goes? Fifty-fifty?"

"There is no usual in this business. In any case, the bank was closed by the time I had the chance to take them. I'll keep those with me. There's no sense in taking them in only to turn right back around and get them."

I nodded. "Makes sense." I chafed inside. That meant that even if Kamal had the tracked drives in his possession, they wouldn't lead us to Dufor's drive. The news just kept getting worse. The only way to salvage this mission was to tail Kamal tomorrow and follow him to his bank and then relieve him of the drives before he was able to hand them off to the buyer. It would have to work.

"You promise you'll give me an advance, and that I'll earn a ton of money?" I twisted one corner of my mouth up.

He nodded. "Yes. I'll get you an advance. Let me know what you need. But you're gonna have to toughen up. There are people who'll want to steal your success. You can't trust anyone. You know, I followed you for a whole day, trying to find out everything about you before I let you join me."

"You did not!" I said, trying to sound totally incredulous. I knew from his conversation with Marni, that even though I was new, I brought in twice as much as the other crew members.

"I did. And you're going to have to do that to any new recruits, too. I'll start training you in about six months or so. No point in giving you too much too soon. Besides, you're still too green." He scratched his nose. He was lying. He thought I was totally ready. "You need to get the picking side of the business down perfectly before we move on." He smiled, genuinely happy with the deal he'd just forged.

I nodded hard once. "Okay. Thanks for listening to me. I'm sorry I went crazy. I'm just really worried, you know."

"No problem. If you ever feel crazy again, just come to me…It'll all be worth it in the end. Let's get you home. It's late, and I expect good things from you tomorrow."

I smiled. "No worries there."

Earlier, while he held me close and I'd sobbed my guts out, I'd put my hand in his pocket, opened his phone, and attached a bug that was not only a listening device, but also had a tracker, inside. Score.

I texted Jeremy after leaving Kamal. *Get to the office. Major change. Heading in now.*

13

When I arrived at HQ, everyone but Summer had assembled in the conference room. I could see through the glass walls that they were seated, probably tired from a hard day's work.

"He looks good, doesn't he?" Summer said into my ear from behind me. "Too bad he doesn't feel the same about you." She left to go into the conference room as quick as she'd come. I followed behind after sighing.

As soon as I entered the room, I announced, "The buy has been moved up to tomorrow morning." Gasps and general muttering filled the room.

"And how do you know this, Agent Hadden?" Siron asked.

"I was just with Kamal and he told me."

Siron's gaze flicked to Summer and back to me. Summer was stone, her eyes fixed on me. A splotchy redness appeared on her neck.

"You were on your way home," Summer accused, her body leaning toward me, the muscles in her neck going taut, her jaw tight.

"I was," I said in a calm voice, "but then I realized I could use the rest of the evening at the fountain to get more info of Kamal."

"You should have told me that."

"I didn't realize I had to tell my shadow where I was going."

Summer's nostrils flared. It looked like she was holding something back.

"Give us the details, Agent Hadden, and next time, let Agent Barnes in on your plans when they change. It does you no good to have a shadow you give the slip. And it doesn't matter if the buy has moved up because we will be activating the trackers later tonight."

"That's the thing," I said. "Kamal is keeping the new drives with him since he's meeting Marco, his drive buyer, tomorrow morning. He didn't see the point of taking the drives to the bank, only to take them right back out again."

"In that case, we pull Kamal in tonight," Siron said, "and use the girl, Marni, to get him to give up the drives. If he thinks Marni is in danger, he'll talk."

"We don't even have Marni, yet. He won't talk without knowing we have her. Even if he did break, it would be too late. I have a better idea and it won't even involve the girl. I'll follow Kamal to the bank and then intercept the drive after he retrieves the rest of the drives from the safety deposit box."

"I think he knows what you look like by now," Summer said.

"That's why I have disguises. I'll go in like a normal day of work, and change into a disguise after I get into the Louvre so I can follow him."

"Now that's thinking," Halluis said. "We can keep an eye on him from the time you enter the Louvre until you exit and then we'll put you back onto him."

"This sounds good," Siron said. "Agent Hadden will keep

to her same pattern so Kamal won't suspect anything. Summer will act as her shadow. Ace will monitor all the tech from a van that will follow Kamal. Halluis will drive the van and Jeremy will provide support. In case she loses visual, Jeremy and Ace can keep Agent Hadden informed over the com where Kamal is, and Jeremy can be ready to help if Kamal gives her any trouble. Rosabella will monitor the mission from HQ.

"Now, everyone, go home and get some rest. Tomorrow is going to be a big day. I'll see you bright and early."

Everyone but Jeremy and I hurried out. I smiled at him. He smiled back, looked at the floor and moved toward me. I imagined him whispering something sweet into my ear and giving me a light kiss, but instead, he put an arm around my shoulders and squeezed. "It sure feels good to be back." It was like he was greeting a guy friend that he hadn't seen in a long time. His arm left me in one swift motion, and he walked out, leaving me feeling deflated.

I made my way to the exit, stopping to get a drink from the fountain in the hall. When I straightened, Summer was standing right next to me, sneering. I couldn't stop my hand from going to my heart. "You startled me." Again, I had no clue she'd been there.

"If you ever make me look bad in front of the team again, I'll have to hurt you."

I held my tongue.

"You made me look bad today, really bad in front of Siron. I'm going to have to make you pay for that." Her voice was firm, set. She meant every word, and I had no doubt she'd follow through.

***

The next morning I got an early start with a fierce cross-training workout that seemed to force sweat from each and every pore in my body. A cool shower rejuvenated me before I got dressed as Eva and packed a go bag with a new disguise that included a silicone mask and a short black wig. I got a text from Division saying the raid on the clearinghouse was a bust. No drives there. Surprise, surprise.

I still had a good half hour before I needed to be on my way to the Louvre when someone knocked on the door. I carefully made it to the door without making a sound. The person on my doorstep knocked again and said, "It's me." Jeremy. A familiar zing zipped through me and hope and longing filled me. I wondered if I'd ever lose that feeling. I had to. I had to learn how I could be with him and yet not with him every day. I wondered if maybe it would have been better had I been given a new handler. That thought sent a terrible shiver through my body. I couldn't imagine not working with him ever again. I held onto the doorknob, frozen.

"Open up. I've got breakfast." I loved hearing him speak French. I took a deep breath and opened the door. He held up two bakery bags. My hero.

"Get in here," I said. "I'm starving." I pretended a casualness I didn't feel. I wished I hadn't had those thoughts only moments before because now they made me feel awkward and unsure. He walked in, and I shut and locked the door.

He cleared his throat. "Thought I'd come by to wish you luck." He seemed a bit stiff.

I wanted to hear that he had come because he wanted to spend some time with me. That it had been too long. That he wanted to put his lips on mine. But, it wasn't to be. It couldn't be. We'd agreed. But seeing him made all my resolve to keep him in the friend zone, crumble. I couldn't live without him. The last four months had been torture. I needed to tell him how I felt. I had to be with him. If it meant not being a spy, then so be it.

We stood, staring at each other, the painful, awkward moment playing out. He cleared his throat again. "I wondered if maybe I'd catch you in bed, you seemed worn out last night."

"Well, you know me, sleeping in is usually not my thing."

"How about you finish doing what you were doing, and I'll set us up on the back balcony."

"Actually, I'm ready, so I'll help you." I started to move at the same time he did and we bumped into each other and jerked apart. "Oh, sorry."

He took hold of my elbow and looked me in the eyes. "It's okay." He was talking about more than the incidental touching. He motioned for me to go first. I did. I'd have to find the perfect time to tell him, when things weren't so weird. We collected dishes from the kitchen and brought them to the balcony. He started to unload the bags. "What disguise are you going to use?"

"I'm wearing a silicone mask and a wig."

"Good. I don't want Kamal to have a chance at ID-ing you."

"Yeah. I will probably sweat to death when it's on, but I can't risk it." I headed back to the kitchen for water and orange juice as well as yogurt. I tried everything to stop the hard, bruising pounding of my heart against my ribs, but nothing worked. When I returned, I found fresh croissants and pain au chocolat on the table. He knew just what I liked. The first little while sitting out there was incredibly awkward. The silence, the stolen glances.

After way too long, he was the first to break the silence. "You're going to be safe, right?"

"Of course. You're here now."

"I'll be there every second making sure of it."

I smiled. "And Summer will be there, for what that's worth." He looked everywhere but in my eyes. Why wouldn't he look me in the eye?

"I checked into her. She's considered one of the rising stars in shadowing. I'm actually glad she's here. Another pair of eyes is always beneficial."

I sighed. "This is crazy. I hate how—"

Jeremy's alarm sounded. "Oh, it's time to go. That went fast." He stood up, cleared away the dishes and took them inside before I could protest. I shuffled behind him, desperately wanting to finish what I was going to say, but I couldn't. I didn't know how to be around him anymore. I knew what I wanted, but he didn't seem to want the same thing. Everything had changed. I'd lost him for good. It wasn't right.

I stood close behind him while he put the dishes into the sink, my mind full of indecision. When he turned around, he bumped into me, his arms shooting out to steady me, pulling me into an embrace and his eyes meeting mine. I thought I saw longing there and then it was gone. I squeezed him tight, enjoying how well we fit together and drawing on his intoxicating male scent.

"Whoops," he said, pulling back and sliding past me. That was all the answer I needed. We were now business colleagues, nothing more. I pulled hard for a breath, but nothing came for several seconds.

"Grab your go bag. We'll go out together." He was already waiting for me by the front door.

I snagged the bag from my bed and plastered on a smile. "Guess this is it." I walked toward him.

"I wish for you every ounce of luck you may need and want. And remember, nothing is worth losing you."

Those were almost the exact words he spoken to me right before he'd kissed me that first, knee-buckling time in New York. I sucked in a breath. Did he know it? Our hands brushed again as both reached for the doorknob to shut the door. Tingles fired through me.

"Remember. I'm here now, making sure you stay safe."

***

Once again, Summer sat next to me on the train. "Did you have a nice breakfast?" How did she know about that? She hadn't been anywhere nearby. She couldn't have been or I would have felt her. I decided the only way to deal with her was to not respond.

"It must be painful to have him reject you over and over."

I had felt it, especially today. She was right he had rejected me. But the words he said right there before they'd left the apartment, was he telling me something? Was he reminding me that he still cared for me, but was unable to act on it? My stomach did a little dance.

"Don't worry about today. I'll take care you. You'll be safe. I'll be watching your stupid little butt. Just know I'm watching." Had Summer really been there? Was I losing my touch or was she as good a shadow as she seemed? Relief slid over me that she hadn't said anything about my feelings toward Jeremy. Summer would certainly report it. Most certainly.

And how dare she come right before a mission and try to rattle me? I had five more minutes on the train to cool off.

I headed into the Louvre, knowing that this time, agents from Division 57 were following Kamal as he left the area. Kamal gave me a new bag to use for the day. It was a fanny pack of sorts, and I strapped it to my waist. Once inside, and certain I wasn't being tailed by him, I went into the closest bathroom and changed into a new person, carefully putting Eva's clothing into my go bag. I had opted for a silicone mask of a mid-twenties woman with tan skin and tastefully done makeup. The mask fit perfectly and there wasn't hint of Christy or Eva in it. With a black wig, glasses, some dark colored contacts and some slacks and a billowy blouse, I was set to go. I pulled out my phone and texted Jeremy. Kamal was in the Tuileries Gardens. He was probably picking up a drop from one of his l'Orangerie pickpockets. I couldn't help but think how much easier it would have been for us had Kamal simply taken the two drives to his bank and left them with the others.

I made my loop through the Louvre before exiting with a jostling crowd. Despite my anxiousness, I felt eyes on me. I stopped to tie my shoe and surveyed the area for this phantom tail. No one. A part of me hoped it was just Summer I was sensing. It would be good if I was finally be sensing her.

Jeremy gave me Kamal's location and then patched me in to his tracker. I hopped on the metro so I could get to Kamal and keep an eye on him.

I never realized just how busy Kamal was until I followed him during his daytime activities. He entered the Jardin du Luxembourg, a sprawling park that had quickly become one of my favorites. I enjoyed sitting in the sun near the gorgeous flowerbeds and reading after a hard run. He walked quickly on a path that was meant for joggers and received several mean stares and comments. Rules governing where and when joggers could run, where cards could be played, where dogs could be walked, and where and when music could be played were hard and fast in Paris. I'm sure Kamal knew that, but I guessed the stress of his meeting was clouding his judgment. Or perhaps he thought the rules were foolish. I wondered if he knew that the park sat right on top of the French CIA. A nervous feeling settled over me.

He met with someone and for a moment I panicked that it was Marco, but when Kamal took a bag from him, I knew I was being overanxious and took a seat. Kamal turned and looked right at me as he passed. An inward burst of relief spread through me that I had put on such a complete disguise today. Sweat had started to pool beneath my latex mask and my head itched, as it always did, under the short black wig. Had I just put on a wig and some different clothes, I would never have been able to pull off following him.

Why wasn't he going to the bank already? Irritation sat on me. I thought he was supposed to meet Marco in the morning. It was almost afternoon. Kamal stopped by the clearing house and then made his way back to a business section of town. My heart leapt. Maybe this was it. But it wasn't. Finally, he entered an area with three banks. This had to be it. Which of the three would it be? I sat in the park across the street to wait as he entered one. The whole time I could feel Summer, which was unusual, but I didn't have time to think about it. I had to focus on Kamal. *I've got my eye on you too, Summer.*

A part of me felt bad for Kamal and how he'd felt trapped into being a pickpocket. I knew what it felt like to be trapped, and it wasn't a good thing. I hoped his girl would get the help she needed. She had to be special if he was willing to do what he was in order to help her. And I knew what it was like to feel like you had to do something you didn't like in order to help someone. The drive and desire could be overwhelming. Time was ticking by too quickly. Again I lamented my choice in putting on the silicone mask. It was hot and uncomfortable.

A dark shadow crossed into my path. I looked up to see the sneering face of a tall, thin man.

"Eva. So nice to see you." His hands clamped down on my upper arms like a vice, capitalizing on my pressure points. An acrid smell filled my nose. I gasped, and everything went fuzzy and then black.

14

I came to, at least my mind did. The rest of my body didn't want to cooperate, but I could see. My go bag was on the floorboard. If I could get access to that, I'd be golden. The men in the front seat were definitely the men from the surveillance photos in Siron's office. The ones who had been following me. The one in the passenger seat was talking on his phone.

"Oui, Monsieur, this is Adolphe," he said. "We have her. You can put your worries to rest. Thank you, Monsieur. Your permanent security detail? Thank you. I'm just doing my job." He was silent for a minute or two. "And you as well, Monsieur. She'll be gone by morning and your investment will be safe...Goodbye, Monsieur."

"Cardwell," Adolphe said as he ended the call and turned to his partner. "We do it tonight."

Who had Adolphe been talking to? Some kind of official? He was obviously showing deference and respect, always referring to the man as "monsieur." I knew for sure now—these guys worked for someone very important. They were hired guns. Who had hired them? I supposed a gang leader might make the people who worked for him call him monsieur, but it also could have been some official he was talking to. There was something about the way he talked to the person that made me think it had to be someone he revered.

Cardwell continued to drive. We didn't go far before he pulled into a garage of some sort. I hadn't realized many homes had garages within the city, but then again, this was the Champs-Elysees area of Paris, a very upper-crust neighborhood.

"Eva, Eva." Adolphe smiled at me. "It is Eva, isn't it?" I noticed the garage door close, and tall, thin Cardwell enter the house.

I couldn't answer Adolphe. My muscles had all decided to go on vacation.

"Then again, maybe not." He spoke in a pleasant, conversational tone that belied the menace behind his intentions. "You're quite the little mystery, aren't you? I'm left wondering—what are you, exactly? Pickpocket? Con artist? Something more? Every time I see you, you have a different face. Quite the mystery. Well, I will just have to unravel you, won't I?" He reached out both hands and peeled off my mask.

I tried to speak and all that came out was a garble of sounds. I groaned—it was as close to a scream as I could manage.

"Don't worry, by the time we get downstairs, your muscles should be able to work on a limited basis. Then the real fun can begin." He opened the car door and dragged me out. Being completely helpless was awful. He carried me over his shoulder with seemingly no effort. His body was hard, like cement.

He brought me down some stairs and then through a door. A chill swept through me. The smell of decay hit me like a sledgehammer and if I could have, I would have shivered. The dank air seemed to cling to my body. My face bounced against his rock-hard back as he walked down the cement hallway. It wouldn't have surprised me if I had had a bloody nose when he let me down. I noted he carried a gun in a holster and a long knife in a sheath, both strapped to his belt. I felt a tingle in my toes and hoped that was a sign that I would soon regain control over my body. The tingle spread up my left leg, but with it came a pernicious ache. I consciously tried to move my leg, but only a tad bit so my captor wouldn't know. It moved!

Within seconds, my whole body set to tingling and aching, and I was able to move again. This was good. In one move I'd have the gun he had shoved into his back waistband. In another, I'd shoot a hole in his leg. Three moves after that, I would have him completely disabled, and I would escape this creepy dungeon. As my hand, which felt sluggish and not truly a part of my body, moved to his gun, he leaned forward and threw me onto a soft surface. But not before I had taken the gun. I used my leg to conceal it as I slid off his shoulder, keeping it out of his line of sight. I all but sat on it as I landed. Before I had a chance to react, the poison was still taking its toll, the prison doors slammed shut and locked into place. He stared at me through them, an almost adoring smile on his face, like someone looking at a beloved pet. I fought back the urge to shudder. I knew he was watching me for signs that feeling was returning to my body, so I kept absolutely still, despite my intense desire to shoot him right then and there. I didn't trust that my body would do as mind told it to. What if I raised the gun and my finger couldn't press the trigger?

"I'm going to make this very simple for you, Eva. We know you took the drive, there is no use denying it. I will admit it took us longer than it should have—that was a clever ruse you pulled, passing the drive to your accomplice the way you did. You appeared to be the victim of a theft, rather than a thief yourself. It was quite the distraction, as I'm sure you had planned." He squatted down to look me in the face, and smiled, satisfied.

"Of course, we did eventually figure you out. From there, it did not take much to inform our network of guards that we were looking for you. When your face popped up again at the Louvre, we were on your trail. But then—oh then! You turned out to be just so much more interesting than we could have imagined. You changed your face, not once, but twice! And who would have thought a simple pickpocket would travel with a bodyguard? It's all so very interesting."

Still crouching and staring eerily at me, he reached to his belt and unsheathed his knife, a wicked, curved weapon with a jagged edge. He pressed it to his smiling lips for a moment, then began slowly tapping it on the bars of my cell. "Now, I'm going to leave you here for a moment—no use talking to you when you won't be able to feel my gentle persuasion. While I'm gone, I'd like you to think—and think hard—about how much you'd like to help me. When I return, I think we'll have just the loveliest conversation. Don't you?" He tilted his head and sighed happily, then sheathed his knife, stood, and turned to walk away.

The shudder I'd been suppressing swept over my body. Revulsion swirled in my stomach, and I fought hard to keep from heaving. I couldn't stop to think about the ludicrous things he'd said. I had to get out of there. I took three stilling breaths, and I was once again in control. I flexed my muscles, ensuring each one was back to working order. They felt a little sluggish, but I knew I could work through that. I had to act fast. I needed his keys, which meant I needed to shoot him as close to my cell as possible.

I stood up and moved toward the prison-like bars,

Adolphe's gun in my hand, hanging by my side. I began to lift the gun to take aim outside the metal bars to shoot. But my eye caught sight of Summer across the narrow hallway, hands gripping the bars of her own cell.

My eyes rounded in shock, and I groaned inwardly. That's what he'd meant by bodyguard. They'd seen Summer shadowing me and assumed she was protecting me. They must have nabbed her first—how long had it been before they'd grabbed me?

She moved only her eyes in a way that told me to look up. I followed where her eyes pointed. Just down the hallway were cameras, one trained on each cell. Judging by the fact that she hadn't just told me they were there, I assumed they had audio feeds as well as visual.

Quickly, I checked the gun to make sure it was still hidden behind my leg. I could hear a door shut above us and bolts slide into place. Each cell was made up of three cement walls and a wall of metal bars that doubled as a door. Summer sat down and leaned against the cement wall of her cell that faced away from the cameras.

I sighed and looked away, moving to the wall in my cell that hid me from the cameras, too. I should have taken the shot. It was most likely our only chance to escape. At some point Adolphe would notice that his gun was missing and would come for it. We would lose our chance at surprise. I had Summer to thank for that missed opportunity. Who cared if there were cameras? We'd have been out of there before anyone could have come. She tapped on the wall. I looked at her. She was blinking, but not looking at me. I opened the Sig Sauer P938 to see how many rounds I had. Summer tapped harder. I swung my head in her direction, and she gave me a bug-eyed look before turning her head, blinking again.

I scowled. Seven rounds. I caressed the gun. It felt good in my hands. Adolphe definitely knew his guns. I heard Summer's insistent tapping again and jerked my head, ready to spout off at her, but she wasn't looking at me. She'd assumed the same position as before and was blinking away. That's when it hit me. She was blinking a Morse code message. At the same time, she spoke. "I'm sorry, boss."

"You can apologize when we're out of here," I said, playing along, speaking French in Eva's Portuguese accent.

"You should just tell them where the drive is," she said. "I'd tell them if I knew." I fought the urge to roll my eyes at her. Did she think that would stop them from torturing her? She was still blinking the Morse message to me, so I focused on figuring it out while also keeping up the conversation for the benefit of the guards.

"I don't know anything about any drive, and I wouldn't tell them if I did," I lied. Why had she admitted to knowing anything about any drive?

"Please, just get this over with, and maybe they'll let us go."

Meanwhile, Summer continued her coded message. Smart. Too smart for the Summer I used to know. I slid the gun into my waistband and pulled my shirt over it. This wall of my cell was too far to accurately see what she was trying to relay, so I moved to the wall that exposed me completely to the cameras. Staring out of the cell like I was watching the door to the prison area, I read the Morse code Summer blinked.

Two guys. Poison. Hole in ceiling.

I forced myself not to look up and find the hole right then.

Killed two. Danger. No way out. Dead.

I ran my fingers over the steel that made up the bars to my cell. Realization hit me. She hadn't made me miss the opportunity to take my captor down, she had saved me. Had I shot Adolphe, his partner, Cardwell, who was most surely watching the feed, would likely have released the poisonous gas and paralyzed both of us, blocking our escape. They would have taken the gun from me, and we would truly have been dead. I moved into position to talk to her. She seemed to read what I was doing and moved so she could see me. I couldn't let her give up.

Escape. Come together?

She didn't move, but slowly blinked that they had only come in once together and that was when they killed the two men.

She started to fake cry.

"Don't cry. It will be ok, you'll see. I'll tell them you had nothing to do with it. Maybe they'll let you go."

They should be back soon. I nodded toward her. *Be ready.*

Panic played across her face. I guess she realized that if they couldn't get me to tell them where the drive was, they'd try to use her against me. It must not have been a very appealing idea to her.

I looked at her. Really looked at her. I couldn't see any signs of physical punishment.

Hurt you? You okay? I blinked.

Fine. She rubbed her left arm.

They had hurt her. I would have to make them pay. I looked up at the ceiling and saw the hole that Summer had been talking about. It was near the far wall of the cell, which worked to my advantage. The cameras most likely wouldn't be able to see me. I had to get that thing plugged up. I took off one of my shoes and then a sock. I blinked out a plea for Summer to do something at the bars to distract anyone looking at the camera feeds just in case there was another camera that could see something. She took hold of the bars and started pulling and moaning. I wondered if she'd done that earlier.

I moved to the back corner of the cell and took a step-step-leap and reached for the hole. I missed. I tried again. Another miss. On the third try, the sock stuck in the hole. I jumped again and pushed it in further. That would give us a few extra, precious seconds. I slid my shoe back on. I took hold of the bars and screamed for them to let me out while Summer removed her own sock and plugged the pipe in her cell. She was taller than I was and was able to get the sock in the hole on her first try. She gave me a smug look. Even in grave danger, she had to screw with me.

Immediately after she got the sock in there, I heard the latch lift on the door to the prison from the garage. I repositioned the gun, pretending to scratch my back. This was it. I glanced at Summer to let her know it was on.

I heard footfalls coming toward me. "Look, I have no idea what you're talking about. That kid wasn't my accomplice, he really stole my bag. It's him you want to find." I had both hands on the bars and pushed my face between them.

"It's a nice try," Adolphe said, the six-inch serrated knife in his bulky hand. "But we know you're the mastermind of this little gang. Just tell us what you did with the drive, and all this will go away."

I stepped back, jerking my hands behind me. One hand cradled the handle of the gun.

"Come on," I spoke with a thick Portuguese accent. "You've got it all wrong. I have no idea where that drive is." At least that much was true.

"Eva, this is your last chance. I want us to play nice. I think we could get along very well, you and I." He flicked his tongue out at me.

I couldn't help but gag.

He laughed out loud, sharp and awful. "All right, if you want to play it that way. I suppose I'll just have to come in there and be a little more encouraging." He started to move toward my cell. I tensed, but didn't pull out the gun just yet. I needed him to open my cell first. He stopped short. "Of course, you do seem to be a bit of a hero type. You'd put up quite the fight, wouldn't you? Yes, I can tell that about you." He took a step back. "I think I'll start with your friend instead. Once you see what happens to her, I think you'll be much more willing to chat with me."

Summer shifted to the back of her cell.

He tilted his head to the side and then raised his eyebrows. He looked toward Summer and then back to me. It wasn't supposed to happen this way. He had to come into my cell.

I'd never forgive myself if he hurt Summer. Josh's square face flashed through my mind. He'd died because of me. Because of what I'd seen. I couldn't be quasi-responsible for Summer's death, too. Summer had been right. I did put others in jeopardy. I had been such a fool. I had to save Summer.

I had to keep reminding myself that Summer was a trained agent and was sure to have driven them mad when they took her. They were probably ruing the day they chose to kidnap her. Such thoughts were the only way to soothe myself and not fall into a pit of despair. I focused on the task at hand. I had to get him to come in my cell.

Adolphe turned, about to take a step toward her, and this

loud voice seemed to speak to me in my head, "Get the keys."

I didn't hesitate, just lunged forward, sliding my hand expertly through the bars and, in my best pickpocket fashion, I relieved him of the keys that were in his back pocket. My hand brushed his cotton button-up shirt as he shifted right toward Summer's cell. He spun back to me.

I did two things at once, faster than I'd thought possible. I palmed the keys into my back pocket and screamed, "No!" then moved my body to make it look like I'd just flung myself at the bars.

He reached for my right hand. I flung it open before pulling it back. It had to register that my hand was empty. I did the same with my left hand. The whole thing deceived him into re-thinking what he thought he'd felt. His eyes told him there was no way I had touched him.

He glanced at his side.

I now had two options for escape.

He narrowed his eyes at me and then pressed the com in his ear and spoke. "Anything I need to be aware of?"

I almost pulled the gun out, but the timing didn't feel right. Hopefully his partner had been anticipating him getting to Summer and was focused on her cell.

Adolphe peered at me. "Did you just take something from me?" His voice sounded almost hurt. His partner had seen me do something. Adolphe moved his hand toward his pocket. Like my hands knew what to do before my brain told them, one grabbed the keys and one grabbed the gun. I crouched quickly and slid the keys across the floor to Summer, who snatched them up and immediately shoved them into the keyhole. At the same time, I whipped the gun out and shot Adolphe in the chest. He sank to his knees as Summer kicked him from behind, sending his face into the cold cement floor with a thud. I heard a hiss and looked up to see a hazy gas leaking out around the sock I'd shoved into the ceiling. I covered my mouth and nose with my shirt and moved as far from the spout as possible.

Two seconds later, Summer had my cell open, and we were fleeing toward the door. I calmed my thudding heart and reached out with my senses. Cardwell was not far. I could hear the slight echo of feet hitting stairs in the house. We ran up the stairs to the garage, and I motioned for Summer to go to the left of the car while I ran up three more steps that led to the house and pressed myself into the wall next to the door.

I wanted Cardwell to rush into the garage, but he didn't. Instead I heard a click and an almost silent whoosh. Summer poked up from her spot, eyes wide. I jerked my head up and immediately closed my mouth and covered my face with my arm. Summer did too. I looked around for a garage door button, but couldn't see one. Summer hopped into the car, shutting the door behind her, and frantically searched for something. She grimaced and then pulled her shirt off, grabbed a water bottle from a cup holder and doused her shirt, bringing it up to her mouth.

I didn't dare open the door to the car and allow more poison to sink in. My eyes burned, and I shook my head, trying to clear it. I blinked hard several times before spotting the red emergency release pull hanging above the car.

I tried to leap down the three stairs but stumbled down them instead, my hands barely preventing me from slamming my head into the car. I pulled myself up using the car handle. I blinked several times.

Summer stared at me, mouth covered with her wet shirt. I pointed up and then slid down the side of the car, my muscles rejecting my brain's call to move. I twisted as my body hit the garage floor. I could hear Summer opening her door, then clambering on top of the car, the metal clanging under the pressure. The next thing I knew, Summer was dragging me out into the fresh air. She threw me to the ground a few feet away and headed back into the garage. I heard gunshots and wished I could curl up and hide, but my body wouldn't respond. The sound of squealing tires and then a door opening and shutting hit my ears.

Summer lifted me into the car, screaming out in pain as she did. She even took the time to buckle me in, then threw herself over me, into the driver's seat and peeled out of the driveway. A part of me wanted to laugh, seeing her drive all crazy without a shirt on. The other half wanted to grab her into a hug and tell her how grateful I was for her. Of course, I couldn't do either. She rolled the windows down, and I tried to breathe deeply. We cruised a good mile away before she pulled off the road and got out of the car. What was she doing?

Not a minute later, she was carrying me to another car and buckling me in. She growled as she moved. She threw my go bag at my feet. The kidnappers must have left it in their car when they took me to the basement. My respect for her at the moment was huge. This wasn't the Summer I'd left behind in Belgium, just as I was not the girl I'd been. Again, she rolled the windows down, trying to get the poison to clear from my body. I wasn't sure if that's all it would take. She made it to the back entrance to her apartment in no time, and dashed out of the car without a word. She was only gone for forty-five seconds before she climbed back in with a go bag. She must have had it stashed somewhere.

She pulled out a phone and with the press of a button, she

was in contact with Division over speaker phone. "This is Agent Barnes, requesting immediate extraction with medical assistance." She pulled a long-sleeved T-shirt over her head.

"Extraction six minutes at PN."

PN was Pont Neuf. Could we make it there that quickly? A sharp pain zinged through my big toe and had I been able, I would have yelled out with joy. My breathing seemed too shallow, and my lungs felt full of water. Hopefully, I hadn't inhaled enough poison to keep me down much longer. Despite my seat belt, I was yanked side to side and forward and back as Summer raced through the streets of Paris like death itself was chasing her. The moment we pulled to the extraction point, a white van screeched up beside us. Summer unhooked my seatbelt, and someone pulled me out of the door.

My head spun as he carried me to the van and slid me inside. Summer disappeared and returned with the two go bags. The whole extraction took thirty seconds. An agent I'd met only a few times—Hamil, my memory never let me down—put an oxygen mask over my nose and mouth and strapped it to my head. Why was he here? Where was my team? Jeremy and Halluis were supposed to have been my backup—where were they? They should be here. Something wasn't right.

Pain, sharp and relentless, started in my toes and fingers. It burst through my arms and legs to my core. With sudden intensity, my heart started to slam into my ribs and my lungs expanded. I sucked in a violent breath that propelled me to sitting position. I screamed out, and the agent put his hands on my shoulders and gently laid me back. I wrenched the mask off my face and sucked in several deep, long breaths.

"Just relax, Agent Hadden. Just relax." He handed me a bottle of yellowish liquid. "Drink that. It will help."

"No time for that, Hamil." I tried to stand, but he pulled me down.

"You aren't going anywhere. Drink that."

I sucked the drink down hoping that would get him off my back. My stomach roiled. "Where's my team?" I barked, grimacing at the bitter aftertaste.

The agent looked away, refusing to meet my eyes.

Then I wretched. Over and over. Hamil shoved a bucket toward me the second I started gagging and only a little bit hit the van floor. Once the desire to throw up subsided, I leaned back on the van wall and breathed deep. I was about to yell at Hamil for making me drink something that made me sicker than I was originally, but then I realized I felt pretty good. Way better than I had when I'd climbed into the van.

"Thanks," I said, wiping my lips with my sleeve.

"Don't mention it." His lips were pressed together in a thin white line and his cheeks flushed. He looked at Summer. "You're going to have to go to Medical when we get to Division. That cut is pretty bad and I think you may have a broken arm."

What? Summer had been hurt badly? She had a broken arm? No wonder she'd been grunting and crying out while moving me. I couldn't focus on that. Hamil was avoiding me. "What is it? What aren't you telling me?"

He shook his head sharply.

"Hamil," I growled, my voice both menacing and desperate at the same time.

He pursed his lips again, then met my eyes. "Your team went after you. There was a big crash. They got taken. They didn't make it."

15

I gaped at him in horror. "What?"

Hamil looked miserable. "We were all listening to the audio feed through Agent McGinnis's phone. We heard everything. They got intercepted and taken somewhere, then they were shot."

"No," I whispered. I wanted to scream, but my body had gone limp—I was powerless.

"I'm so sorry."

"Where are they?" I swallowed hard. "What did Siron do with the bodies?" My ragged, rasping breaths strained my lungs. My heartbeat crashed in my ears, making it hard to concentrate on the people around me. And yet, it seemed everything was louder, faster, slower, and softer than it ever had been. I needed to move, but I was frozen to the spot. I forced deep breaths into my lungs. *Move. Get going. Find Jeremy.* My mind cleared, and my heart slowed. I realized that this threat was merely an echo of my own. I closed my eyes. A burning focus settled over me. I had to find him.

He shook his head. "They've been disavowed. Their bodies won't be recovered." Hamil laid me back down, and I didn't fight him. My mind refused to work—I could not function in a world where my team was dead. Where Jeremy was dead.

We pulled into one of the hidden entrances to Division. I knew that hours of debriefing lay ahead of me, but I wasn't about to let that happen. I needed to talk to Ace. I needed answers.

Hamil tried to help me up, but I pushed him firmly aside.

"I'm fine. I can walk now. You don't have to baby me."

He shrugged and left the van with the others. "If I were you, I'd go to Medical and get checked out." Not even. Whatever had been in that drink had seemed to pull all the poison right out of me. I climbed out of the van last, leaving a gap between myself and the other agents, pulling my go bag over my shoulder. My mind churned, trying to formulate a plan. I refused to believe Jeremy and Halluis were dead. Not until I saw them myself.

I peeled off from the group and said, "I'll meet you guys up there. I need to visit the bathroom." I really just needed some time to digest the information.

Hamil's eyebrows knit together, but he let me go. I guessed he wasn't under orders to babysit me. Siron probably thought I was incapacitated. I rushed to the bathroom, making sure to keep my stride capable and strong, so Hamil wouldn't feel the need to worry and wait for me. Or worse, come after me. Once in the bathroom, I took the moment to wash my face and arms, placing my forehead on the mirror and pounding my fists to the sides of my head. "You can't be dead. You can't be dead." I spoke the words to no one. Then drank thirstily from the faucet.

When I dragged myself into the conference room, Rosabella was there to comfort me. I sobbed in her arms until I heard someone else enter the room. Siron. Immediately, I turned to her. "They can't be dead. I have to see them for myself."

"I assure you, they are gone."

"Then I'll go retrieve the bodies. Just tell me where they are. Let me make this right."

"No. I'm sorry." Siron left the room.

"Rosabella, you can't leave me hanging. I know you have access to the recordings. Let me listen to them and form my own conclusions."

"Not now, Christy. Let's focus on the drive and then we can get them."

"Come on. You adore these guys as much as I do. They could be alive. If they are alive, we have to save them."

"I get it. But, what about Siron? She's positive they are gone."

"Come on."

"Alright." She motioned for me to sit at the oval table. She plugged in an extra pair of headphones and handed them to me. She stood and shut the door. From where we were sitting, we could see out the glass wall of the conference room, but no one could see what we were looking at. A small screen popped out of the table, showing a map highlighting their location while we listened to the audio feed from Jeremy's phone. I heard my team's running report of me getting kidnapped ending with Jeremy's words, "They've got her. Follow them. Do not let them get away."

"Tell Siron to send backup to go for Kamal. We are going after Agent Hadden." Halluis's voice.

"Don't you lose them."

"No chance of that." I heard Halluis gun the engine. The dot on the screen followed them as they drove. No one spoke for several minutes until Jeremy said, "We've got a tail. They're coming up on us pretty fast."

"Can you do something about them?"

Jeremy called for backup and then it sounded like he put his phone in his pocket and opened a window. Gunshots filled the mic. He must've been hanging out the window.

Jeremy called out, "Crap! Bulletproof glass and reinforced metals. I can't stop them."

There was a crunch and then some louder crunches.

Rosabella sat stiffly in her chair. "That's when the accident happened."

I nodded. "They had to be injured."

"Most likely, some of them."

Unfamiliar Frenchmen spoke. The voices were muffled and it was impossible to hear what they were saying.

"Do our guys ever speak?"

She shook her head.

"Then how are we supposed to know if they're alive?" I slapped my hands on the table.

"By the mere fact that Jeremy has his phone transmitting."

I nodded. Rosabella pointed to the screen.

"This is the last location the phone transmitted from."

"That's definitely not the same place they took Summer and me."

I could hear rustling and low, muffled voices speaking in French. My head felt like it was about to explode, and a ball that was too big for my throat seemed to lodge itself there. I listened more intently.

It sounded like the phone was still in Jeremy's pocket. Fabric seemed to be brushing and rubbing up against the phone making it all the more difficult to understand the voices outside of the pocket.

I took a deep breath, saying a little prayer that they were all right.

The foreign voices accused them of being spies. It was obvious Jeremy and Halluis were being hit, whether by a fist or some other object, I didn't know. Then there was a scuffle and everything got louder. The captors' voices came through loud and clear now, but only for a moment before a gunshot rang out and the feed went dead.

"Listen to the gunshot. It's like in our trainings when you had to listen to the gunshots and be able to discern from which direction they came."

"Oh, yeah. I totally remember that." She rolled her eyes.

I gave her a look.

"I mean I remember it, but I don't remember what we learned exactly." Rosabella back-pedaled.

"Look. Right after the shot, the phone goes dead. They shot the phone. Yes, everything was muffled. They discovered the phone, removed it from his pocket, and shot it."

"Could be. The voices did suddenly become clear for a few moments before the shot."

"Yes!" We listened to the recording again. Rosabella was nodding.

"You could totally be right."

"I'm going to convince Siron of that." I ran to Siron's office. "They aren't dead. We need to go rescue them."

"Agent Hadden, what are you talking about?"

I told her my conclusions.

"That's not what I heard."

"Come listen again with a new context."

"No. They are not alive, and I won't risk sending any other agents out there to collect their bodies. Not with the drive still out in the open. The drive must be our top priority, and we are running out of time to retrieve it. We are bringing in Kamal's girlfriend and interrogating him. It's the only way. We can talk about retrieval after we have the drive."

"We haven't lost anyone, though. They are alive. Most likely being tortured as we speak. We are going to lose them if we don't go after them. Think about it. Why would they kill them without getting the information they needed first? They are alive."

"I'm sorry. I know this is hard. But there will be no rescue mission. Not now."

My insides burned and my hands curled into fists as Siron dismissed me, her hand going to the headset over her ears. I went back to Rosabella more determined than ever.

"Siron won't help. We have to rescue them on our own. I can't imagine what is happening to them, but I'll bet my life they are still alive and will remain so until they uncover who our guys are."

"I will go with you, Christy. You need backup." Rosabella looked terrified beyond belief, and I loved her for the courage it took her to volunteer despite her fear.

"No, someone needs to be here in case our guys somehow manage to check in. If any new intel comes in, I'll need you to tell me where they are so I can get to them faster. I'll bring Ace and Summer." Asking for Summer's help would not be easy.

"Summer's at Medical. She's not going to be able to help and Ace is out with the team getting the drive."

I nodded. I hated that I would be on my own, but I could do this. I had to. "I only need one more thing from you then. I've got to get out of here. I need you to make sure Siron doesn't know."

"I think I can do that."

My team—my friends—were in danger because of me. I would never abandon them, no matter what Siron ordered. I did not look back as the door to headquarters shut behind me. I knew Rosabella would keep the garage feeds from Siron as long as she could. The cars were the perfect resource to quickly refresh my go bag and get supplies for a new disguise. Each car was equipped with small makeup kits and limited hair and clothing choices.

I took a few minutes to disguise myself. I wanted to pay homage to Cort, my handler in Florida, who had taught me so much about disguise, but I would have needed more time to be that amazing. I would be a bum for this mission, and I hoped it would be the last disguise I'd have to use in Paris.

Since all Division cars would be tracked, I chose to go on foot. I pushed my number into the keypad and let the optical scanner identify me so I could leave the garage. If Siron didn't already know I was going after Jeremy and Halluis, she would shortly.

16

I slipped out into the twilight, one address and the best routes to get there spinning through my mind. I stuck to the subways, the most appropriate transportation for my disguise. I hugged my go bag to my chest. If only my original alias had been a bum here in Paris, I wouldn't be in the position I was now in. No one would have ever tried to pick me. I huffed and used my burner phone for Internet access as I hid under the ratty blanket I had wrapped around me. I was glad I'd never bothered to get a new Division phone when I'd been let back into Siron's graces. If I had, they'd be able to find me, just as they'd found Jeremy. The train seemed to become uncharacteristically packed as we got closer to my stop.

I memorized every detail of the area around the house I was heading to. It was in the Marais neighborhood, a trendy, busy, and fashion conscious area of Paris. I could see the lure of it for the boss of a pickpocket gang. It was so busy, no one would ever wonder why so many people entered and exited a particular building all day long. The building appeared to have five different entrances disguised as separate apartments and a business front on street level. It was also the area where the Bastille was found. The history of the area had probably spoken to such a corrupt and villainous person. Plenty of people had lost their heads here. I hoped Jeremy still had his. No, I was not going to think like that. He was alive, and I was going to rescue him.

To my surprise, when I climbed out of the train, the platform was packed. Many were dressed as if going out on the town, while others were dressed in costume as if going to a street festival. I puzzled over this until I stepped out onto the street, brushing against a woman dressed as a sexy Marie Antoinette, and saw the banners and fliers all over the place. I was smack-dab in the middle of the Marais Art Festival. A man in drag with excessive sparkles and massive plumes of feathers cut in front of me, the feathers tickling my nose as he passed. Surprisingly, no one snickered or stared at me in my bum attire. I seemed to fit right in with the partygoers.

A large section of rue Beaubourg had been shut down to accommodate all the revelers as well as a large stage where a band had just finished playing a song. The French words of one of the band members boomed out over the crowds.

"Yes. It's true we have our very own Prime Minister here today. Why don't you come up and say a few words to all your loyal subjects before you continue on with your art tour?"

The crowd cheered, obviously loving the idea. I saw hands wave above a head, and I wondered if it was him.

The band member sighed loudly into the microphone and said, "Just one sentence would suffice, Monsieur. We don't need a full speech."

After almost a minute of near absolute silence, only a few intoxicated revelers shouting out here and there, the crowds parted and the Prime Minister, second only to the President of France, walked up to the makeshift stage and took the microphone, "Vivre le festival artistique de Marias!" His hands shot up in the air and behind him, my eyes found something I wasn't expecting to see: Cardwell. He stood behind the Prime Minister, acting as some type of a guard, his eyes sweeping the area. I shrank back into the crowds, as if he would be able to pick me out of such an enormous group of people. Cardwell had had a busy day today. He looked upset. I would be too if I'd lost the two people I was supposed to have locked in my dungeon.

Suddenly, my brain registered what I was seeing: Cardwell worked for the Prime Minister. There was no way this was a coincidence. The kidnappers were tied to the Prime Minister, and by the looks of things, they worked directly for him.

I gasped and felt my way back to a building, any building that I could press up against. My mind reeled. Pieces cascaded into place, suddenly making sense. Adolphe and Cardwell had been looking for the drive, and Dufor had said the drive contained incriminating evidence against a powerful public official. The Prime Minister must have somehow been implicated by the information Dufor was planning to give us— but what could it have been?

A perfect image of Dufor's agitated drawings flashed through my mind. The man with the knife in his back— betrayal. *Liberté, égalité, fraternité*: the national motto of France, crossed out. Prime Minister Alden had betrayed the people of France? Then the twisted quote, "Poverty is the mother of crime and he is the father." *He* could mean the Prime Minister. *For Henri, I must.* Dufor's nephew, Henri, had died as a pickpocket on the streets of Paris. Suddenly, I understood, and my blood boiled.

Dufor must have found out that Prime Minister Alden was connected to the crime rings of Paris. That was what was on the drive—evidence that would take down Alden, and the crime rings with him. "This cannot go on", Dufor had written. He'd risked, and ultimately lost, his life to stop the Prime Minister from sponsoring crime.

I stared up at the Prime Minister's face as he waved to the crowds and exited the stage, Cardwell following close behind. I truly wanted to rip his eyes out.

A church bell tolled, a stark reminder of the ticking clock on my friends' lives. My friends were in the middle of this mess because of me, and now that I knew it involved high levels in the government, fear nested in my chest. I needed to get them out, as fast as possible. As soon as they were free, I'd deal with the Prime Minister. I felt a slight tremor go through me, and my hair stood on edge like I was being watched. Had Cardwell or the Prime Minister seen me as I stood frozen, figuring out what was most likely going on? That had been a completely stupid idea. I scanned the crowd but saw no one, and the feeling subsided after I took a couple deep breaths. I made my way down the packed sidewalks to my destination.

I leaned on the stoop of a nearby house and watched the building that was my team's last known location, looking for security, alternate entrances, and anyone who seemed to be watching the place. I made out five cameras on the front of the building, and the green sheen on the glass told me it was bulletproof. A man sat on the porch swing, but the bulge at his hip betrayed his weapon. He got up and went inside. I bet more guards were waiting inside. With security so tight, I could see no easy way in from the ground floor. I slipped into the alley on the other side of the neighboring house and hunched down like I was just finding a place to bed down for the night. After two minutes, a good pathway up the exterior of the building presented itself.

I carefully shed the blanket and started up the brick wall of the neighboring building, using window ledges and anything sticking out to help me move more quickly. It was nice to have so much distraction on the main street. Hopefully, no one would bother to look down a semi-dark alley. My fingers burned, but I knew this was the only way to gain entrance to the house. The ground level was too fortified with security and henchmen for me to consider trying to break through without some support.

By climbing the sidewall of the neighboring house, I'd have access to the roof of the target building without having to get past anyone. The guards and the cameras paid it no attention. Major security flaw, in my opinion.

Once on top, I stuck to the edges of the building where there was the most support and hopefully most absorption of my careful footfalls. I made it to the back edge of the building, away from the street, and leapt. I landed on the very edge of the target building, hoping to have the sound of my impact absorbed into the walls and across the roof instead of having a loud thud hit the building. After the initial hit, with ballerina feet, I took two more steps to the side to further disrupt any noise that had come with the jump.

I then scanned my surroundings and let myself down the back side of the building and climbed into the first window that someone had neglected to shut completely. I'd dreaded having to get in the window and disable any alarms attached to it. If the window was slightly ajar, then the alarm was already out of the equation. I was only two stories from the roof and obviously in someone's apartment. This wasn't a business building after all. I stood in a bedroom that most likely belonged to a teenager. No wonder the window was ajar.

Posters of rock bands and their lead singers along with bare chested movie stars hung on the walls. With that clue and the bright pink and yellow colors, I assumed it was a girl's room. A lucky break. I crossed quickly to her wardrobe and rifled through the girl's clothing, pulling out some black leggings and a black turtleneck. I shed my bum costume—it had too many pieces dangling from it that could get caught as I tried to move stealthily through the house. I slipped into the girl's clothes and stuffed my discarded costume under her bed. I guessed it wasn't my last disguise after all. The turtleneck was a bit snug, and a slice of my stomach showed no matter how hard I tugged down on it. This was Paris, though, and I needed no luck to find a scarf that I could wrap around my waist. It was burgundy with gold stripes through it and with a couple of creative knots, it didn't look half bad used as a belt. I flung the go bag over my shoulder and moved to the door.

I surveyed the hallway as I opened the door. Empty of people and no cameras. Maybe the cameras were only on the exterior of the building. I needed to get to the basement. In my experience most people kept their darkest secrets in basements. It probably had everything to do with keeping noises from the streets, but I liked to think that dark things belonged in dark basements. I guessed which direction would lead me down and lucked out finding a staircase. I was about to descend after discovering that the only cameras in the entryway were facing the front door, but two men appeared from behind the steps, just below where I was. I peered down at them, hiding myself as much as I could behind the wall that opened up to the spiraling steps.

"Gonna have to go big to break them," the voice said in French. "They've got to be serious professionals. They've been trained hard in interrogation. We've worked non-stop for almost three hours now, and neither one is showing signs of weakness. I think we've got some undercover government agents here."

"Not our government," a second man laughed. "They're our pals, aren't they?"

The first joined his laughter. "Man, they love us. We're keeping them fat and happy. No—these guys must be foreign. We'll figure it out."

They walked through the foyer and left out the front door. I didn't see or hear them lock the door. They must use cameras and a central security team somewhere in the building. If I were to make it to the spot I'd seen those men, I'd need to take the cameras out, but I had no backup. I needed a distraction or another way down.

I searched the upstairs and while I found no cameras in the living quarters, I did find my way into the ducting through a bathroom vent. It was already a snug fit, and I wondered if the old ductwork would support my downward travels. Keeping track of my go bag presented its own difficulties, too. I snagged a couple of towels and tied them around my knees and elbows to help with the noise. I moved quickly while horizontal, then slowed considerably as I hit a spot where I'd be totally vertical. I pushed my hands and feet hard into the metal hole as I lowered myself. I had counted one hundred steps on that staircase with my quick glimpse earlier, and I estimated my progress by them. Each time I readjusted my position, I figured I'd gone down one step, so I counted down from one hundred.

By the time I hit fifty, sweat dripped profusely into my eyes, and I had to keep telling myself that I was in the Swiss Alps, enjoying the crisp air that beat against me. I decided to move a bit faster because the ache in my arms was starting to bother me. I hoped this run didn't continue to the basement without having any arms leading out from it. I wasn't sure I'd have the stamina to make it otherwise.

My leg slid the requisite step, and the wall seemed to disappear. I let my other leg slip down and found the run had split two ways. I had to push both forearms into the metal to ease down. I slipped, but since I had my feet angled out they landed in the side runs. A gong sounded around me, and I pushed again on the sides trying to absorb the sound some. I hoped the noise had gone unnoticed or that it would be blamed on old-house sounds. I crouched and then sighed as I lay in the horizontal ducting, rubbing my upper arms and legs to relax them. I only allowed myself ten seconds of rubbing before I searched for a vent opening. I found one, but it had long since been closed off with a board over it. I used some pliers from my go bag to yank the board off. I could see out, but apparently I was still too high up to see what was in the room.

I placed a magnet on the vent and then set to removing one screw. Instead of falling to the ground when it came free, it clung to the vent because of the magnet. Whew! I repeated the process with all four screws. Before I took out the last screw, I bent a twist tie through a metal slat in the vent to prevent it from falling to the ground. Once it was totally free from restraints, I pushed it out, holding onto the long twist tie and lowering it slightly before grabbing the vent and pulling it inside the ducting. I could hear the intermittent clinking of chains.

I then used a mirror to look down. A completely empty cement room lay below me with no soft items anywhere. No rugs, no curtains, no furniture that wasn't metal. A true dungeon. That's when I saw them, my coworkers, my friends.

17

Jeremy and Ace were chained to the wall right beneath me. Where was Halluis? And how did Ace get here. I thought he was on assignment for Siron. I scanned the room for him, but I couldn't see him. I also looked for cameras and found none. Did the bad guys really only have cameras around the front door, but nowhere else? I chirped like a bird, and Jeremy tilted his head to the side and looked up. Terror crossed his face, and he shook his head almost imperceptibly before circling his head around as if he'd just been stretching.

Both my team members stood with their arms chained above them. They wouldn't be able to free themselves with paperclips or any of the supplies I had in my bag. I scanned the room again. There had to be a camera somewhere or he wouldn't have risked warning me. No cameras were visible to the naked eye. Silently, I took out my binoculars and searched the three walls I could see, one by one. Nothing. Absolutely nothing. I leaned just out of the vent and, still using the binoculars, I found the embedded cameras. They were hard to spot, but a glint from a light on one of the cameras put me onto them.

Jeremy was right. This was not the right move. First, I had to find out where the guards were located in the house. Then,

I'd need to come up with some distraction to get them out of their hidey-hole and in position to take advantage of that distraction to escape. I wasn't looking forward to climbing the ducting. In fact, I decided I wouldn't climb.

The security team was most likely on the first floor and not on the same floor with the family's personal quarters. I shimmied over the vertical ducting to the other side of horizontal ducting, and heard a slight scraping noise. I stopped to listen. I heard it again. It sounded like something was in the vent with me, and it wasn't a rat or mouse with their tip-tapping claws. It was a dragging, scraping noise. A snake? I shook my head at the idea. What was I thinking? Just because I hated snakes didn't mean they could climb into ductwork. No. This was something much worse. It had to be someone following me. Summer had been right. Someone always followed me. Yet in this case, I realized, they were out in front of me, and I was following them—the sliding, scraping sound was coming toward me from the direction I wanted to go.

Had the security team somehow discovered me? I had to believe the guard had no idea I was so close to him or he wouldn't be coming toward me, making noise like he was. Trying to move at the same time he was and hoping I was moving twice the distance he was, I made it to the vertical opening. Up or down?

He was most likely on his stomach, so I'd do better to climb up a little bit and then surprise him. But if he was trained at all, he might flip just before reaching the opening and be face up, giving him a quick glance at me at the same time I saw him. I'd take my chances and go up. A quick kick to the head would knock the guard out so that I could disable him and escape.

The guard came quickly, and my foot was poised to take

him out. As the head slid out, I shoved my foot down, but had to hold it back at the last second. Summer's face looked up at me, gasping, her hands flying to cover her face. My foot tapped her forehead, and her hands hit into my shoe.

"Summer?" I whispered, my nose scrunched up in confusion.

"If you had kicked me, I would have been forced to hurt you."

I shook my head, my arms ready to move my body up or let me down. "How did you get here? I thought you were in Medical with a broken arm."

"Partial dislocation, whatever that means. And the same way you did. I really appreciate being led in here. Ducting is my favorite." I couldn't miss the sarcasm in her voice.

"Mine, too." I wanted to laugh, but Summer's face did not invite humor. She was mad. "What are you doing here? Did Siron send you?"

"You've got to be kidding, right? I was forbidden from even thinking about y'all. But I wasn't about to let you get all the glory on this one. Not after everything I've been through. I thought you'd be going after the drive, but no, it turns out you are going after the other agents."

"I figured it wouldn't take me long, and then I could snag the drive from Kamal right after. No big deal."

"And if he passes the drives on?"

"Then we'll have Marco's coordinates while he carries them around. And if he takes them somewhere, we'll have those coordinates too. The drive situation is under control. However, as you will soon find out, Jeremy and the others are in deep trouble, and they need us right now."

"Are they that way, then?" She pointed to the horizontal

191

ducting that led to the other agents.

"Yes, but there's no way to save them from there. Cameras everywhere."

"So that's what those guys are watching. I couldn't see the screens, I just knew they were the guards on duty."

"The guards are in a room at the end of this ducting?"

"Not at the end, but somewhere in the middle."

"How many guards?"

"Two."

I let myself down, putting one foot on the opening to the horizontal ducting opposite Summer. I let out a harsh breath of air and shook out one arm at a time. "Do you think they have a view of the street?"

"Most likely. The room was pretty big. I didn't notice a window, but I wasn't looking for one."

"Let's get out of here. We need a distraction." I started shimmying up the ducting. I heard Summer sigh before she also headed up.

Once on the roof, we looked over the edge of the front of the building, watching the crowds enjoying the festival. It would be great if they could act as a distraction. There had to be a way to use them without truly putting them in danger.

On the sides of the building, we could see garbage bins.

"How about encouraging the festival goers to use this building's bathroom? With the gallons of wine they've drunk they must need a toilet," she suggested.

"Perhaps several different distractions. Maybe a fire in the alley and several invitations to a private art showing in this fine house *and* a few invites to use the nice, clean bathrooms?" I raised one eyebrow and chuckled. "I'll get a bit spruced up," I said, waving over my black blank slate, "and go looking for some interesting characters to invite into the house. Then I'll pretend to be a bit tipsy with a full bladder and join a group that I can lead here to use the bathroom."

"And you want me to pick the lock?"

"No need. The front door is open. I watched two meatheads leave earlier, and they didn't lock up. They use the cameras to control entry. I need you to set the fire in the bin, but make sure you get an audience. Better yet, talk some drunk guy into setting it. That will divert the guards' attentions."

She gave me an exasperated look, and I remembered that she didn't typically lead missions, but followed everyone around. "Use your womanly wiles, you know, the ones that make everyone follow and worship you."

"I'm not that girl anymore."

"You are tonight." Without giving her a chance to respond, I slinked my way to the side of the building and jumped to the neighboring one. Summer followed.

We checked our watches and marked the time on them. In ten minutes flat, the fireworks would begin. I would be one of the revelers looking for a party and use the others as my cover to disappear behind the stairs and down to the dungeon to free my captive teammates. My stomach felt queasy, and I swallowed over and over again.

Summer would be the second wave, coming in full force with several weapons to clear our exit if needed. I was nervous about counting on her since we'd never worked together before, so I went forward thinking it was all up to me. If she happened to contribute something, all the better. I had to be ready and prepared for the worst. And the worst on this rescue mission was to be alone. Minute movements of the crowds caught my attention and for the first time that night, I smelled the sweet and savory smells associated with a festival.

I didn't know if I could live with the loss of Jeremy and Ace. That's when it hit me again that I hadn't seen Halluis. They must have him in a separate room, interrogating him. I couldn't stand the idea that he was being tortured as we spoke. Especially since he was there because of me.

I slipped into a store and grabbed some items to create a crazy outfit: feathers, a rainbow scarf, and a bright yellow, tight-fitting dress. I also picked up some knickknacks to give out as invitations to the "party". Then I bought some sparkler-like fireworks from a street vendor, lit one, and went to work. I found the loudest, most outrageous group of party-goers and ran in front of them. "You all look like you would appreciate a private showing and party! What do you say?"

They all looked at each other and then said, "Yes! Yes!" I handed out ten purple Eiffel Tower key chains as invitations.

"Show up at that building with the white stoop in exactly five minutes." I pointed to the building where my team had been chained up." Don't be early and don't be late. The owner of the gallery is very picky. Don't make me look ridiculous for inviting you."

Their eyes widened.

Then I laughed and said, "He will totally love your outfits. I think they just might earn you the pass into the Dungeon. Only about fifteen people make it into the Dungeon each year. He never issues invites until a half hour before the event, and he sends me out to find the best and brightest. I choose you. Now I only need to find five others." I consulted my watch. "Oh, shoot. Now I only have four minutes." I hurried away and invited another five to the "event" and then put on my drunk persona and joined up with some awfully drunk people walking down the path on a collision course for the pickpocketing boss's house. "You guys know anywhere I can take a pee?" They all shook their heads.

"Not around here. Just pee in an alley." They laughed.

"No way! Oh man, there's a good building. I think I went there last year. Really nice and really great, clean bathroom." I had a lot of fun slurring my French words like a drunk would as I linked my arms through two other people's and led them up the stairs of the white stoop just as the groups of gallery hopefuls showed up. Once they realized this place had no art gallery and no public bathroom, they'd be gone in a flash, so I'd have to be fast. "See, you guys, they love to open up their doors for the festival." I pushed on the door and everyone flooded in. "Head upstairs, everyone," I called out. Once they were all inside, I let myself be pushed to the back corner of the stairs, but there wasn't a staircase going down, and I couldn't see a door that led to one. I'd overheard those men when they'd been in this exact area, and stairways were typically stacked in these old houses. The entry had to be along one of these walls.

As the partygoers started to climb the stairs, I took the opportunity to push along the stair wall in hopes of finding a way to the hidden basement. I was sure security would be at the top of the stairs and stop their progress, so I didn't have a lot of time. In the far back corner, I pressed on the wall, searching for a hidden switch. It finally paid off as I pressed on a particular spot in the faux wood paneling, and a false wall opened. The door swung inward. I watched as the last of the visitors headed up the stairs before I went through the doorway. Surely the guards wouldn't hurt the party-goers. They'd simply escort them out.

I made sure no one was on the steps then disappeared

down the stairs to the basement. Just as I reached the bottom, I heard a huge boom, and the ground shook a little. Summer did not go small, that was for sure. At least I hoped the boom came from her fire. The two guards in the guardroom had to have been lured out by now if they hadn't already. That meant no one would be watching me go to the basement.

I sprinted across the cold cement floor to where the agents hung on the opposite wall and immediately set to freeing Jeremy.

"You made it," he said, his voice weak.

"Nice outfit," Ace croaked. "Sorry. I didn't bring any sweets with me."

I grinned, then cried out in dismay as Ace's eyes rolled back in his head and his whole body went limp.

"I'm going to get you guys out of here. Where is Halluis?" I asked as I worked on the last shackle holding Jeremy. To my surprise, he leaned into me when he was free, not because he was happy to see me, but because he was having a hard time standing. All I wanted to do was hold him and comfort him, but I had to stay in operative mode.

"If we're going to make it out of here, I'm going to need your help, Jeremy." Jeremy shook his arms out as I freed Ace. I tried to give him a determined look as I passed him a couple of lock picks. They'd been tortured and spent hours tied up in that position. I'd been naïve in thinking either of them would be able to help with the escape.

"Halluis is upstairs somewhere," Ace said, his voice a faint croak, as he sank to the ground once he was free. "We have to find him. I tried, Christy, but I couldn't save them. I'm sorry."

So Ace had defied Siron again and had gone to save his team members instead of going for the drive. A lump formed in my throat. "Thank you for trying, Ace, and don't worry. We will find him." I immediately wrapped his arm around my shoulder and dragged him toward the stairs while Jeremy followed slowly after us. That's when I noticed the blood dripping behind us, but I couldn't worry about it right then. First, I had to bring them to safety.

I prayed Summer would come through and give us another diversion to get out of the basement. As we rounded the pillar where the stairs wrapped around, I heard the door open. I motioned for the agents to lean against the pillar, out of sight of anyone looking down the stairs.

The footfalls were heavy, most likely not Summer's. She was light on her feet. I glanced back at Jeremy, who was now helping to support Ace. I leaned over and sat him on the step, readying myself with the switchblade and a few safety pins from my go bag. I closed my eyes, not liking my odds.

The hulking guard saw me at the same time I saw him. I chucked my knife, and it embedded itself in his thigh. He grunted but didn't go down. Instead, he shot a silenced gun at me. I felt the heat of the bullet as it brushed past my hair just above my right ear. After the shot went off, he doubled over. I lunged, overestimating the debilitating effects of his injury. He raised the gun and shot again. This time the bullet hit the stairs and ricocheted off the wall nearby.

I couldn't stop. He fired again, both hands on the handgrip, steadying it. The shot hit Ace in the foot, and he cried out despite his weakened state.

"Come any closer, and he's dead." The guard bit his lip, obviously in a lot of pain.

I didn't move, but my mind was calculating the many possible actions I could take along with their outcomes. The only chance we had was for Summer to show up and give us our exit. The gun the guard brandished was definitely a Kahr K-9. Seven bullets in the magazine and one in the chamber. He'd shot three. That meant there could be five more bullets in that gun. I had to get it from him.

An explosion rocked the room above us. I held on to the wall for support, but the guard fell to his knees. Apparently, Summer had decided to bring the distraction inside. That was not what I had in mind, but I'd capitalize on it. I jerked forward, pushing the guard's gun up above his head, another shot digging deep into the ceiling plaster. I wrestled the gun away from him and shot him in the foot, the foot attached to his uninjured leg. He yelled out in pain and fell on the cement steps. I slammed his head into the wall, making him black out. I took everything from his pockets and removed the com in his ear. Then I quickly retied the rainbow scarf around my waist and shoved the gun into the makeshift belt.

I turned back to my friends. "Jeremy, can you carry Ace?" I asked. "I need to be free to take on anyone who tries to stop us." He nodded, then pulled Ace's arm up around his shoulder and started up the steps.

I kept one hand on the gun as I climbed the stairs. This rescue was all on me. At the top, I peeked around the corner. Tapestries and fine rugs were on fire, the room filling up with smoke.

"The place is on fire, Jeremy. I'm sorry, but we're going to have to hurry."

He did, grunting louder and yanking poor Ace up the steps as fast as he could.

"Where up here is Halluis?"

"Not sure. But they had me in there." Ace pointed to the

opposite side of the large foyer. Huge crowds had gathered in front of the burning building. Just then, the masses of people who had ascended the stairs to the second floor came screeching down. So the civilians hadn't already escaped. I hoped none were hurt. I flagged several guys down to come help my two injured friends. They came readily, helping each of them out despite how drunk they were.

I darted over to the door Ace had pointed out, picked the lock and pushed through it. Halluis sat tied to a chair and was choking on the thickening smoke. I rushed over and untied him, then yanked him toward the door, crawling.

"Hey now, no call for that sort of behavior." Halluis smiled wryly, though each word was strained and hoarse. "Just point me to the exit, and I'll find my own way." He started crawling forward, just to prove he could.

"Oh, thank goodness," I sighed. He'd be able to get out on his own. I pushed him toward the door. "Go—I'm right behind you!"

I searched for Summer, but she was nowhere to be seen. She'd come inside to set off that explosion—had she made it out? Something told me she was still in the building, a feeling I couldn't deny. I heard voices above, yelling. The yelling got quieter as time passed. They were going up. Was Summer with them? I had to work on the premise that she was. I could not leave anyone behind.

18

I pulled the Kahr K-9 out of my scarf-belt and held it at the ready as I began to ascend the stairs. I paused for a second and hastily tied the scarf around my nose and mouth—it would help at least a little. I heard a noise just behind me, and whirled around to find one of the tall, crazy-outfitted partygoers crashing back through the entryway.

"Get out!" he cried, shielding his face from the smoke. I took the opportunity to hide the gun behind my back. "You have to get out, now!"

"I've got to help my friend. She's upstairs."

"I'll come with you."

"No. It's too dangerous. Make sure everyone outside gets the help they need. Don't let anyone back in."

He didn't seem happy about letting me stay in the building alone, but he nodded anyway. "I will."

"Wait! Did you happen to see a tall blond girl, gorgeous beyond compare, out there?" I hollered down at him.

"Only about a dozen." He disappeared out the door.

I raised my gun. This time no one would be following me, I would be following them. I carefully made my way up the inside of the steps, my gun pointing up and ready to fire at anyone who dared to look over the rail. The fire seemed to be losing its power, but it released smoke with a vengeance. I was grateful for the scarf.

That's when I heard Jeremy calling my name. I turned, trying to make him out through the smoke.

"Get out here, Hadden. That's a direct order," he sputtered. The guy who'd called to me to get out earlier was holding him up.

I was halfway up the stairs already. I couldn't respond or the bad guys would be able to pinpoint my position. Instead, I leaned down to see if I could find a visual pathway to the door to alert Jeremy to my precarious position. As I did, I caught sight of Summer up the stairs by way of a mirror. Our eyes locked in the reflection. A man had a gun pointing at her temple, her upper arm held tightly in his hand. At the same time, I noticed a guard with a gun in his hand coming up behind Jeremy. I had enough time to save one. But only one.

I made a quick assessment. It had to be Jeremy. I didn't have a direct line on Summer and even if I did, she was too entangled with her captor—if I shot I would risk missing my target and hitting Summer. Instead, I spun and shot the man coming up behind Jeremy in the only place I had a direct shot, his head. The guard fell back, and the man holding Jeremy up gave a shriek, throwing his hands in the air and letting go of Jeremy, who immediately slid to the floor without the extra support.

I turned quickly and aimed opposite the mirror, but the people from the reflection were gone. I moved like a cat up the stairs, almost silent and with a speed I didn't know I had in me. I wasn't sure anyone but Summer knew that I was there. I'd seen her in the mirror, and the man holding her captive had been looking in a different direction. At the top of the steps, I found an empty landing area.

I carefully made my way through the floor, clearing each room. They were not there. I heard hard steps on the ceiling. The roof. There must be a secret passageway up there. I didn't have the time to waste to look for it. I climbed out the same bedroom window I'd climbed in earlier, and made it to the edge of the roof and carefully peered over. Three guards stood on the roof. One talked into his com. The other two talked to each other, one with his hand tightly on Summer's upper arm and a gun pressed against her temple. All three were within six feet of Summer.

I thought about the shots I'd taken with this Kahr K-9 and the shots the previous owner had taken. Added up, it was a total of six. That left two, maybe three, if he hadn't taken any shots before he came into the dungeon, and still had one left in the chamber. I prayed for more ability than I had so that Summer could be saved and the bad guys would pay for their crimes. I dug the tips of my toes into the grooves of the bricks and threw myself up into the air. Like my whole body somehow slowed down, I was able to steady my hands as though I were standing on solid ground. I pulled the trigger twice in quick succession and landed on the edge of the rooftop.

The first shot whizzed through the small opening between the guard and Summer, hitting the guard's gun startling him into dropping the gun over the edge of the building. His hand released Summer's arm, and he spun in the direction the gun flew.

The second bullet whizzed toward the guard on the com. The bullet hit his shoulder, and he bent over in pain. I shifted to aim at the third guard. *Click.* "No!" I yelled, pulling the trigger again and being rewarded with more clicks instead of the bang of a bullet leaving the barrel. The guard leveled his gun at me. I flew to the side to avoid the bullet. It hit something behind me with a loud zing.

Summer took advantage of her freedom and flew through the air, kicking her legs up and smacking that third guard in the face. The hit forced him to his knees and he pulled the second guard down with him, sending his gun skittering across the roof. She put her hands together and slammed the second guard in the face. He lay still. I stood, using the ledge of the roof to help me up.

The guard who had been holding Summer's arm regrouped, snagging the skittering gun and sent another shot my way. It grazed my shoulder, and the surprise of the shot and the searing heat twisted me, making me lose my balance. As I shifted, my foot caught on a piece of metal sticking up from the roof and sent me careening over the edge. I reached out with my hands, grappling for a handhold. I cried out as pain shot through my injured arm as it scraped along the ledge. There was only the asphalt below me. With a final burst of energy, my fingers snagged the edge of the building. I pulled hard, trying to get my injured arm to allow my hand to grab the roof, too.

It took more strength than I thought I had, but I managed to keep hold of the lip of the roof, first with the tips of my fingers and then to my second joint. I hung there, feeling spent, but dug deep, reaching inside me for strength. Not for myself, but for Summer. I had to help her. One guard was out, but there were still two others who could overpower her. I pulled hard, sucking breath and crying out, trying to use my screams and grunts to give me more power, more ability.

As my eyes crested the lip of the roof, I could see a body coming toward me. Summer. She must have overpowered the two guards. Good for her. She walked, slowly, carefully. Her eyes met mine, and they narrowed. I grunted with the effort of keeping my fingers rounded over the edge. She reached me and I lengthened my arms, knowing I was about to find relief. It didn't come. She looked over the edge at me, her ponytail hanging nearer me than her face. I tried to find purchase with my toes, but could not.

"Summer. Please."

She sat on the edge. "You know, I could let you fall, and no one would be the wiser." Her voice was soft, silky, evil.

My heart sank. She did want me dead.

"It wouldn't reflect poorly on me, and you'd have a hero's funeral." She closed her mouth and took a deep breath through her nose. "It's a win-win."

I kicked at the wall, my fatigue and panic preventing me from getting what I wanted. What I needed.

"You let him take me," Summer said, looking off at nothing. "You had the shot, and you chose to let him take me."

"I didn't have a clear shot. I saw your reflection in the mirror and you were blocking most of the guard." I grunted against the pain. "I could have killed you. I had the shot to save Jeremy. I took it. I turned to you second, but you were gone. I didn't abandon you."

"I felt abandoned. I think Josh felt abandoned. Do you feel abandoned? Do you?"

"I do." I knew it was what she wanted to hear. Sweat dripped from my chin, and my fingers started to feel slick. If my feet did not grab something soon, I would fall with certainty.

"You're not a murderer, Summer. Help me."

"You don't know what I am."

"I do."

She stood up and screamed. "No! You don't. You are not the star child. You don't know everything. You are not special. Life is uncertain, but death is not. We all face it. Perhaps this is your time."

A shadow grew over us. Someone was there. "Summer!" I yelled. "Behind you!" My toes finally found purchase as a rush of adrenaline coursed through me and catapulted me over the ledge of the roof. I lunged directly into the knees of one of the guards. We toppled to the roof, his head slamming into the rocky base. Still brimming with power, I bludgeoned his head until his eyes rolled back and he lost consciousness. I twisted and looked back toward the other two guards. They did not move. Summer had completely disabled them.

I looked up at Summer, who remained still on the ledge of the roof. Fierce anger boiled inside of me until I saw the tear drip from her chin followed by more, and then her whole body shook with sobs. I would have moved to her and consoled her had I been able to, but it seemed the adrenaline rush had passed and left me near-dead. Instead, I joined her, tears trailing down the sides of my face too.

19

I'm not sure how long we stayed like that, frozen, mourning together, but separate. After what seemed forever, an extraction team took us from the roof into a helicopter and to a hospital where we joined the rest of the team, injured, frazzled, and completely drained.

At some point, I startled awake. I was dying of thirst. I looked around the room. Definitely a hospital room. It was only me. The visitor's chair was empty, and no one stood around my bed gawking at me. It was dark; only a thin light came from the moon outside and the crack under the door. An IV dripped something into my veins from my scraped up hand, and something was clipped to my index finger—a pulse monitor. I went through my own little health check, starting at my head and moving to my toes, wiggling and moving all my body parts. While I was sore, certainly not pain free, I felt surprisingly good.

"Agent Hadden?" A voice came from the door.

"Director." My body tensed as she entered. I wasn't sure what Siron was about to say, but I wanted keep my temper in check so I could ask some questions.

"I'm so glad you are safe. And, I owe you an apology. I'm sorry. I was wrong about Jeremy and the others on your team. They were alive and you were right to go after them. I misread the evidence."

That little speech was an utter surprise. "It happens to the best of us."

"Yes, it does. You did an amazing job."

"Thank you." She was being so nice, I thought I finally dared ask the question I had to get an answer to. "Director, have you been able to see what was on the drive yet?"

She sighed. Well, the sound was something between a sigh and a huff really. She licked her lips. What she was about to say was very uncomfortable for her. "With all the commotion, with the kidnapping and the aftermath, we weren't able to keep up with Kamal. We don't have the drive."

"Seriously?" My heart dropped and a sick feeling tore through my gut. Immediately, I thought of the Prime Minister.

"No."

"Well, if you're up for one of my crazy ideas…"

"I don't know that I'm up for that, but you can pitch me."

"I think the Prime Minister is involved in all of this." Siron was already shaking her head in dissent. "Listen. We've known all along that it was someone powerful who was involved with this. I thought it had to be some rich guy or a big corporation that could throw money at people, but it isn't. I'm certain of it. One of the men who kidnapped Summer and me was at Marias Art Festival and he was protecting the Prime Minister as he spoke."

"Private security firms are hired for that type of thing all the time. Just because they were together at that one event, doesn't mean they are always. It's too flimsy. There's no proof. It's all conjecture. We can't follow up on assumptions when it comes to the Prime Minister and the President. We need concrete proof for that. But, I don't want you to worry about it.

I've got men on it. You need to rest. You've done an amazing job. I'll have you know, I plan to put it in your file. Your loyalty is to be commended."

"Wait. What about the tracked drives?"

"They didn't work as we'd planned. Someone discovered them and disabled them. We followed them until they went dark."

"Let me tell you one more thing to try to convince you the Prime Minister is involved. I promise to drop it after you hear this."

She nodded, but rolled her eyes.

"I know he's involved in this whole thing. Dufor's doodling told us everything. His nephew was killed, executed, because he picked somewhere he shouldn't have. Dufor must have connected information Sécurité Un was storing with his nephew. That's why he thought it was worth it to go against his company's mission statement of protecting all information."

She was shaking her head again.

"Put a tail on the Prime Minister. That will tell us the truth." I swung my legs off the bed to show her I was still strong.

"Your accusations, while intriguing, are unfounded and without proper evidence. To go up against that man, we would need more. I'm sorry. Besides that, I've met him, and he's an upstanding citizen. The scrutiny he's under every day considering the investigation around the President right now tells me this couldn't be true or someone would have uncovered it already. Maybe it's the stress and confusion with what has happened to you that has clouded your thinking, making your conclusions off. It's okay. I understand. We know where Kamal is, and we are in the process of detaining Marni. We do believe

Kamal would not fold without having an imminent threat to his girlfriend. We'll arrest him and force him to tell us about Marco and the drives."

"You mean torture him."

"If that's what it takes. I appreciate your dedication to this. Leave the rest to the backup team. You rest. Heal with your team." With that, she left. I growled in frustration.

"Why won't anyone ever listen to me?" I said aloud to the empty room. She didn't have concrete evidence, but all of the circumstantial evidence was overwhelming. Besides, she didn't know Kamal at all. Siron had stuck her hand in the viper's nest. From what I knew, he would not respond well to threats against Marni. He'd somehow find a way to set up Siron and get her killed. I was sure of it. Echoes of Kamal cutting into that boy haunted me. I had to get to Kamal before Siron.

I spotted my go bag on the floor next to the visitor's chair. I turned the machine off and removed the pulse monitor, then the IV, pressing some tissues on the insertion site to stanch the bleeding before heading for the en suite bathroom.

After relieving myself, taking handfuls of water into my mouth, and making a vain attempt at fixing my matted and frizzy hair by forcing it into a ponytail, I opened the bathroom door. I was met by a large, scowling nurse.

"Let me help you back into the bed," she said in sweet but somehow condescending voice. She put her hand on my back and pressed, forcing me in that direction. "I'll get someone in here to put that IV put back in and make sure you have some water next to your bed."

A bit shocked and not wanting to cause a scene just yet, I allowed her to guide me. After I sat, she pulled up a remote looking thing that appeared to be attached to the bed and said,

"If you need anything, feel free to press this button here. It alerts us that you need something. That's why we're here, to help you get what you need."

She nodded as if in silent direction to lie back and get covered. I did, and she left the room. While shutting the door, she said, "Someone will be here shortly to help you with that IV."

I sputtered a laugh as I swung my legs off the bed to get to my go bag and some clothes. That nurse had learned to school her emotions, even if her boiling point was right under her calm exterior. I had no idea where my other clothes had ended up. All I knew was that I couldn't or wouldn't be held up at a hospital any longer than I had to, and this flimsy gown had to go. I changed into the only outfit left in my bag, too-big black slacks and an extra-large white button up shirt. I topped off the ensemble with a chauffer's cap and found my shoes from last night tucked under the small side table to the left of the visitor's chair.

Sliding my go bag on my back, I cracked the door and watched for the robust nurse to go answer a call. The moment she did, I slinked out of the room, easing the door shut with a tiny click instead of a bang. I took off toward the first exit signs, not even wanting to wait for the elevator even though I was five floors up. I practically slid down all the flights of stairs, determination burning in my chest.

I started out of the stairwell and quickly stepped back. Siron had placed operatives at the doors. Had she discovered that I'd left my room already? I spotted Summer. Her head was in her hands, and she looked a bit dejected. Her head suddenly popped up, and our eyes met. It was over for me. She'd gladly report me to Siron and get the two dummy operatives to take me into custody. A deep sigh rushed out of me as I eyed the doors and then the hallways, calculating my chances of escape.

I glanced back at Summer, who was still looking at me. She stood, and I readied myself to take off, but she gestured with one of her hands and shook her head slightly as if warning me to wait.

What? Wait to give her time to alert the guards and turn me in?

She walked over to the guards.

I turned to take my chances with the hallway. Before I took off, she had everyone facing completely away from me. She was distracting them. Go figure. I didn't have time to dwell on the weirdness of her helping me after what happened on that roof.

Despite my confusion, I made my way to a restroom where I found a hinged window. After a few swift kicks, I was able to free the window from its hinges, creating a space big enough for me to throw my bag out and slip through into the black night. I was free.

I took the train to Kamal's. I checked his tracker just to make sure he was actually home. His dot sat right on his address. I made it to his apartment in twenty minutes, rehearsing in my mind what I might say to him to convince him to give Marco up. I stood watching the building from a block away, a few street lamps lighting the area.

Aside from the front door, there were two windows through which I could gain access to his apartment. One was by the front door and the other in the alley. I flicked my gaze at my fellow agents who were watching that front door, then I looked at the brick wall that led to the window and veranda that I would have to get to and scowled. My fingers were still red and sore from climbing last night, but if there were operatives watching the place, this was definitely my only way in. The dark night would help camouflage me. I snuck over to the narrow alley and rolled the too-big pants several times at my waist and used elastics from my go bag to control the hems. I dug my fingers in, and after wincing and stifling a cry, I climbed. At the top I sat on the veranda and shook my hands a bit, closing my eyes and wishing the pain away. I tied a rope to the metal veranda for our escape. At least, I hoped we would be leaving together. Then I freed the screen and window from its housing, glad I'd oiled it the other day. I set the screen inside on the floor without hearing Kamal stir. Apartment life had apparently taught him to sleep soundly.

A faint scent of spices hit me as I wove my way through the easels, without the aid of any light and without disturbing any of them. I was more than thankful he hadn't moved anything since the last time I'd been in the apartment as I crept up next to his bed and stood over a sleeping Kamal. His breathing was even and shallow. I grabbed him into a fierce embrace, using his sheet to wrap him up like a burrito, so tight that his arms and legs were useless. Sitting on his stomach, I whispered in his ear.

"It's Eva. I'm not here to hurt you, but others are coming to do just that. I am whispering because they are listening and if they knew I was here, they'd break in and take you. I am an undercover agent, and I bring down the bad guys. I know it sounds crazy, but it's true. I can't answer your questions here, but I have a way out for us through your window. If you struggle or signal the people outside, I will not be able to help you. They know about Marni and are going to use her against you. If you are ready to trust me, wiggle."

He did, and I slowly released my hand and whispered, "Not a sound."

Much to his credit, he remained silent. I don't know that I would have been so trusting had the same thing happened to me. I released the sheets and helped him stand. I had him stand with his back to my chest, and I walked him through the maze of easels without bumping anything. One thing I knew for sure, people were not truly aware of the surroundings they were in each day. They tended to stop noticing things and would not remember where things were without sight. His heart pounded hard.

I shimmied down the rope and had to trust that he would follow. A part of me was surprised at his compliance. After the knife incident, I'd thought he would at least try to fight. We stayed close to the building and after jumping a fence to a neighboring yard, we headed out behind the apartment building. He followed me in silence to a park where we could talk in private.

We straddled table benches, facing each other. I checked my watch. Four a.m. In about an hour, dawn would hit and we would lose the cover of darkness. I had to hurry. As quickly as I could, I explained everything—the stolen drive, my place as an undercover agent on his crew, and how I'd been watching him from the beginning.

His eyes went wide when he heard that news, and I could tell it pissed him off royally, but he stayed still as his body tensed.

"There were...unforeseen circumstances, and I wasn't able to get the drive before you delivered it to Marco. My director took over, and now she's doing things her way." I took a deep breath before telling him, "They found your girl. They're planning to use her against you to get you to give up Marco."

His leg bounced and a twitch developed over his left eye as

he clamped his jaw tight. He was trying to stay in control.

"I'm here to get you to help me get the drive from Marco without involving my boss and your fiancé."

Air burst out of his nose, and his posture became stiffer.

"I know how important this job is to you and why you need the money. I'm not asking you to help me for nothing. The man who was giving us the information on that drive was going to be paid for it. I will see that you get that money instead. You will be able to get Marni well and live comfortably while you build up your art clientele."

His shoulders rounded slightly, but his eyes were narrow and his brow furrowed.

I waited. And waited. I was right on the edge of nudging him to speak, when he did.

"You mean to tell me that your boss has my girl. You mean here—away from her caregivers—the people who are keeping her alive until her surgery?"

I nodded.

He spoke through his teeth, the veins in his neck protruding. "She wasn't to be moved for her own safety." His Arabic accent seeped heavily into his French.

"I had nothing to do with it, but I'm sure they took every precaution possible and that she is safe and comfortable. Otherwise, they wouldn't be able to use her as a bargaining chip."

His eyes seemed to pounce on me. "Have you seen her?" Pain was etched in his face, his posture, his voice.

"No, when they told me they had her, I came straight here. I wanted to get to you first."

"Why? Why? I never did you any favors."

"You were kind to me when others weren't, and you tried

214

to help me stay safe. And even though I disagree with you choosing to become a pickpocket, I sympathize with your motives."

He cocked his head to the side.

"It's awfully romantic." I gave him a slight smile.

He shook his head.

"Besides, I knew you'd flip a lid when you heard about Marni, and they'd have a heck of a time getting any help from you, since you don't know or trust them. I thought my best chance was to come to you directly. Was I wrong?"

"No. You did the right thing. I'll help you. But you have to guarantee that Marni and I will get that money and be able to disappear."

"I guarantee it, but we need to move fast. They may have discovered my absence and have guessed at what I intended to do. We need to stay one step ahead of them."

He was looking at his hands sitting in his lap.

I took a chance and put my hand on his. "Let's end this.

20

Kamal nodded and looked me in the eye. "What do we do?"

"When did you get Marco the drives?"

"Yesterday, around six."

"Why didn't you do it in the morning like you planned?"

"He got held up at the airport." He shrugged like it was nothing.

"What does he do once he gets the drives?"

"I don't know."

"You told me he tests them, runs some kind of a program on them..." I tried to make him think.

"Yes. He does."

"Where does he do this?" I couldn't understand why the signal from the drives had gone dead.

"I'm not sure, but maybe at his apartment near Versaille..." He looked off into the trees. "One time I gave him some drives and after he took off, I discovered he left one behind. I followed him, and he stopped at an apartment that I think is his. I don't know for sure, but we could try there."

"Good. We'll go forward with that information. If we discover the drives aren't there, we'll have to improvise with whatever we find."

"If anything happens to Marni, I don't know what I'll do, but it won't be good for you or your gang of agents." His body shook as he spoke.

I believed him. I'd ensure that nothing happened. I hotwired a small green Peugeot, and Kamal climbed in the passenger's side, giving me directions as we drove to what he believed was Marco's home. I called Halluis, hoping against hope that he'd recovered enough to give me some electronic support, but he didn't pick up. He was probably still recovering in the hospital. Instead, I called Markay.

"Hello? Christy?" It was almost four thirty a.m., but surprisingly, his voice was not thick or groggy.

"Yes. It's me."

He started to speak before I could say anything else. "Tell everyone that I am working hard to get the tracker on the drive to give us the information we need. I've achieved a one-one-hundredth of a second pulse. From that information, I have narrowed the possible target area to five kilometers—down from the fifty we had only fifteen minutes ago. I should have it narrowed even further in the next ten."

Apparently, Markay had assumed I was back in Siron's good graces. And there was still a live tracked drive? I thought they were all dead. "I'll tell everyone, Markay." It wasn't really a lie. I did plan to tell the team—after I had the drive back. "Siron wants to know if you could tell us which direction from the hospital we should send the advanced team."

"Ah, yes. Direction. Versaille, perhaps rue de la Convention. That is smack dab in the middle of the pulse area. It would be a great place to set up an advance team. Yes." Kamal had me heading in that very direction. Maybe he was on to something.

"Thank you, Markay, and when you get the information in ten, just call me. I'll be directing everyone." It calmed me to know that Markay was on the tracker problem.

"I will. And I should have that information in eight now."

"Excellent."

A soft coolness fell over me thinking about seeing Jeremy after I had completed the mission. I wanted that. What I didn't want was to get fired. I had to complete this mission and make it impossible for Division to fire me. Which they easily could do for insubordination.

I turned onto rue Lecourbe, the anticipation growing as Kamal told me to turn onto Convention. He pointed the apartment out to me as we passed it, and I got a call from Markay.

"Christy?"

"Yes, Markay," I said, trying to keep my calm.

"I narrowed it down to a half km stretch when the signal went dead."

"What are you saying, Markay?"

"Whoever has that drive finally discovered Ace's plastic tech for real this time. There's no longer a glitch in the programming. It is dead now."

So, they discovered the tracking program wasn't executing the search for the tracker earlier. That's why Siron thought they were dead. "Wow! They are too good. Have you seen Halluis? Or is he still at the hospital?"

"Yes. I see him at his computer. He got here a few minutes ago. Would you like me to tell him to call you?"

"No. No," I sputtered out, not wanting to alert Siron if she was anywhere near, that I was talking to anyone at Division. "It's fine. I just wanted to know if he was okay."

"All right. And one more thing. The way the signal disappeared leaves me to believe it was being worked on right that moment."

A car sped out of the drive of the apartment we were about to enter. Kamal jerked.

"That's him. That's Marco."

"Thanks, Markay." I hung up.

My stomach got all fluttery, and adrenaline coursed through me. I followed the car, figuring he must have the drive with him. He drove across town to the Eiffel Tower area and threw something in a restaurant dumpster as we passed. We stopped, and I jumped into the dumpster with my flashlight to add extra light. I shoved big bags to the side and shuffled papers and miscellaneous trash around the bin in an organized fashion until I finally uncovered two drives—the ones Ace had made. I searched further. There was no sign of any other drives being tossed. Our tracking link to Marco was gone.

A hard rock seemed to take up residence in my gut. I hopped out of the bin, discarding the drives, ignoring the grime I was now coated with, and jumped into the car with Kamal.

"Which way did he go?" He pointed, and I sped off in that direction. I checked the clock on the car console. It had taken me seven minutes to search the trash bin. He had a seven minute head start on us. He'd been driving pretty fast. He could have gone seven kilometers in any direction. He probably wanted distance between himself and the tracked drives. The most logical route would be to drive on the straightest path, so I stayed on rue Saint-Dominique, curving around the Army Museum. I'd miscalculated. He wasn't just trying to put distance between himself and the drives, because we caught up to him right before he turned onto rue de Bourgogne, a mere three kilometers from the tower. Perhaps he had a second apartment where he also checked the drives out. However, when he turned on Varenne, my heart almost stopped.

It couldn't be. He must have lost his mind. That or he must have no clue that we were following him. Perhaps he wasn't headed where I'd thought. He could have a home near the Hôtel Matignon, which was nothing like a hotel, but instead was the residence of none other than the Prime Minister of France. He could, but the chill running over my bones told me differently.

And when he pulled up to the huge black doors that opened to allow cars inside the compound, he had to wait because the bulletproof glass guard shack was empty. I pulled the car over to the side of the road about a half a block from the residence to watch. There was no one to radio to security to let him in. He honked and then honked again.

"If nothing else, he's persistent." I chuckled.

Finally, a guard in full regalia came out to greet him. I had no idea what was said, but Marco slammed his hands on the steering wheel and peeled out of the short driveway.

Marco cruised around the corner. I started the car and followed him, but was forced to drive past the road he'd turned on because he had pulled to the curb just around the corner. Light from a cell phone lit up his face. So far he had obviously been driven by anger and was not even considering the idea that he was being followed. Now I couldn't risk that he would start paying attention and realize a suspicious car had been following him. We drove a few blocks and swapped the Peugeot for a black BMW sedan. It took me two minutes to override the security using my phone. I worried it'd been too long, but I thought we needed to have a fast, reliable car.

When we circled around to where Marco's car should have

been standing, it was gone. It was my turn to slap my steering wheel. I drove around past the glass guard shack entrance to the Prime Minister's residence and was surprised to see a car leave the "hotel" and turn the way we'd just come. I took the next street and made an abrupt U-turn to follow that car. It didn't hold any official markings, but the car leaving the Prime Minister's residence before five in the morning after what we'd seen Marco do was too suspicious.

The question was, was it the Prime Minister, and was he going to meet up with Marco? Was I about to get my hands on the drive *and* put a nail in the coffin of the pickpockets?

We followed at an extremely safe distance not wanting to risk detection. Light had just started to fill the sky, and any stars that had been visible, were no longer. "Did you ever hear anything about political leaders being involved with your boss?"

"No."

"Are you sure?"

"I'm sure. But I was low on the totem pole. I wouldn't have known anything. Do you think the Prime Minister is somehow involved with the pickpocket gangs?"

"You know," I said, continuing to follow the other car, "after being here four months and watching pickpockets get away with so much, I wondered why the government hadn't cleaned up the city. Now I understand. The Prime Minister is sanctioning the pickpockets, and who knows what else, and filling his bank account at the same time. And this drive is going to help me prove it."

He shook his head and sighed. "A man with that kind of power and connections, you are nuts if you think we can do anything about it. You should get on that phone of yours and call in reinforcements."

The car pulled off the main road. I sped up. "No. The director would call me back and then spend too much time wringing her hands. I know her. She's terrified to go after the Prime Minister." I couldn't keep the bitterness from my voice. "No, if he's going to be stopped, I'm going to have to do it."

Once we turned the corner, we saw the car's red brake lights shine and then turn off as it pulled into a little inlet at Champ de Mars, the park butting up to the Eiffel Tower. It had pulled up next to none other than Marco's car. We inched up the street, still a block away. Marco got out of his car and jumped into the Prime Minister's. When he did, the lights turned on for a good two seconds, and I was able to confirm the identity of the Prime Minister and watch Marco put a box into Alden's hands.

It also confirmed to me at that moment who Marco sold his digital information to. The Prime Minister himself. He was double dipping. He was probably receiving bribes from the various pickpocket gangs on the front end, and on the back end he was using the information he bought from Marco to do all kinds of nefarious activities that I could only guess at. The power of this one man as an underworld mob boss was incredible, and he was operating as the second most powerful man in France.

21

I pulled binoculars out of my go bag and tried to lip read the conversation using the light from the park lights. Prime Minister Alden and Marco sat in the back seat of the big car. The driver sat attentive in the front seat. It was obvious that Alden and Marco were angry, but I couldn't make out what was being said. Was Marco mad about getting a drive that was tracked? Did he think the Prime Minister could somehow stop that? He opened the box and shook it. Metal and color glinted in the sparse light. Flash drives.

"Did you give him the drives in a box?"

Kamal nodded. I handed him the binoculars.

"Is that the box?"

"I think so. Marco just got out of the car."

"How many were in the box?"

"Twenty. There should be eighteen now that he threw out two."

This was it. Not only was I about to get my hands on the drive, I was also about to expose the Prime Minister for the evil man he was and hopefully release Paris from the strangling grip of the pickpockets. This would be like taking candy from a baby. "Kamal, would you like to help?"

"With what?"

"I need someone to document the confession of the Prime Minister." I smiled.

"I don't know."

"All you have to do is put this phone on Record, get a good picture of the Prime Minister and record his voice as I get him to confess. No biggie."

"You mean I'd have to be in close proximity to Marco and the Prime Minister? Are you nuts? I'd like to live to be with Marni, thank you. I'm out."

I nodded. Fair enough. "You're just going to have to act as my lookout then. I'll have my phone on Record as I walk up to the car. If you spot a problem, then call me." I changed the phone's ringtone to one of me yelling, "Get out! Get out!" I laughed.

Kamal still looked through the binoculars. "Uh, Marco just drove away."

It was time. I checked the area and found my calm spot after saying a heartfelt prayer for courage to do what was necessary. Deep heat spread throughout my chest.

I slinked my way over to the car and grinned when I saw the Prime Minister had neglected to relock the doors after Marco had climbed out. Too bad everything couldn't be so easy. I yanked the door open and flew into the car, my gun on the temple of the Prime Minister before he could even register my presence. I recognized two things right off the bat. Number one, the red light was flashing on my phone, letting me know the conversation was being recorded. Number two, in the ashtray, a small fire burned what used to be a flash drive. I was too late. I wouldn't be able to retrieve the information.

"So you're the one who's been giving me heart attacks. You're such a little thing."

"It doesn't matter that the drive is gone," I said. "I know what was on it. I know you're helping the pickpockets."

He leaned back. Next thing I knew, something was coming right at me. I lifted my arms to cover my face. The box of drives hit my arms and drives flew everywhere. Now Alden had a gun pointed at me.

"Go ahead my dear, drop your weapon or you die."

I had no doubt he'd use it. I let my gun drop to the floorboards.

He told the driver to get going. "We need somewhere less visible and accessible, with a nice spot to dispose of a body."

A trickle of fear passed through me, but I shrugged it off knowing Kamal was watching what was happening. He'd follow us. Then I remembered pocketing the keys to the car he waited in. He would see me leave, but would not be able to help. He didn't know how to contact Division. Fine. If I was going to die, I had to at least find out if I had been right. Maybe I'd get a chance to send a recording to Division and they would get the Prime Minister anyway. I had to stay on target. I needed to get him to talk.

"I don't get it," I said. "As Prime Minister you earn great money."

"There's never enough money and never enough power."

He liked the power of it? This was about to get easier. People like him liked to boast, so I'd get him to boast. "Why did you kidnap my shadow and me?"

"Oh, that's an easy one. I figured you had the drive or that you'd given it to someone. I wanted it back." He chuckled. "I should have known you didn't have it or you would have used it against me already, blackmail, you know. A miscalculation on my part.

"Yes. The second Marco had the drive, he called me. You see, I'm much too powerful for a little girl like you to bring down." He wanted me to know he had always been a step ahead and had the upper hand. I'd let him keep talking, burying himself. "You did give it a noble, valiant effort. It simply wasn't enough."

I wanted to wipe the smug look off him. The driver pulled onto the main road.

"Too bad I can't keep you around. You wouldn't want to change sides, would you?" He'd started getting comfortable with me and was waving his gun around as he talked instead of holding it steady. I let my shoulders slump a little too, to encourage his relaxation, but also to give me access to my knife. Now I needed the right moment.

"You know, I saw the feed of you escaping my men. You were pretty good. Last chance to join me. I'm sure I'd pay you better than whatever agency you are working for." He smiled and rested the gun on his lap. I gripped the knife tight in my hand and stabbed him in the leg and took his gun from him in two seconds flat. Prime Minister Alden screamed out in pain and clutched at his leg as a large spot of blood blossomed on his pants. I pointed the gun at the driver's head, and told him to pull over. I retained the knife in my left hand.

"So, Prime Minister," I said in the most mocking tone I could manage in the French language, "Would you like to bind that wound?"

He nodded.

"Well, tell me what a bad little boy you've been. I want every last detail. But do it quickly." I stabbed the air with the bloody knife, directing it toward Alden.

He didn't speak, so I added, "A cut like that, bleeding like that, you could be dead in a few minutes. Do you believe in the afterlife? Judgment and all that jazz?"

He didn't speak. Sweat dripped along his hairline. I pressed the knife to his cheek and he yelled out, "Okay! Okay! Yes, I hired those men to kill you. I couldn't have you messing with the pickpockets."

"What were their names?"

"Adolphe and Cardwell, among others."

"How did you pay them?"

"I paid them as security consultants."

"And why couldn't you have me messing with *your* pickpockets?"

I kept an eye on the driver as he looked through the rearview mirror, flashing him a menacing look here and there to let him know he wasn't safe either. Prime Minister Alden's face was pale, and copious amounts of sweat dotted his face and neck. His hands pressed hard on his injured leg, blood pouring through his fingers.

"Can't you see this man needs a hospital?" the driver yelped.

"Minister?" I said, pushing the knife even harder into his cheek, drawing blood.

His whole body shuddered "Yes! I was taking bribes. They would bring them every second Wednesday with a bouquet of flowers delivered to my office."

"So, I guess what I'm hearing is that you profit on the front and back end of the pickpockets' activities, Prime Minister. Is this true?" My heart pounded.

He nodded.

"I didn't hear you." I glanced quickly at the phone. The red light still blinked.

"Yes." He exhaled hard.

He had spilled the beans. All of them. I slipped my knife back in its holder near my ankle and pulled out my phone. "Thank you for that." I waved the phone in front of him, so he could see I had been recording, and then I jumped out of the car.

Luckily, we'd only driven a few blocks. I stole a black bullet bike just down the road.

22

I blind texted Kamal as I drove, telling him to be ready to jump on the bullet bike that was about to swing by the car he was sitting in. He did. We were gone in a flash, passing an ambulance that was most likely heading for the Prime Minister. They were quick. In my rearview mirror, I could see two police officers standing on the driver's side of the car and someone on the other, wildly gesticulating. It did surprise me that no one seemed to be following us. I calmed myself and reached out, making sure I wasn't letting the excitement and craziness of what just happened keep me from noticing tails or danger.

Once we were far enough away, I blindfolded Kamal and took him in to the interrogation wing of Division HQ, had someone bring him some food and water as well as a blanket, and then removed the blindfold.

He blinked hard and looked around the room before zeroing in on me. "Is she here?"

"I don't know." I didn't want to give him any false hope of Marni's whereabouts and left it at that. "But it shouldn't be long before you know." I sighed. "And, I think it only fair to tell you that I may not be able to come and see you again. I just might lose my job after this little stunt." I slapped my hands on my thighs and stood up. "In any case, I wanted to thank you for helping me get the drive. You're a good guy, Kamal. You're set now, and I'm happy for you and Marni. I hope you have a great future together."

He closed his eyes and curled his bottom lip over his teeth. I stood to go.

He reached out and took my wrist. "Thank you."

I smiled at him, "I hope you never let desperation make you a criminal again. Many never get second chances in life."

"No worries there."

Once outside Kamal's interrogation room, I took a deep breath and headed straight for Siron. No, I hadn't retrieved the drive. It was gone forever, but I may have gotten something even better, right from the horse's mouth. A confession in all its beauty. Siron would still probably be completely irate and send me to Division Central with a terrible ding to my record for insubordination, but I didn't care. All I wanted was justice for Dufor, which I would get with this recording.

Siron was in her office on her phone. When she saw me, she waved me in and hung up. This was it.

"Shut the door, please," Siron said.

I didn't want to let Siron prevent me from telling her everything, so I started in before the door was even shut. "Kamal is in a holding cell. I told him he would get the money that would have gone to Dufor had he not been killed, for him and Marni to get set up somewhere safe."

"All right," Siron said in a much too calm voice. What was going on?

"I believe the Prime Minister is at a hospital somewhere."

I held out my phone for Siron to take. "I recorded a full confession from him on my phone."

"Keep it," Siron said.

"But—"

"No!" Siron said, cutting me off. "It's your turn to listen to me."

I closed my mouth.

"We heard everything that happened. We used your phone."

"Wait. What?" Then it occurred to me what they'd done. "So, that was how Summer did it. She tapped my phone."

She nodded. A myriad of feelings washed over me. I felt violated, but also glad and mad. But mostly relieved. Then I remembered what I'd said about Siron to Kamal and a furious blush hit my face. I was dead.

"Agent Hadden, while I would have done things differently, you showed remarkable skill and ingenuity and that must be commended. Especially considering all the obstacles you had to face. Paris owes you a lot. While the pickpockets won't totally disappear, they will be severely crippled. Perhaps the police will have a chance of eradicating them.

"The Prime Minister will be taken care of by our men so there can be no chance of corruption. The connection between him and the President is also being scrutinized to see if the President knew about what the Prime Minister was doing. I'm hoping the public was confusing the Prime Minister's corrupt actions for that of the President. Not only will the Prime Minister be finished with politics, but hopefully, he will be in jail for a very long time and everyone will know what he did.

"And, Paris will be a safer place for people to be. Maybe I'll even be able to keep my belongings from now on." She chuckled.

I'd never seen Siron laugh, let alone chuckle. It was nice.

"Rosabella has asked to be transferred back to Italy. I've

known for some time that she wanted to go back home, but she's so good, I didn't want to lose her. She deserves it, though, don't you think?"

I nodded.

"And, I'm sure you'll be happy to know Summer has returned to her training in Germany. I know there's more to the story of you two. Maybe one day you'll trust me enough to tell it to me." She raised her eyebrows. I said nothing. I wouldn't even tell Jeremy this little secret.

"As for the rest of your team, it's still being worked out. I hope you'll be happy in the end. I know you are anxious to move on."

"Thank you, Director."

She nodded. "Now, I do believe you have a hospital full of team members who would love to see you and hear the latest."

"Thank you, Director," I said again, and left.

***

Finally, Halluis and Ace were getting their prize as we sat in a café in Montmartre near the Sacré-Cœur two days later. The view seemed to stretch on forever, the Eiffel tower appearing small in the distance.

"Wouldn't you say this was worth it?" Halluis held out his eight-euro soda as he looked over the beautiful city.

I nodded. My rich dinner left me feeling satisfied and relaxed. "You were right. It is worth it. Nothing compares with this. In America, the waiter would have been dragging us out of the restaurant by now. It's been what? Two hours?" I tapped my glass into his and then Jeremy and Ace joined in.

"Three," Ace said. "Not that I've been counting." He looked relaxed, leaning back in his chair, his foot still bandaged.

"We should do this every day." Halluis's look was wistful.

"I'm afraid that would ruin it. No. This is a moment to be cherished and repeated only sparingly to keep it from being commonplace."

They all nodded. "I want to thank you guys for believing in me. I can't tell you how much it meant to know you had my back." There was a tickle in the back of my throat and a burning sensation assaulted my eyes.

"I've learned that working with you will never be boring," Ace said. "Yeah. You make this spy business more fun than work."

"Hey," Halluis said. "Take that back. I think it was a lot of work. It was the hard work that made it fun."

"That's something I'd never say," Ace said, screwing up his face, making everyone laugh.

Halluis punched him. Then he glanced at me and his face turned serious.

"I'm sorry I didn't answer your call. I wanted to, believe me. But Siron was standing right over me."

I shook my head, "It's all right. I understand. Siron's orders have to be followed. They are paramount."

"If she'd only told me to cut you off, that would be one thing, but she had me transmitting everything your phone heard to her. I couldn't pick up or it would cause terrible feedback, and you'd have known we were listening."

"Wait." I grimaced. "When did you make this connection?" I wondered when she started listening. Maybe she hadn't heard what I'd said about her.

"I had a bad connection about the time Markay called you. I was able to get a better connection where we could hear everything about the time you hotwired the second car. I'm so sorry. I hated every moment of it. I never wanted to do that to you."

"You were just following orders, Halluis. I would never hold that against you."

Jeremy was oddly quiet throughout the entire exchange.

I thought maybe I should pull him in. "Jeremy, you came back at just the right time."

"Had I been there earlier, maybe a lot of the chaos could have been averted."

"Are you kidding?" Ace said. "And miss the whirlwind? The excitement? All I can say is they better keep us together as a team from now on."

"I second that," Halluis said. "We are fast and forward thinkers and we are extremely quick on our feet."

"Not to mention our total awesomeness," Ace interjected. Both Halluis and Ace had excited looks on their faces. Jeremy looked up from the spot on the table he'd fixated on. "Siron has already put in that recommendation." Despite the happy news, he looked sad somehow.

"We wouldn't have it any other way," Halluis said.

"For sure," Ace said. "The Fearless Four. Together forever."

"Forever!" Halluis said and lifted his glass. We all followed suit, clinking our glasses together again and repeating *forever*. It seemed Jeremy whispered it. Then we all drained the remaining liquid from our cups.

We had to hail the waiter to bring us our checks. In America, the waiter would have left it a half hour after he brought the food and scowled at us until we left, but not here. Here they expected you to stay for forever. Ace handed me a bag of something.

"My favorite French candy. You'll have to tell me what you think."

I peered inside to see brightly colored hard candies dusted with sugar. "They look fabulous. I took a dark red one and popped it into my mouth. Jeremy, Halluis, and Ace each took one as I held the bag out to them. We stood and walked to the metro, Ace using crutches, all going our separate ways.

***

As I fiddled with the door lock to my apartment, I felt him. "Need some help with that?"

Just then, the key slid in and I turned the knob, opening the door. "Got it," I said, opening the door up wide and indicating I wanted him to go in. He smiled and entered. I watched Jeremy walk to the couch and take a seat before I shut the door and joined him. How I wanted things to be different between us.

"You were really quiet today." I kept my eyes on my fidgeting fingers.

"Yeah. Well, I had a lot on my mind."

"Care to share?" I glanced up at him.

"It's not a good idea. I shouldn't."

"Not fair!" I said in a loud whisper, looking at him full on now. "Share with me," I pleaded.

His eyes held a troubled look. "I'm so glad I'm back with you."

I glanced at my new phone and had to resist the urge to check it again for bugs. I didn't want anyone hearing my conversations again. "Me, too. This is hard on me too. It doesn't have to be awkward between us." I swept the room with my eyes to make certain there were no listening devices in the apartment.

"That's just it. It does have to be awkward. I can't stop how I feel about you and yet we can't be together, but we have to be near each other all the time. That full three hours at the restaurant, my mind was fixed on finding a solution. How can I be your handler and be with you all the time and not be able to touch you, feel your soft skin, your incredible lips, your embrace. It's too hard. I'm going to ask to be transferred. Maybe then they'll let us be together." He looked exhausted, dark lines visible even in the dim light of the room.

Hot tears pressed on the backs of my eyes as the raw emotion I'd been suppressing threatened to escape. He did still care for me. I worked hard to speak. "No. That doesn't work. It can't work. Like you, I can't be away from you and I can't be with you." My voice sounded strange, pinched.

"It's a hell of a spot to be in." His head hung low and shook it in short, clipped motions. He looked at me and slowly, his hand moved to my cheek, my tears washing over it. My skin tingled where he'd touched me and a burn settled in my chest. "I have an idea." The words tumbled out of my mouth, loud and broken. I sniffed. His fingers brushed at my tears again. His deep, intense gaze was probing, but he didn't speak.

I brushed at the tears with the heels of my hands and then took a deep, shuddering breath. "We are spies."

"And?" He ran his fingers fleetingly over my lips.

"Our jobs. Who we are." Excitement burst out of me at the realization. "We pretend to be people we aren't every day. We can pretend not to be together."

He nodded, slowly. "We are good at what we do. That's why we can't be together, remember?"

"Don't you see?" I said, standing up, energy filling me.

"We can be together and they don't have to know." I had no idea why I hadn't thought of this earlier.

He still looked puzzled, so I forged on. It seemed so obvious now. "We are not only good at what we do. We are amazing at what we do. And because we are amazing at it, we most certainly can have a relationship without Division knowing. How many times a day do we do something in secret? Things that no one knows about? We can do this."

His eyes suddenly sparkled. He must've finally understood. But he was shaking his head instead of nodding. "I don't know. I don't know if I can be around you and not touch you. My face will betray me."

"You don't betray yourself when you're on a job. Ever. You have to see us as a job. A most wonderful and perfect job."

He chuckled and his eyes beamed into mine as he stood. I followed.

I needed him. He had to agree. He had to see it would work. "You won't betray yourself now. And if they discover us, what are they going to do? It's not like they would expel their two best spies."

"Actually they would." He grimaced. "I've seen it happen."

I put my hand up to his mouth. He sighed and I moved my hand.

"Do you really think we could pull it off?" he asked. "I'm your handler. I'm supposed to stop you from doing reckless things like this." His hand brushed down my arm.

"Instead, we can make it happen." I closed the small distance between us.

"You're the one thing I'd never imagined when I became a spy." He took my hand and caressed the top of it with his thumb. His eyes burned into mine. His other hand drifted along

CInDY M HOGAN

the back of my neck. Nice and slow.

My heart beat hard. Shallow fast breaths filled the space between us until his eyes closed and our lips met. My insides were on fire, whipping and roaring about. There was no distance between us, and yet, I wanted him to be somehow closer. This would have to do for now. He pulled back at some point. The smile that split across his face instantly brought a smile to my own. I desperately wanted to kiss him again. To distract myself I said, "I'm so glad that they are honoring my promise to Kamal. He gave up everything to help me."

Jeremy must've noticed the distraction because he dropped his hands and sat down on the couch again, then patted the empty spot next to him. I grinned and sat.

"Yes," he said. "And the reunion was amazing. I wish you could have seen it. Kamal and Marni are going to be okay. Thanks to you."

I threw my arms in the air as I let out a loud squeal. He laughed and continued speaking.

"The Prime Minister will be resigning tomorrow around noon at a special press conference and a coordinated operation taking down all six of the major pickpocket gangs will occur at the same time.

"The police department will be going through a major overhaul to rid itself of all the dirty cops who willingly took part in furthering the Prime Minister's agenda. Siron finally came around to the fact that just bringing down the Prime Minister's gangs wouldn't afford the cleanup that was needed. She is in a secret meeting with key players in the government as we speak."

"How did you get him away to interrogate him? He was talking to some police, and an ambulance was on its way when we left." This had been bugging me for a while.

"Meet paramedic Martin." I burst out laughing. "Unbelievable. You were one of the paramedics? Who were the cops?"

He named a few agents and explained how they put the Prime Minister in the ambulance and then took him to Division where he was told what was going to happen. "It's not like we could use the recording you made, in open court. His confessions were made under certain duress. However, he could see that its release would condemn him either way and chose to resign."

"Good choice." I grinned.

"He'll be in prison for a long, long time for a few murders he had his cronies commit. The President was clean. He had no idea about what the Prime Minister was doing." My cheeks were hurting from smiling so big. I had to bite on them and make a fish face to relieve some of the ache.

"Now," Jeremy said. "Fill me in on a few things that I'm not really clear about. How did you get out of the hospital?"

The smile flew from my lips and I spoke through my teeth, a bit embarrassed. "Summer."

His head jerked back and he blinked in disbelief. "What?"

"Summer distracted the guards so I could sneak out of a bathroom window."

"Hmm. That surprises me for some reason."

I nodded. "It surprised me too." I thought about filling him in on what happened on the roof, but I wasn't sure if I wanted to ruin the moment with that information. It was like my throat squeezed around the words.

"I know I told you to let her surprise you, and I'm glad she did."

I nodded. I wouldn't tell him. He would feel way too bad

about it. No, Summer would continue as an agent for Division for another day.

"So Dufor did not die for nothing." My hand pushed on my stomach trying to stop the flutters that awoke.

"That's for sure. Good job. The team did an amazing job."

My mouth twitched into a hopeful smile.

"Looks like you're getting all your wishes from this mission. You get out of Paris, and the pickpockets will be hurt in a way that will most likely prevent a revival for a long, long time."

"When are we leaving?"

"The day after tomorrow."

A bit of regret seeped into me. I wished I'd been able to see Paris through the eyes of romance—like movies and books portrayed it. I looked at my watch and yawned. It was eleven p.m.

"Yes, sleepy head." Then he yawned. "Ah, you made me yawn."

I chuckled. "So we have a day to spend here, together as tourists?"

"I think that's a correct assumption, but only if you agree to see it with new eyes." His smile lit up the room.

"I think I can do that, but only if I get to sleep first. I want to not only see Paris with new eyes, but with open eyes."

He laughed. "Heaven forbid we don't blend in." I leaned on him, taking in a deep breath before closing my eyes and falling asleep.

***

The next morning, I woke early. I even had time to catch up on my favorite book series as I waited for Jeremy to show up.

His knock sent me running to the door. His eyes gleamed and he reached out and pulled me into a much needed hug. I lost myself in his embrace. I tucked my head against his hard chest and breathed in his manly, musky smell. His chin rested on my head for a few moments before he pulled back. I wasn't ready and pulled him closer, tighter. We stayed like that, frozen in time with no problems shadowing us, no sorrow hanging over our heads. He stepped back and took my upper arms in his grip before searching my face.

I squished up my nose, but did not look away from him. The excitement in his eyes made it almost impossible to keep my eyes off his mouth.

Our day together was just like the movies. We even got into disguises, dressed like actors playing a part. Totally dreamy. And that night, I didn't dream about Division Central and whether they would allow me to be a spy, dirty pickpockets feeling me up, scary dungeons, sore fingertips, or flash drives. No. My dreams were all about Jeremy and me climbing to the top of the Eiffel Tower together, screaming with pure delight as our stomachs dropped, going to the catacombs and grabbing his arm in fear and disgust, and walking through the Tuileries Garden eating a turkey panini and then a lemon tart and finding excuses to bump into him until he took me behind a few tall, leafy, beautiful trees to put a sweet, soft kiss to my lips. And then more.

Oh, and yes, I still had a knife tucked into my boot and a go bag sitting at the base of the tree, because as you know, a spy never really has a day where she stops being a spy.

MORE FROM CINDY M. HOGAN

Thank you for leaving a review online!
It helps me more than you know. Big Hugs!

If you missed the first two books in the series, pick up *Adrenaline Rush* and *Hotwire*.

If you loved this book, try these fun novels and series by Cindy M. Hogan:

Jump into the exciting adventures of the *Watched Trilogy*
And *Kate Unmasked*
Dive in to great mystery in *Gravediggers*
Laugh and cry with Brooklyn in *Sweet and Sour Kisses.*

Know Cindy's news before anyone else by signing up for her newsletter http://eepurl.com/GL2HL Get sneak peaks and free stuff!

Visit Cindy on her website:
cindymhogan.com
and on Google plus: Cindy M. Hogan

For series trivia, sneak peeks, events in your area, contests, fun fan interaction, like the Watched Facebook Page: Watched-the book

Follow Cindy M. Hogan on twitter: @Watched

ABOUT THE AUTHOR

Cindy M. Hogan is inspired by the unpredictable teenagers she teaches. More than anything she loves the time she has with her own teenage daughters and wishes she could freeze them at this fun age. If she's not reading or writing, you'll find her snuggled up with the love of her life watching a great movie or planning their next party. Most of all, she loves to laugh.

She is the bestselling and award-winning author of the *Watched trilogy*, a YA suspense series with a dash of romance and three in a spy series, *Adrenaline Rush, Hotwire,* and *Fatal Exchange.* She has since branched off to write a mystery, *Gravediggers*, that won Best YA novel of 2013, a contemporary romance, *Sweet and Sour Kisses*, and *Kate Unmasked*, the first in her new thriller series, *Code of Silence.*

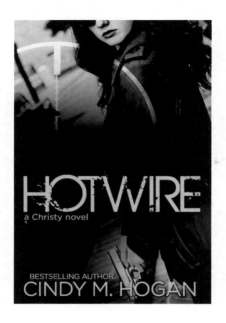

Division spy Christy Hadden can't wait for her latest assignment posing as a student at a prestigious New York City academy and car thief extraordinaire.

The best part of the mission is her attractive handler, Jeremy, and her new team. The worst part? The sociopath masquerading as the academy's most popular guy.

But soon she realizes the car thieves are much more than they seem. Her simple spying mission becomes more dangerous than anyone imagined. If the organization discovers her true identity, they won't hesitate to kill her, and if she fails, others will suffer the same fate.

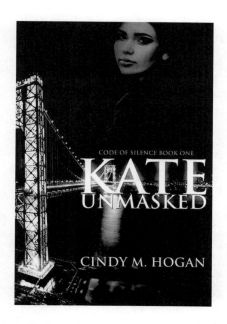

CODE OF SILENCE BOOK ONE

KATE UNMASKED

CINDY M. HOGAN

The mysteries of her past consume her.

Seventeen-year-old Kate has never stopped searching for the secrets of her past--the secrets that began with her missing birth parents. After years of every lead drying up and every hope turning false, Kate finally lucks onto a promising lead.

Determined to find the truth once and for all, Kate travels to the gritty New Jersey shore. But what she finds is worse than she ever could have imagined. She can't hide from who she is, and now she must face the awful consequences of finding the very people she should have been hiding from.

Seventeen-year-old Billy thinks his father's murder will never be solved until he stumbles across an old ammo box while digging a grave in his small-town Tennessee cemetery.

What he finds leads him to question everything he knows, and his search for answers will uncover more than he bargained for: lies, secrets, and conspiracies and behind them all, a dangerous truth.